Tea

Tea

a novel

by

STACEY D'ERASMO

Algonquin Books of Chapel Hill

2000

Published by
Algonquin Books of Chapel Hill
Post Office Box 2225
Chapel Hill, North Carolina 27515-2225

a division of
Workman Publishing
708 Broadway
New York, New York 10003

Printed in the United States of America.
Published simultaneously in Canada
by Thomas Allen & Son Limited.
Design by Anne Winslow.

A short excerpt from early sections of this novel was first published in different form in *Venue* 3, "Boy/Girl," 1998.

Library of Congress Cataloging-in-Publication Data
D'Erasmo, Stacey.
Tea : a novel / by Stacey D'Erasmo.
p. cm.
ISBN 1-56512-243-7 (hardcover)
I. Title.
PS3554.E666T4 2000
813'.54—dc21 99-33337
CIP

10 9 8 7 6 5 4 3 2 1
First Edition

Tea

MORNING

On Saturday, they found a house. They drove far past Philadelphia, into the country, the newspaper with the circled ad between them on the seat, the radio playing. On the news, the talk was of Vietnam.

"Will Dad have to go in the army?" asked Isabel.

"No," said her mother. "He has a family." A wide headband held her hair back, and she had pushed her sleeves up as she drove. She sipped from the mug of tea she always brought with her in the car. She seemed almost happy, as the countryside spun by. "This is like where I grew up," she said. "Look for cows, Isabel."

Isabel counted several cows, not a single one walking anywhere. They turned down a road, then another, passed a little store, then rumbled onto a road that led to the top of a hill, where the house was. The agent's name was Madge, and she met them at the peeling front door, seeming cheery. Everything about Madge was wrinkled except her feet, which were beautiful in white slingbacks. She led them around, pointing things out in her raspy voice. She was skinny as a piece of celery.

The house wasn't particularly nice, in Isabel's opinion. There was an enormous water stain cascading down the living room wall, and the kitchen wallpaper was peeling. Pairs of boots of different sizes sat up on a muddy shelf in the kitchen, close to the floor. The living room was full of books stacked up like firewood, none on shelves. There was an intriguing small door cut into the side of the staircase. Isabel rattled the handle, but it wouldn't open.

Madge sent them up the steep wooden stairs alone. "You break it, you buy it!" she rasped out, then laughed a deep laugh, as if she had told a very hilarious joke indeed. Isabel wanted to tell Madge how stupid that was, that they weren't going to break anything, but didn't, following her mother up the stairs.

"Oh, look at this," her mother said when they reached a narrow room with a painted floor and a small desk set all by itself in the middle, like an island. Against one wall was a mattress on the floor, covered by a chenille bedspread. From the desk, out the odd, oblong window, Isabel could see a field. In the field, there was a car up on cinder blocks. All its doors were gone. There wasn't anything else in the room but the bed, the desk, the desk chair, and the window with the field and the car in it. Beyond the car, the land sloped and fell away into woods. Isabel, squinting, took a picture of it with her mind so she could think about it later.

Isabel's mother sat down at the desk; her knees didn't quite fit under it. She lifted the lid.

"Mom," said Isabel.

"I'm just peeking," she said. Inside, there were maps, a messy notebook, pens, pencils, some thread. A yo-yo. A book about the birds of South America. "They must travel," said Isabel's mother, opening to a photograph of a bright lime-green bird that seemed to be hugely tall, with bulging eyes. "The people here travel." The bird's eye bulged unpleasantly at Isabel.

Isabel sat down at the very edge of the mattress. Why, she wondered, was there no furniture in this room besides the bed, the little desk, and the matching chair? "Are we near Springston?" she said.

"Springston?" said Isabel's mother, dropping the lid back down with a hollow bang. She leaned back in her chair, stretching out one long leg. "We're not moving to Springston. That's your father's big idea. What do you think of this house?"

"It's okay," said Isabel. She passed her hand over the country of the bedspread. There were the mountains. There was the sea. There was a farm where she lived with her friend Ann. "Mom. Have you heard of The Doors?"

She wrinkled her forehead. "Who?"

"The *Doors*. It's a group."

"Chiggy-wiggy music?"

"Yes," Isabel giggled.

"What kind of group?"

"I just told you. *Rock*-and-*roll* music. They're really good."

Her mother was quiet for a minute. Her lime-green bird mood seemed to have passed suddenly. She leaned her head in her hand at the little desk. Her two rings shone in her hair. "You know, Isabel," she said, "sometimes I want to die."

Isabel retied a shoelace, light-headed. The room seemed to get brighter for an instant, then faded to normal again. Maybe that was a sunspot. The sea roiled as the sunspot blazed, overturning a ship sailing over the sea past the farm where she and Ann lived. "Why?" she said, staring at the sea.

Isabel's mother pressed her long fingers into the corners of her eyes, squeezed her eyes shut, shaking her head. "I just do," she said. "I just want to die."

Isabel flicked the farm off the planet. "I don't know what you're talking about," she said, and she tried to sound cold, like a cold girl in a book. "It's Saturday. We're looking for a new house. You drove us here in our car. You'll drive us back. It isn't that hard."

Isabel's mother shook her head again, as if in response to a silent question. She looked like a stranger to Isabel for a moment, and that was worse than seeing her get upset. "How would you know what's hard?" she said quietly, her dark blue eyes wet, turning in the small chair to face Isabel. "How would you know, Isabel?"

Isabel had no reply. She picked at the chenille bumps, which were in a feather outline. What town were they in, then, she wondered, if they weren't in Springston. Several minutes went by. Isabel's mother stood up, and looked out the window.

"Hey," called Madge from downstairs. "Look out that window. Do you see the rosebushes?"

"Madge," said Isabel's mother loudly. "I'm in love with this house. It's perfect. What are they asking?" She turned around, no longer crying, and gave Isabel the little pinch that meant *I'm back*.

Madge came up the stairs, slingbacks making a fast Morse code Isabel couldn't quite read. "Twenty-five," she said, lighting up a cigarette and opening the window. "They'd probably take less."

"Oh, let me sneak a puff," said Isabel's mother.

Madge handed her the pack. "I've gotta quit anyway."

"Who lives here?" said Isabel.

"Renters," said Madge. "Three or four girls all live out here together. Hippies. One of them's a mechanic, if you believe that. The owners are in Florida."

"A lady mechanic?" said Isabel's mother, blowing smoke up into the air.

Madge shrugged, tapped her ash out the window. "She's the only one I've dealt with. Big friendly girl."

Isabel stood up. "How are the schools?"

Madge laughed, exhanging a glance with Isabel's mother, who shrugged. "The schools?" said Madge. "They're all right, honey." She stubbed out her cigarette on the windowsill, closed the window. "They're just fine."

Isabel decided that she would never smoke as long as she lived. "I'd like to see the rosebushes, Madge," she said.

The three of them went back down the loud wooden stairs, Isabel in the lead, the winner. Outside, on the tilting porch, there was an orange cat with one chewed ear.

"What's his name?" said Isabel.

"Kitty," said Madge. Isabel, despising Madge, resolved to be superpolite to her for the rest of the day.

Madge walked them through the backyard, proudly pointing out the rosebushes, which were little more than a few stringy bundles of thorns. "How lovely," said Isabel loudly to Madge.

They walked past the car, Madge, in her slingbacks, giving it a wide berth. "They'll take that with them," she said. Isabel peered at the car, wondering if there was anything interesting left in the glove compartment. She attempted to excavate it with X-ray vision, but nothing happened. These people, she thought, were poor, and not nearly as smart as the Romans, who built aqueducts.

The March air tipped all of their noses with red as they walked, bit their cheeks. The marks of Isabel's mother's tears faded away into a general flush. She put her arm around Isabel, and Isabel held her breath. Then she couldn't help it. She moved closer, hard. "Whoa," said her mother, stumbling. They walked together into the wind, awkwardly, hip to hip. Isabel noticed that her head was not so far from her mother's shoulder when they stood side by side. She would be so much taller than her mother when she grew up. Isabel put her hand in her mother's pocket and felt crumpled Kleenex, some change. A quarter, a nickel, she figured out. Two pennies. From the yard, Isabel could see the peaked window of the room that would be hers, because this was going to be their house, and they were all going to live there, and paint it over. Isabel's room had eaves. Jeannie's room didn't. From her window, Isabel would look out over the yard and muse on the empty car until she grew up, and moved away.

Sitting in the living room, in chairs covered with Indian

print bedspreads, Isabel's mother discussed prices and taxes and land with Madge. The book on the top of the stack nearest to Isabel was called *The Diary of Anaïs Nin, 1931–1934.* Isabel began reading it, but the person didn't seem to have any friends, so she put it down, bored. The house came with fifty acres, Madge informed them, and Isabel's mother said that they could have a pool, back in the forest, down a path. Isabel and Jeannie would learn to swim. She stretched her arms over her head. "I just feel *right* about this one," she said. Isabel noticed a stain on the Indian print bedspread her chair was covered in, and wondered what had made it. The stain was the shape of Texas, more or less.

When was it, Isabel thought later, much later, long after her mother was dead and she herself had grown up and moved away, and visited Philadelphia only reluctantly—when was it that she began to feel so full of dread? When, in other words, did she know? She knew that the exact answer hardly mattered. She knew that the exact answer was *from the beginning* and *never.* She knew that her question was really a screen for a deeper and more troubling question, which was, When could her mother have been saved? Again, the answer was *at the beginning* and *never*. When her mother finally did it, she did it at the hospital where she worked, locking herself in a supply closet with a vast amount of pills, as if to say:

This is the size of my hunger. It circled outward: a pill, in a hand, in a room, in a hospital, in Philadelphia, in April 1968. As she got older Isabel increasingly referred to her mother by her first name, both in conversation (proprietarily) and in her own mind (ritually); her first name, Cassie, made her mother small, like a nesting doll, circled inward.

For every day of the seven days of the shivah, Isabel wore a black dress with a stiff bow on the back supplied by Nana, white ankle socks, patent leather shoes, and her mother's high school ring on its fine gold chain. The dress began to smell, but she wouldn't wash it. She wore the same dress at the unveiling a year later, her wrists extending past the wrists of the dress, the material tight across her shoulder blades, and at the elbows. She ripped the sleeves, pushing them back as they drove in from Springston, where dirt was piled up next to the open pits that would be houses. Heavy in her hands was the paradox her mother had left her: Cassie, a woman so hungry she couldn't eat, so tired she couldn't sleep, so lonely she couldn't speak. Cassie landed awkwardly on her shoulders, and pulled at her hair. Cassie had a keen, crude, innate sense of irony, saved from being entirely lethal to her children only because her lack of education made her somewhat overblown in her dramatic presentation. Toward the end, she often seemed like a girl playing a mad scene in a high school play; she walked

Riding home, they were happy. Isabel explained who The Doors were.

Later, a fight ensued. Isabel's father, jiggling his leg, said, "That is not a commuter neighborhood, Cassie. That's rural. They don't need a dry cleaner out there." Isabel's mother picked up her plate, and sat alone in the kitchen, staring at her food, while the three of them silently ate dinner. After a while she put on her coat and walked out the front door into the front yard, in the dark, leaving her food behind. There was a flash as she lit a match. She stood there a long time, the lit end of the cigarette marking where she was, like *X* marks the spot. It was as if she were refusing to move back into the house they already had. Isabel, eating peas one by one, wondered if her mother could live in the backyard, maybe in a tent, with a lantern. They could bring her dinner in a basket. At night, from the house, they would see the lantern light, shining through the walls of the tent.

March was supposed to come in like a lion and go out like a lamb, or in like a lamb and go out like a lion. The formula was reversible, like a reversible jacket. This March hadn't come in any particular way. It was just cold. So maybe that was a lamb. Isabel and Ann sat at the dining room table at Isabel's house, doing their Roman projects. Isabel's project was a Roman house; Isabel looked at the sheets of cardboard, brought home by Isabel's father from the dry-cleaning store. They were flimsy. The two precious gray ones would have to be glued together, for the stone floor. The rest were dull red, a dusty, clouded red, like clay. That was history: Romans did make their houses out of clay, and limestone. Plus, they weren't even houses. They were compounds, with fountains in the center. They had bathhouses, and wine-pressing rooms, and temples. Isabel's Romans were wealthy, with many children. They would all have their own rooms. Isabel planned to make the fountains last, out of shredded Kleenex. On the corner of one of the dull red sheets, Isabel wrote the date in tiny letters, then cut it out in a little square, to be glued down later.

Ann unrolled a long sheet of white paper. Her project was a mural of Christians being fed to lions. Authoritatively, she picked up her paintbrush, dipped it in red paint, and began painting a long, seeping spot, like a red shadow, along the lower edge of her paper.

"Aren't you going to draw it first?" said Isabel.

"No," said Ann. "I know what happens."

Isabel began measuring out the lines where the walls of the compound would go, drawing them with a pencil against her ruler. The pencil marks were silver, nearly invisible, on the gray cardboard. This, thought Isabel, is the floor. This is the floor now.

From the living room, there was the faint smell of cigarette smoke, the sound of the TV. *General Hospital.*

"I just love Jesus," said Ann, and sighed.

"I know," said Isabel. One of her lines seemed to be leaning; Isabel tried to erase it, but it smudged instead. She regarded the smudge for a moment, thinking. Maybe there could be a little inside garden there. Romans could have that.

"I'll baptize you later if you want," said Ann, cracking her knuckles. Ann was spectacularly double-jointed, and a Baptist. She had been reborn last year at Bible camp; since then, she said, she took Jesus with her everywhere, even to the bathroom. She could say the Lord's Prayer as fast as if it were one continuous word, like *supercalifragilisticexpialidocious.* She had taught the Lord's Prayer to Isabel over the course of one long afternoon that left them both feeling mesmerized. Ann was also extremely good with glue, even though she herself seemed to be held together with string. Isabel did not love Ann, but she was fascinated by her.

"I don't know," said Isabel casually. She did not say what she privately believed: that getting baptized might cause her to disappear, or become a zombie. They would begin it as a game, and then it would be terrible.

Ann did not reply, starting on her first lion. His yellow tail curved energetically several times, whiplike. Through the window, Isabel could see her little sister, Jeannie, and Jeannie's friend Donna, who always had tomato soup in the corners of her mouth, dropping orange seeds in the bushes outside. The March wind blew in their hair as they bent their heads together, teaspoons in hand, planting oranges. From the living room, there was the sprightly sound of a commercial.

"I got this line wrong," said Isabel.

"Just keep going," said Ann intently. She bent over her mural, painting abundant fur.

The smoke in the other room freshened. Isabel knew that her mother would be lying on the sofa in her nurse's uniform but with her white shoes off, nyloned feet on the sofa, her arms crossed over her chest, as if holding herself in. She would be watching for her favorite character, Nurse Audrey, who always wore a scarf. The scarf was like Audrey's shadow.

Isabel made a corner. Strands of dark hair would be falling across her mother's face. Isabel thought: Marmee, Bertha, Ma, a ghost. But Cassie was her name.

"I'm hungry," said Ann. "Ask your mom if we can have something."

"I don't have to ask," said Isabel. She went into the kitchen and came back with crackers and a slippery plastic pile of American cheese on a plate. Ann unwrapped her cheese a bit at a time, holding the slice by the plastic, taking a bite of cheese, then a bite of cracker, dropping crumbs into her box of paints. Isabel folded her cheese into squares, fit the squares onto circles of cracker, then crunched down quickly, surprising them, the rough and the smooth together. She wondered if that was religious, to eat the way Ann was, keeping things apart. She wondered if that was a way to get to heaven.

Jeannie and Donna ran inside, giggling. The front door slammed as they began clattering up the stairs.

"Shut up, you guys," said Isabel, going to the foot of the stairs. "Mom's resting." They continued laughing, hands placed theatrically over their mouths, clattering into Isabel and Jeannie's bedroom.

Ann leaned over, peering into the living room, as Isabel returned to the table. "No, she isn't, Isabel. She's sitting up."

"No," said Isabel. "She's resting."

"I don't think so," said Ann, still peering. "She's watching TV. Look."

"She's *my* mother," said Isabel, not needing to look. "I would know."

Ann, cheese wrapper in hand, considered Isabel. "I have to go home now," she said. She dropped her paintbrush in the water jar. The yellow made a streaky swirl, then vanished.

"All right," said Isabel.

At the front door, Ann said, "Good-bye, Mrs. Gold," and Isabel's mother, leaning her head in her hand, said, "Oh, good-bye, Annie. See you." Ann, holding her mural by two corners, gave Isabel a distinct stare.

"Thanks for the crackers," said Ann, as Isabel opened the door for her. She held the unfinished mural over her head as she walked away, her half a lion undulating above her in the breeze.

Isabel closed the front door and returned to her Roman house, which wasn't anything but silver lines so far. Who were the Romans to her? Who was she to them? They couldn't see her, huge and in the future, reaching in to rearrange their furniture. She loved the Romans, and she hated them, too. When she actually read about them in her book, she tended to fall asleep. The smudge on the left was still unresolved. Isabel pondered it. If it was going to be a garden, the master bedroom would have to be either extremely small or moved somewhere else. Isabel went into the living room, and flopped into a chair.

On *General Hospital*, Doctor Steve was kissing Audrey. Isabel's mother, watching, lit a cigarette. It made her look busy. Under her eyes, there were dark lilac circles of fatigue. It was because she was heavy, or so she said; her insides were pulling her down. To Isabel, she didn't look that heavy. In fact, her uniform had begun to pucker at the shoulders, to sag at the waist. The two rings she wore—the ornate antique engagement ring, the plain wedding ring—were loose on the hand holding the cigarette. After the doctor left, Audrey took off one scarf, put on another, in a way that seemed to be significant. Isabel knew that one day her mother might go back to being an actress and join Audrey on *General Hospital.* One day Isabel might turn on the TV and there her mother would be, next to Audrey at the gift-shop counter, wearing her own scarf. Her mother would be famous.

"I did a line wrong," said Isabel.

"So just turn the paper over," said her mother in her low afternoon voice. In the afternoons, she was dreamy and distracted, like someone floating on a lake. The sofa was her afternoon raft. She rested there, surrounded by important items: her pack of Pall Malls, her lighter and ashtray, her fat book of Green Stamps, and her chipped glass of what she called her afternoon tea, though the tea was always cold, which was strange, Isabel thought; the tea was strange and tangy and adult, like anchovies, or smelly cheese. Her mother sipped the tea slowly, as if it were hot.

Isabel got up and went back into the dining room. She flipped around the cardboard sheets so the grays were back to back on the inside, shiny white on the outside. Now the floors looked like marble instead of gray stone. That was altering history, which you were never supposed to do when you went back in time, even if the Romans would have been ecstatic to wake up and find they had shiny white marble floors. It would be wrong, like giving them a car. But then, reconsidering, Isabel thought that maybe it would be all right: the marble, the stone, Audrey's scarves, fluttering in the winds of time. They were all a kind of team. She looked at the foundation of her house. It was just a big empty marble square, and it made her extremely happy, although now she would have to start her lines over again. That made her tired.

She walked into the living room to tell her mother this, that flipping the foundation inside out was fine after all, but her mother had finished her tea and fallen asleep in her usual way, her cigarette stubbed out in the little dish beside her favorite chipped glass on the floor. Isabel turned off the TV and let in the silence, the way you'd let in the cat. Her mother lay on the sofa, breathing quietly. Her white shoes, like two white lions, guarded her. An afghan covered her. The lamplight on her face froze her in time. Isabel secretly touched her mother's sleeping body with her gaze, touched it all over, because ever since that day at the house that was not in Springston she had not wanted to touch her mother in real life at all. She thought that probably it would be dangerous never to touch your mother again, never to lean against her or hug her or kiss her good-bye, so she touched her all over now, with her eyes, for good luck. Her mother had long, dark hair and a strong brow that suggested she possessed more than the usual number of thoughts. When her eyes were open, they were what you looked at: dark blue, hooded. She talked with her hands, and her hands were long, her feet were long; sometimes, in particularly animated conversation, they seemed to be getting away from her. But they were quiet now. Her knees, in their nylons, were large and perfect, smooth L's. Her uniform was white with gathers just below the waist that seemed nonsensical to Isabel. The collar was round. She had unzipped it a little at the back, revealing freckles, and a gold chain under her uniform that no one ever saw. At the end of the chain was her class ring, and inside the curl of the ring was written *Drama Club President 1954 Oh, Susanna!* Isabel knew that secret, that mysterious refrain. Her mother's elbows were rough, the victim of many sleeves impatiently pushed past them whether the sleeves would go or not; her forearms, resting on the afghan, still looked strong from winning at tennis, which was what she used to do continually, in the past.

Curved in sleep, she reminded Isabel of Cleopatra, which was the part she was playing in a little theater in Peterborough, New Hampshire, when she met Isabel's father. Now the sofa was her barge. The cigarette was her snake. Her shoes were her lions. Her glass of cold tea was mead. Isabel studied her mother's brow, wondering if she had seen anyone die at the hospital today. Upstairs, Jeannie and Donna made subtle skittering, thumping sounds. Isabel mentally hushed them. With her gaze, she touched her mother's crumpled pinky toe, hidden under the afghan. She touched the top of her mother's head, touched the waves of her hair. Then she was done.

Isabel wandered over to the living room picture window and looked at her own face in the glass, her face that was just becoming visible as the daylight waned outside. Her hair was wavy. Her eyes were dark spots on the glass, transfixing. She looked for her mother's face in her own, found it, lost it, found it again. After a while, she began to slide away from the inside. At first it was interesting, like purposely unfocusing your eyes, but then it became terrible. She had made a mistake, she realized, too late, as she began to burn from within. Her heart began to race. The burning crept over her and covered her like a second skin or a caul, which babies used to have when they were born, and it meant they were either lucky or unlucky, Isabel couldn't remember which. She stopped looking at herself in the window and sat down. Isabel, covered, burning, sat very still within the strangeness of the sensation, and her brain began to open like a dark flower and a wind blew through her stomach, and she began to feel blind, although she could still see. She bent her head. An elevator inside her plunged to the basement, then beyond that. The house was utterly, completely quiet. Isabel knew that she would not return, that she would be lost there in the afternoon, forever, as her mother slept on the sofa. The elevator went to hell. Isabel wanted to speak, but she knew no sound would come out, and that would be worse, to be trying to speak without sound. Her scalp burned; darkness rushed along her spine. She felt sick at her stomach and as if she wanted to cry, but it was hopeless. The dry dark had her. Isabel held her cool fingers to her eyes, as if she had a fever; the dry dark drew away slightly, then slightly more. Like seasickness, she thought. This is what seasickness is. Her balance began to return, and a minute or two passed, and then she lifted her head, and then she felt victorious. It was all right now. In fact, everything was even better, much better, than it had been before. Isabel exhaled loudly.

Isabel's mother, on her barge, stirred. The white lions remained immobile, still asleep. "What? What?" She was back in time now, and would age quickly.

"Nothing," said Isabel. "The wind."

Isabel sketched a rectangle for the bathhouse, an octagon—daringly smack in the middle of the cardboard—for the temple. Nana would like that, a temple right on the property. Her mother, at breakfast in the morning, or at dinner in the evening, pushed her plate away. Her dark bl under her strong brow were serious. There were creases at the corners of her mouth, and these creases, to Isabel, seemed medical and important. The March wind blew, sometimes like a lion, other times like a lamb. Isabel counted how many rooms her Romans would have: ten, exactly.

Isabel wrote, *My mother's face is as pretty as snow,* then underlined *snow.* That was poetry. Everyone was doing the exercise; Isabel was finished. At the top of her paper she added: *March 9, 1968*. She added: *Philadelphia, Pennsylvania.* She looked at Ann, sitting next to her. Ann was writing, in large letters, *Jesus is the ligt of the world.* Isabel felt a pang, because that was spelled wrong. Plus, you were supposed to compare something to something else, using the words *like* or *as*. You couldn't just say it that way: *My mother's face is snow.* That wouldn't make sense.

Isabel looked at the clock. She looked at her paper. *My mother's face is as pretty as snow*. In Philadelphia, in the winter, it always snowed. That was different from countries below the equator. In one of these countries, Isabel thought, and it gave her another sort of pang, they might not have snow, so they might not understand her. There would be a little blank in their minds, there, where the last part of her sentence was supposed to be. *My mother's face is as pretty as* ____. Isabel began to feel worried. She erased *snow* and wrote *music.* Ann had finished her poetry and was drawing a picture to accompany it, Jesus with little rays of light coming out of his head, like the Statue of Liberty. But did Isabel's sentence make sense now? Because you couldn't see music. Isabel erased *music* and put *snow* back. Snow was right.

Isabel's father stood at the head of the table, holding a suit jacket. Unclaimed clothes from the store covered the table and the floor. They did this now and then. Everyone in the family was allowed to pick; the rest went to charity. The rhyme was: Choose what you can use. Isabel had already commandeered a provocatively gold curtain to be cut up for Roman flags. It lay next to her at the table in a glamorous, exhausted heap. Isabel paused in her search for the other curtain to admire her father's slender pale neck, and the chain around it. Even in the summer, he was pale from being in the store all the time. As always, his hair was precisely parted, with exact comb marks. His wrists were delicate; he wore a thick gold chain on the right one. My father, thought Isabel, is like a *bracelet.* Or maybe a *bureau,* with three strong drawers.

"I've been refining the plan," he said, and cleared his throat. He sat down, jiggling his leg.

In the living room, Isabel's mother sat watching *Carol Burnett,* wreathed in smoke. Her face was impassive, the creases deep and intelligent. She absently pulled a checkered scarf back and forth between her fingers. It was the only thing she had wanted.

"Let's move *soon,*" said Jeannie. "Let's have dogs." Next to her place at the table was a tangle of pants, and a monogrammed ski hat.

"We can't move until school's out," said Isabel.

In his soft voice—he never raised his voice—Isabel's father explained that there was a very expensive, special machine he wanted that could clean your clothes in forty-five minutes: you, the customer, the commuter, in at 7:15 A.M., out by 8 A.M., sipping your coffee and listening to the radio, your freshly cleaned clothes hanging inside your car, encased in long, beautiful sheaths of transparent plastic. Once he had enough money for that machine, which wouldn't be too long now, probably by the summer, they could move. They could leave Philadelphia, where the neighborhood had gone downhill, and live where the neighborhoods were all new, everything in them new, new school, new friends, new families. They could buy a brand-new house, instead of living in this old and dark and tilted one, which belonged to Nana, whose feet overflowed her shoes.

"I don't want to go to school anyway," said Jeannie. "I want to work in the store."

"Well," said Isabel's father. "That's very flattering, Jeannie."

Jeannie loved machinery, loved going down to the store

and getting the same tour from Ari of the dolly, the steamer, the ancient washing machine with the mangle in the back. The presser: that was the machine, with its thick, padded arms, but Ari, the person, was also the presser. Lifting Jeannie up, Ari would put his hand on top of hers on the big presser and together they would push the bar down, enveloped in steam. Anything that the presser put into the presser came out dampish and amazingly flat. The impression that the person had made disappeared completely. Jeannie had a scar on her hand from the time that talking, talking, she got too near the big presser and it bit her. But her hand did not become flat. Isabel didn't care about the boring presser; she preferred the Suzy, a headless dress form clothed in a white nylon shift that was attached to a thing that looked like a bicycle with levers instead of wheels. Ari put shirts or dresses or jackets on the Suzy, making her different people, pulled the levers on the bicycle, and the Suzy exhaled a wild burst of steam. You could also pull the levers when the Suzy had no other clothes on and her white nylon shift would blow up. Isabel was very fond of the Suzy.

Jeannie took after their uncle Dave, who was the mechanical brother. She liked to hit the buttons on the cash register as if she were ringing up sales, and if she managed to hit the button that opened the cash drawer, she liked to remove the drawer and peer up inside the machine. Isabel took more after their father, who was the chemical brother. He read about chemicals at night, because there were always new stains being invented, and new ways to get them out. Isabel, looking over his shoulder at the densely printed dry cleaners' newsletter, felt that she understood the articles, too, even if she couldn't have explained them, entirely.

"Are Ari and Louise coming to the new store?" said Isabel, sensing a flaw. Louise was the shirt person. She had hazel eyes with long eyelashes, and was very nervous. Her only son, who also had hazel eyes with long eyelashes, was in Vietnam. His picture hung over Louise's table in the back, watching over the shirt boxes. He was in the infantry, and that was apparently good, although sometimes it was also quite bad, the worst. Louise was a kind of barometer of the infantry. She showed Isabel her son's letters, and together they decided where he must be, from clues, because he couldn't say. "I think they've gone north," Isabel might announce to Louise as Louise snapped open the day's supply of boxes. Whatever direction he went in, Louise said, "Oh my." The air was always humid around Louise's worktable.

Isabel's father waved his hand in a sweeping motion. "There are jobs," he said. "I'm not the only plant in town."

"But Uncle Dave—" said Isabel. Dave ate potato chips and Slim Jims and drank RC Colas all day with Ari and Louise in the back. Not Isabel's father. He ate dried apricots and yogurt for lunch, sitting in a broken chair out behind the store at exactly 12:30 every day, reading; he cut the fat off the meat at dinner. He did not believe in going to temple, which exasperated Nana so much she wouldn't say a single word about it. It was because he had never finished his education and so there were things he had to do now, to change.

"Of course, he's coming," said Isabel's father. "I've been trying to convince him to move, too. Get his own place." Dave lived around the corner with Nana in a house where canned soup and tuna fish tumbled magically out of any closet you opened. Dave found that, and many other things, very amusing. When Isabel's mother met Isabel's father in New Hampshire, it was because he was there with Dave, for the skiing, and Dave was the one who spoke to her first. He told her a joke. Isabel's father didn't know she was a nurse; he thought she was Cleopatra, but Jewish. She didn't know he was a dry cleaner; she thought he was a skier. Isabel always imagined their meeting like that: her mother all made up like Cleopatra, her father trim and neat as a bureau, on skis. That was like a little play itself. "Hello, Cleopatra." "Hello, skier." She went back home with Isabel's father and Dave to Philadelphia, and had Isabel, and that was a generation. Her mother was the first generation. Her mother, the first generation, stopped acting so she could be a nurse, but Isabel, the second generation, would be an actress forever. (Ann and Isabel were already making a script about runaways and quicksand.) Seen from the perspective of generations, it made sense to move, like people on the prairie moving west. If they moved west, they could live underground, in a sod house with goats running around on the roof. They would have to whitewash the walls every spring.

Isabel's father took a ballpoint pen out of his pocket, got a yellow legal pad off the sideboard. "All right, then," he said softly. "Let's make a list of what we have to do."

"We need three big dogs," said Jeannie. "Their names should be Larry, Curly, and Moe."

Isabel said, "That's so dumb, Jeannie," but she said it gently, her attention drawn by the unclaimed suits and ties and dresses and sweaters and blouses on the floor. One blouse was lilac, with ruffles everywhere. It lay on top, the queen. Who had not come to claim it? And why? Isabel felt sorry for the forgotten blouse, tossed into a pile of rude strangers, the suits with voices like old men. Maybe the sweaters were nice, if a little stupid, the thicker ones the stupidest of all. The gold curtain was all Isabel had wanted, although she was frustrated not to have found the other half; the rest of the heap seemed dismal and forlorn and haunted, all the unclaimed things on the verge of rising up again, full of people.

"Boxes," said Isabel's father. "We should all begin collecting boxes. Sorting our things. And Nana wants us to paint. She's going to use this as a rental."

It was oddly exciting to Isabel that soon other people, other families, would live in their house, people who might find a barrette of Isabel's, a drawing of Jeannie's, and say, *Look, this was who lived here long ago, in history.* The thought made Isabel feel simultaneously ill and happy and strangely powerful, as if she could spy on them, the new people, after they moved in. She could learn everything about them, one of them looking up from her book to say, *What was that? Did you hear that?*

Isabel's father said, "Masking tape. Newspaper."

Jeannie said, "A map."

Isabel smoothed her gold curtain over her knee. Maybe she wouldn't cut it up, after all. Maybe she would hang it in her room, in the new house.

"You know—" Isabel's father tapped the pen on the table. "Maybe we should look into building something entirely new. They're doing that a little farther out. I think Dave knows a guy." He wrote down on the list, *Contractor?*

Isabel said, "I want a window seat. Put that on to ask Dave."

Jeannie said, "I want a blackboard."

He wrote it down. "Cassie?" he called out brightly, the

comb marks all flowing toward her as he lifted his head. "Any requests?"

There was no reply. They waited a moment for her to speak, the three of them poised around the table like three people in a diorama. Jeannie put on the ski hat. A laugh crested and fell on the television. Perhaps, Isabel thought, she hadn't heard him. But no one asked her a second time.

Isabel's father jiggled his leg again, writing things down in neat block letters.

Isabel, collecting her curtain, said, "I'm going to do homework."

Upstairs, Isabel sat on her bed on her side of the room, satisfied to see that Jeannie's side was a total mess as usual, pictures of dogs pasted up on her wall, broken crayons scattered around, the insides of the music box she had taken apart smashed here and there into the carpet. If you ever ventured onto Jeannie's side, which Isabel assiduously, almost superstitiously, did not, you would always end up stepping on a tiny spring or a little crank handle, and hurting your foot. Jeannie also had a multicolored collection of puppies, stuffed animals, who lived in a plastic princess castle. Instead of princesses combing their hair, puppies crowded at the windows, reclined on the turrets, and were half-stuffed by their back legs down the chimneys. Jeannie's side of the room was like a cave.

Isabel's side, where she sat now, with her gold curtain on her lap, was neat, with certain things arranged in a particular way on her bookshelf, a way that told the story of her life: a green plastic dreidel, a note from Ann, a small ivory box with two tiny white ivory elephants inside, a string of amber Mardi Gras beads brought back for her by Dave, a papier-mâché knife, the blade curving optimistically upward, from the first play she and Ann had ever put on. Jeannie was not allowed to touch these things, ever; if Isabel caught her touching them, and that had happened, the punishment was an Indian burn. If Jeannie surreptitiously added some old junk—usually from the yard—to Isabel's collection, the punishment was worse.

Running between these opposing sides of their room was a force field, broken at the doorway by a wooden gate with a bell on it that leaned against the wall. At night, they put the wooden gate up to keep Jeannie, who sleepwalked, from tumbling down the stairs in her sleep. If you heard the bell ring, you were supposed to get up and gently, without startling her, lead Jeannie back to bed. It was important not to startle someone who was sleepwalking. Isabel sometimes awoke at night to find Jeannie standing by the gate, just standing there, her eyes half open, her hands fluttering. She never fussed. It was really quite easy to take hold of her small shoulders and steer her back into bed, back into her cave. It was easy, but it meant going onto Jeannie's side, so Isabel was more inclined to say "Jeannie!" in a purposely startling way. One time when Isabel did this, Jeannie opened her eyes, frowned slightly, and said, "Why did you wake me up, Isabel? I was flying." This annoyed Isabel so much that she pulled the covers over her head, and cried, even more enraged for not knowing why.

The gold curtain, reclining on Isabel's lap, had the faintly scorched smell of dry-cleaning fluids. At the store, her father put on long yellow rubber gloves to pull the clothes from their chemical bath and put them in the big dryer. A heady chemical mist swirled around him; he made everything new. After a while the smell would fade away, but Isabel always liked it where it still clung here and there in the grain of sweaters or the deep folds of pleated skirts. To herself, she called the smell *Kentucky,* even though she had never been to Kentucky, which was in the South. They were in the North. Kentucky, to Isabel, was just the name of the place where her father was: there, in the pleats, in a chemical mist, busy, busy, making his endless lists.

In the new house, so much would be possible. It seemed clear to Isabel that they traveled, as a family, like hurdlers, over a series of increasingly dim horizon lines. It seemed clear that every moment was important; it was part of history. The Romans hadn't known that. They had carelessly dropped their things behind them as they conquered what they thought was the whole world (and they thought the world was flat), never suspecting that anyone modern was going to dig their things up and put them in museums. Isabel, folding her curtain, resolved to leave something telling in the house for future excavators to find. *The Gold family,* they would say, nodding. *Yes.* The excavators, who would be bald, as people in the future were, would think that someone had left it there by accident, and that they were so lucky to discover it.

Isabel and Ann, living on a farm and near a river and near a sea in the basement of Ann's house, watched *Get Smart* from underneath the Ping-Pong table.

"I love Max," said Ann. "I want to marry him." Max and 99 were trapped in a room that was painted psychedelic colors; the walls were getting closer and closer together.

"Max!" said 99. "I think this room is getting smaller!"

"Him?" said Isabel. "I don't think you should marry him."

"Why not?"

Isabel looked at Max, who was pressing against a swirling orange spot with his legs. "I don't know," said Isabel. She was keeping the fact of their impending move a secret for a little while; having a secret made her feel superior.

Ann unwrapped her leg from behind her neck. "You have to know," she said.

"I don't trust him," said Isabel.

Ann cracked her neck, studying the little Max figure on the screen. "I see what you mean now," she said. "He has shifty eyes."

"Yes," said Isabel. "That's it." But she had just made that up, just that second. She felt dizzy from the lie.

Max and 99 got out of the room by talking on the shoe phone. "Hey," said Ann. "I know what let's play."

"What?" said Isabel, still dizzy and giggly.

"Come in the yard," Ann said. They went upstairs, past Ann's small, happy, Baptist mother washing dishes, and out the concrete porch steps into the backyard, not even pausing to put on their shoes. The ground was cold, like needles. Isabel stood shivering on the concrete path, but Ann rushed ahead into the damp yard in her stocking feet, looking around excitedly. "There!" she said, as if a ship had suddenly appeared.

They went into the green plastic-sided shed Ann's family called the barn, although it was only about the size of a garage. Ann's family seemed, somehow, to be rural despite living in Philadelphia; they all had an accent and went to the dog track on Saturdays, where Ann, aided by God, often won. Ann pulled Isabel inside the shed. The walls were ridged, with shallow wells between each ridge. There were a few bags of mulch piled in the corner, a wheelbarrow, engine parts, an old kiddie pool standing up on its side.

Ann wedged herself into one of the wells. "Get in the one next to me," she said. Isabel squeezed herself into the well, which felt nice.

"Pressure," said Ann happily. Then she popped out of her well. "Wait, wait." She dragged a bag of mulch over to right in front of them. "Okay, now," she said, wedging herself back in. "You be 99. Push!"

They pushed with their feet against the bag of mulch.

"I think this room is getting smaller," offered Isabel, and Ann screamed, "It is!"

"Oh, Max!" lamented Isabel. The plastic walls made her voice echo strangely, with a kind of peculiar bounce, like men walking on the moon.

Ann pushed harder against the mulch, grimacing. "I'm getting weaker, 99. Help me."

Isabel concentrated. In dreams sometimes, she could not get her eyes open. The light pressed against her eyelids from the outside, full of shapes, and though her eyelids struggled to raise themselves, they would not fully open. She had that same sensation now, wondering what she was supposed to say next. "Oh, Max," she said again. "What do we do?"

"Let's pray for Jesus to help us," said Ann, putting her hands together. "Oh, Jesus, 99 and I are having a terrible time. We cannot get out." She paused, as if listening. "Okay," she said, nodding. "Okay. Uh-huh. We will."

She turned in her well to face Isabel. She held up her hand to Isabel's ear, cupping her fingers. "Here," she said. "Call Jesus on the shoe phone."

"Help, help," said Isabel. She turned in her well to face Ann. "You try." She held her hand around Ann's ear and Ann whispered into her hand.

"Let us out, let us out," said Ann softly, breathing into Isabel's palm. "Let us out."

Isabel, turned in her well toward Ann, had that same dream-feeling of not quite being able to open her eyes. But the shoe phone seemed to be working, because as she looked at Ann she found she could see her much more clearly than she ever had before: the gentle open angle where her nose met her forehead, the punctuating dark fleck in the iris of her right eye, the faint down along the edge of her cheek. Ann's lips were always red, from biting them. Her skin was so white, and her hair was so black. One thin hip jutted out of her well. But was Isabel still 99, or was she Max? And why weren't Max and 99 married? Ann, carried away by the game, was singing "Go Tell It on the Mountain" into Isabel's palm, dampening it. Isabel's shoulders were beginning to ache. She was no longer sure who anyone was in this game anymore. The shed was cold, and the light inside was pale green, a pale and damp echo of green, flashing over the walls. If Ann let go of her hand, Isabel knew, they would both go shooting up into the sky.

Ann finished her hymn with one prolonged note, and hung up Isabel's hand. Then, biting her lip, she held her hand around Isabel's ear. "Now you say."

Isabel decided where all the doors would go. Here, here, and here. Some more, all around. In the other room, *General Hospital* clicked on, then, abruptly, off.

The sealing wax was scented and magenta and it burned a little if you stuck your finger in it before the seal was dry. The little burn felt strangely good, like an ordeal. Isabel's seal had written on it "IG" in letters that Isabel thought of as courtly, because they were curly and feathery and swanky in a way that would be pleasing to a member of a Roman court, sealing a letter for a messenger to carry. Ann's seal was a large cross. Isabel and Ann sat at Ann's kitchen table and sealed their script, which they were going to send to Julie Andrews, who figured in the plot. They took turns: first Isabel would make her seal, then Ann would make hers. They folded up the script, then began sealing all around the edges, pushing hard. Sealing wax seemed to put them in a bad mood, which was why they liked it.

"Would you ever want to be perfect?" said Ann.

"No," said Isabel.

"I would," said Ann, taking a break from sealing to deftly

pull a marshmallow into long, white strands. "Then you would know everything."

"Okay, but if you were perfect nobody would like you," countered Isabel.

"If they were perfect, too, they would."

"There aren't that many perfect people in the universe," said Isabel, feeling annoyed. Because of being double-jointed, Ann was, actually, perfect at jacks, but Isabel decided not to say that today.

"It doesn't matter how many perfect people there are," Ann pointed out, "because if you're perfect you don't care. Plus, a person can't be perfect anyway, because only Jesus is perfect. It would be a sin." She finished her marshmallow with confidence and picked up her sealing cross again.

"It's a free country," said Isabel.

"Not free to hurt Jesus," said Ann, making a series of magenta crosses laid end to end, in a chain. She raised an eyebrow at Isabel in the way that meant: *Your people.* "Baptism," she said airily, "only takes one minute and a half."

Isabel shrugged. The wax dripped and stank, slowly made a pool of magenta with black streaks in it, then Isabel pressed the seal down into it. One corner of the "I" had a tendency to smudge. But overall it worked quite well. Isabel tore a piece of paper out of her notebook and began making a whole row of seals on it: IG IG IG. That was almost a sentence.

"Would you ever want to go back in time?" said Isabel.

"It would depend," said Ann.

"You're not allowed to change anything when you go back in time," said Isabel.

"Not me," said Ann. "I'd kill Hitler."

"I don't know," said Isabel. "Then something worse might happen."

Ann, blowing on the wax, didn't disagree for the first time that day. They passed easily from irritation into hope.

"There," said Ann after a while. "Get the stamps, Isabel. It's all sealed up now."

Because her thumb hurt from cutting out dusty red walls, and because it was Saturday again and her mother would certainly be getting up soon, Isabel put down the scissors and went into the kitchen for a snack. There, left amid the scattered sections of newspaper, she noticed one of her father's lists. It had a grease spot in the upper-right-hand corner. In small, neat capital letters, it said:

1. SHOELACES
2. TAX FORMS
3. ¼ LB. AMERICAN CHEESE
4. ARI: SWITCH TO JACKETS; FIND HELPER FOR PANTS
5. DAVE: BIRTHDAY CARD

6. 1 WHOLE CHICKEN, CUT UP
7. WINDEX
8. 1 GROSS BLACK THREAD
9. BOTH GIRLS, DENTIST
10. CASSIE'S SHOES: NEW HEELS, TAPS FRONT AND BACK
11. NEW COMB, SIX INCHES OR LESS (POCKET)
12. #605: DAY-GLO REMOVAL; OTPR? CALL FRANK IN WESTMINSTER FOR ADVICE

At the bottom it said, ASK CASSIE ABOUT DR. BALABAN. Isabel read the list a few more times, then folded the piece of paper in half and put it in her pocket. The list was private, his private thoughts, and she was glad to have taken it. She got a piece of bread and started pulling the crust off as she strolled into the dining room. But then, picking up the scissors to resume her task, she realized that this was what to leave for the excavators. From this list, they would be able to reconstruct America, although they'd have to put some work into it, particularly for number twelve. Isabel unfolded it, wrote *March 24, 1968* and *The Gold Family* at the top, put it back in her pocket, then rolled the crustless bread into a doughy ball and began snipping sharp corners on her walls, happy.

Night was falling around Isabel and Ann when they realized that they had somehow missed "Raindrops Keep Falling on My Head" on the countdown and would now have to wait until next Sunday. In despair, they kicked at the shiny floral bedspread on Ann's bed.

"Do you want to go home?" said Ann.

"Not yet," said Isabel.

"Do you want to watch TV?"

"Uh-uh," said Isabel. "Let's do pressure."

"It's too late," said Ann. A black curl hung over her forehead in a disappointed way.

"We can go under the Ping-Pong table," said Isabel. "I have a new idea." They hopped off Ann's bed and went down into the basement.

"Let's take cushions with us," said Ann, pulling the basement sofa apart. Isabel crawled under the Ping-Pong table and Ann followed, dragging the two long sofa cushions, which were rough, slightly strawlike, and dark orange. It was dark under the table. Ann arranged the cushions in a line, then wiggled on top of them, crossing her legs Indian-style.

"Okay," said Ann. "Now what?"

"Lie down," said Isabel.

Ann stretched out and closed her eyes.

"Take your shoes off."

"You do it," said Ann. She was smiling with her eyes closed.

Isabel lifted off Ann's shoes, leaving her socks on. Ann's feet were warm and small; she waved them back and forth in their thin white socks. The underside of the Ping-Pong table was like a roof, covering them. Upstairs, Ann's mother ran water in the kitchen sink.

"Now—" said Isabel, taking a breath.

"Wait," said Ann. "What's this called?"

Isabel thought for a moment. "This is called—matching."

"All right." Ann looked pleased.

Isabel lowered herself slowly, slowly along the length of Ann's body: first her shins, then her knees, then her belly, then her chest. Ann's legs pressed into her legs. Their hip-bones bumped, then Isabel shifted over and they fit. Isabel stretched her arms along Ann's, stretched each finger out to cover each of Ann's fingers. Ann opened her hands out flat, so the pads of their fingers touched at the peaks. Isabel lowered her head next to Ann's, burying her face in Ann's hair. Ann breathed in, then out. She smelled like crayons. Their shoulders, Isabel could feel, were more padded than their hips; their shoulders could rest on top of each other very easily. Beneath their shirts, their flat nipples met. Neither of them spoke. Dishes clinked upstairs. Ann turned her head away from Isabel's head, revealing her neck, her ear. Ann's wrist pulsed against Isabel's.

"Okay," said Ann. "Okay."

"Okay," whispered Isabel. Her entire body felt warmly liquid, even the knobs of her knees. "We're moving away," she said, and Ann lay perfectly still, saying nothing, moving not one muscle.

They lay like that for two minutes more, and then they got up. Together, they put the sofa cushions back on the sofa. Ann walked Isabel to the door, stood there silently while Isabel put on her coat, her scarf, her boots. Ann leaned against the doorway, one foot up on the other knee of her red hip-huggers. "Good-bye," she said, biting her lip.

"Good-bye," said Isabel. She turned away into the cold. She ran her hand along the black rail next to Ann's three front steps. It was cold, too, like a black tube of ice.

After school one day, Isabel went into the yard with a spade. She was wearing her favorite corduroy jumper with the flower-power appliqué. The pink tights she liked most to wear with the jumper were full of ladders and bits of leaves from kickball. Isabel was torn between her sadness that the tights were ruined and the desire to pull at one of the intriguing ladders to make the run lengthen. She didn't dig where Jeannie and Donna had sown their absurd orange seeds. She dug next to the small, gnarled tree in their front yard, which was too low for a swing. In the new house, maybe they would have a huge tree with wide, spreading branches and many, many leaves. She had put the list in a plastic bag, which was cheating slightly, but perhaps the excavators would think people did that, in the past. She dug for a long time: past a root, past a rock, her spade chinking. Her hands were cold. A bug scurried away, suddenly homeless. The afternoon wind shook the little tree; it creaked faintly. Isabel looked up between the low branches, toward the sky; up near the sky, there was a swaying movement. How strange that was, she thought, pausing with her spade, that the tree would sway in one place and not in another. She was getting tired of digging, but dug some more anyway, her elbow twinging. And beneath the tree were the roots, and beneath that was darkness, and then when you got to the center of the earth there was lava. And it was that way all over the world. And then, up off the top of the tree, there was blue sky, and then clouds, which were really ice, and then the universe, which was dark, until you got to the sun. So, really, Isabel thought, shifting the spade to her other hand, it was the same in both directions: the earth, then crumbly or leafy or icy things, then darkness, then a tremendous fireball of heat, hotter than the hottest oven. How lucky they were, to be people with eyes and ears and noses, and not worms or fish. Worms did not have eyes. That was evolution.

Isabel decided she had dug far enough. The ground had

gotten very cool in this part, and dark. She dropped the plastic bag with the list inside it into the hole she had dug, pushing it down and putting a rock on top. She scooped the earth back in, patting, pressing. The excavators, bald and smart, were going to be so happy. Maybe they would even fight over this find, and one of them might sneak up on another one and kill him. Isabel stood up, dusting dirt off her pink tights. She pulled at one of the ladders, and it lengthened all the way to her ankle.

She stood for a moment contemplating their house: brick, two stories, the porch on the front, the number slanting up the doorjamb. Their house was both like and unlike the others in their row, each one like a different face in the same family, some prettier, some uglier. The silent man who never took off his raincoat came out of his house three doors down, and waved to Isabel. She wasn't afraid of him. She waved back, feeling terribly sorry for him suddenly, alone in the world with his too-big raincoat, like Audrey, alone in the world with her pointy scarf. How would the excavators know about him? Maybe she should have included a picture or two. Maybe she still could, in another spot, she thought, and she made a plan to do it but then she forgot.

March must have come in like a lion, because it had grown softer. Isabel opened the dining room window an inch as she considered the courtyard. Fountains: five. She drew five small circles. It was Saturday again, the last Saturday of March, March 30. Her mother was having a bath. After Isabel was done making the circles for her fountains, she was going to get up off her history book, which she was sitting on, and read about the Romans, sitting up very straight in her chair so she didn't go to sleep. That was her schedule. Next to her elbow, a stack of dusty red walls sat waiting.

The sharp March sun illuminated the dining room, giving the shadow box hung on the wall a rainbow shimmer on the beveled edges of its mirrored shelves. Dave had built that, as a wedding present. It held small, delicate glasses—aperitif glasses, they were called. The set was dull, little used, and always minus one, the one with the chip in it. The shadow box, which was the only ornament on the dining room wall, had a spare beauty. It ruled the room; it made their house their house. The wallpaper was blue, and stopped at a wooden rail halfway down the wall. Isabel felt as if she were on a train, traveling across a landscape in the dining car. One by one, she lay glue tracks for her Roman walls, then set the walls in the glue four at a time, so they wouldn't fall over: the library, the dining room, the bedrooms, the wine-pressing room, the bathhouse, and the octagonal temple, which wasn't easy. But everything was coming out right.

Isabel stood up, pleased. She walked upstairs to get the Kleenex for the Roman fountains. Jeannie's gate was leaning, folded, against the wall; Isabel flicked the bell on the gate with her thumb as she passed. They were the same: a bell and her name, which she loved. Pausing before the half-open bathroom door with her box of Kleenex, Isabel could see her mother's hand, slowly shaving her calf. Her leg was white, and her foot looked large and ugly. Isabel thought, *That's her foot,* and she watched it for a while, propped up on the faucet. From where she stood in the hallway, she could smell the soapy smell of her mother, and she imagined she could smell her foot, too, damp and soapy and fleshy. Isabel moved closer until she saw her mother's knee and spread of thigh, the edge of her face, blank as she slowly finished shaving one leg and began shaving the other. Isabel couldn't see it, but knew that there was also the darkness of the hair between her legs, underwater.

"Isabel? Could you bring me some tea? I'm sure Daddy left water on the stove."

Isabel went back downstairs, dropped her box of Kleenex next to her project, and walked into the kitchen, which smelled of toast and margarine. The kettle was lukewarm, so she turned the gas on. She watched the second hand sweep around the yellowed face of the kitchen clock—noon and thirty, thirty-five, forty seconds—until the kettle began to whistle low, under its breath. Isabel made the tea in the one china teacup, which wasn't very big, but it was painted, and it had its own saucer. She carried it upstairs on the flat of her hand, like a Roman messenger with an important letter to deliver.

Isabel opened the bathroom door.

"Set it there on the sink." Her mother's eyes looked large, the blue deeper and closer. Her arms were thin as the hands of the kitchen clock downstairs; they crossed and recrossed her body, uncomfortable, fidgety, as if time were racing where she was.

"Nana called before," said Isabel, sittting on the closed toilet seat. "She said you should call her when you got up."

"Really." Her mother leaned forward, soap clinging to her wide back, and picked up the teacup. "Thank you, Isabel. I needed this." She sipped her tea, her wet dark hair spreading all around her on the soapy surface of the water. "I could just be so lazy all day today," she said. "I didn't sleep one minute last night, I don't think. So much on my mind." She smiled. "Does that ever happen to you?"

"Sometimes," said Isabel.

"What time is it, anyway?" She pulled the plug and leaned back against the tub, bending one knee. As the soapy water ran out, the contours of her body gradually appeared: the freckled droop of her chest; the C's of her ribs, holding her; her hipbones, sharp and distant from one another; her thighs, like spears. Soap clung here and there as the water swirled away.

"I don't know," said Isabel.

"I have such a headache. Hand me an aspirin?"

Isabel reached into the medicine cabinet, then dropped two aspirin into her mother's hand, careful, careful, not to touch her. "I think it might be noon," she said.

Her mother set the china teacup on the tile floor. "Well," she said, "I'm going to get dressed and then we'll get in the car and go out to dreadful Springston, make your father happy. Is it cold outside or is it spring yet? This cup is so small, Isabel! Fill it for me again, honey, would you." Her brow was very pronounced this afternoon.

A plan occurred to Isabel. "I'll have it for you in the kitchen," she said. She addressed her mother from the doorway in a slightly too loud messenger's voice. "The tea will be in the kitchen." Her mother nodded absently, closing her eyes. "I'll put sugar in it," added Isabel, as a bonus. She stood there for a moment more, but there was no return letter to carry. She gathered up the cup and saucer, and went back downstairs. She spread bread with jelly, poured orange juice into the chipped glass, which she had to rinse out, and, last, made the hot tea. It was so much better hot. She spooned in the sugar.

She laid everything out on the kitchen table. She folded a paper napkin into a triangle, and tucked it next to the plate.

Isabel sat down at the dining room table to wait. She could wait all day, she thought sternly. Keeping a watch on the china teacup out of one corner of her eye, she began shredding Kleenex to make her Roman fountains. She twisted and glued the cottony ends, concentrating, and then there it was, at last: her Roman house rose inside the dining room, a walled city. Its dusty red right angles rhymed with the mirrored ones of the shadow box. Isabel laid a sheet of newspaper over her Roman house, to let it dry overnight. Covered, it stopped rhyming. She looked in her history book to see what kinds of houses the Greeks had, but they were practically just the same: another rhyme. Isabel considered giving in and bringing the tea upstairs again, but then decided, No, she wouldn't, after all, because that would be altering history. Isabel made a tent with her overturned book, as if that were reading it. She listened for footsteps. The kitchen clock ticked. In the other room, the tea was all ready.

AFTERNOON

Years went by at Lottie's house. First Isabel, then Lottie, turned over in the sun. Tea bags bobbed silently in the glass jar of sun tea that Lottie was brewing on the corner of the patio. There was a smell of boiling apples; they were making applesauce in the pressure cooker. They were stoned. They had the arm up on the stereo so that the first side of *Court and Spark* would play over and over. They were supposed to be watching Bettina, Lottie's deaf sister; Lottie had sent her out to the driveway with her basketball and turned the stereo up. Not that it would bother Bettina anyway. Lottie misted herself with the spray bottle. She encased herself in mist. Lottie had a thick scar that ran straight down between her breasts. It bisected her. On this side: Lottie. On that side: Lottie. She was a Libra; everything had to be even.

Isabel retied the straps of the black bikini Lottie had shoplifted for her from Woodward & Lothrop. Isabel was a Gemini. She was all uneven, like fraternal twins. In that way she was very much like Joni Mitchell: no two sides of her precisely matched. One breast (the left one) was larger than the other. Her right foot was bigger than her left foot. Her hair was one color in the front, but a slightly different color in back, and a choppy blond streak fell across her eyes. She and Lottie had dyed it with some of Lottie's mother's peroxide. It didn't look right. Lottie didn't say so, but they both knew it was true.

Lottie was the rule giver.

Isabel was attentive.

Isabel had had hopes for the streak as some sort of unifying force, because when she looked at her face in the mirror, she found that it changed constantly. It slipped from mood to mood: these Isabel eyes, those Isabel lips (too big), the small Isabel ears assembled themselves differently when viewed from different angles. Isabel held mirrors up to the side, the back, the front. Some of the faces were the right ones; others weren't. The streak did nothing to explain or enhance any of them.

"Are there any more cookies?" said Isabel.

on her ward who had had the same heart operation she did had died, one by one, while she was waiting her turn. The nurses and doctors didn't tell her. The other children just disappeared. Lottie, sitting on her bed in her hospital gown, not knowing that she had been born with two small holes in her heart, made a village out of paper cups. She wrote herself letters, although she couldn't actually write. She sang little songs. She felt her heart lagging behind, like Peter Pan's shadow, when she walked. The doctors took the chance; she had the operation, then lay in the hospital in her enormous stitches for several weeks, humming to herself. She was the nurses' favorite. After a while, she was sent home. She was a child then. She didn't know that her life had been risked. All she knew was that before the operation she couldn't go five steps without sitting down and after she could walk and run, too, although there was still some question about how much she should, even now. Because the few other patients who had survived this childhood operation had then died before reaching twenty-one. Lottie, like Isabel, had made it to sixteen. She went running; she went ice skating; she danced. Isabel was always impressed that Lottie was engaging in brinksmanship simply by allowing her heart to continue to beat. Lottie's scar bisected her, but it also drew her together, like a seam. And it was also a flag. It marked the spot where one Lottie—a Lottie who couldn't go five steps without sitting down—had disappeared, and a new Lottie—a Lottie who didn't apologize, didn't explain—had arisen.

Bettina, who had Lottie's eyes but was thicker and already taller, came to the screen door, bouncing her basketball. Lottie flapped her hand: *Get out of here.*

Bettina wanted Lottie to drive her to the mall. Lottie said, "No," soundlessly. That was the way they talked to Bettina so that her lip-reading would improve. Bettina wasn't allowed to sign at home anymore.

Bettina said, "Come on," her O's distended. Her hearing-aid string, grimy with sweat and dirt, ran down inside her shirt, mysteriously.

Lottie mouthed, "Forget it."

Bettina bounced the ball hard against the door. "Lottie!" It sounded like an alarm of some kind.

Lottie whispered, "You're a baby. Leave us alone."

Bettina said, "Fuck you, Lottie," the words stretching out like words written on a balloon. She turned away, kicking the screen door, her footsteps punctuated by hard bounces.

"Asshole," said Lottie, remisting.

Isabel, eating her third pecan sandy, said, "When's your mom coming back?"

"Not for a while," said Lottie. "She went to the pool." Lottie's mother went to the pool a lot. She was tall, and bitter, and smelled of chlorine. She spent hours in her king-size bed, making phone calls and listening to the classical station on the radio. She attended Parents Without Partners meetings and knew all about the life of Mozart; she frequently made comments to the effect that her teacher's certificate, like her marriage, had given her knowledge without power.

"Do you want to stay over after the dance?"

"I can't," said Lottie. "My father's coming tomorrow."

After five pecan sandies, plus a half, Isabel had a cigarette. The smoke was rough and dark and grating; smoking imparted the sensation that she was passing over to the other side of something, or that the other side of something was passing through her. It also made her feel thinner.

Lottie often told Isabel she should quit, pointing to her mother as an example of someone who hadn't, as if divorce and general unhappiness were a consequence of smoking. But Lottie also, indulgently, gave Isabel a silver cigarette case for Christmas; Isabel kept it at the bottom of her bag, filled with cigarettes, and flipped it open at parties. Isabel enjoyed smoking. Pot made her feel two-dimensional; once she had crawled under a bed after smoking too much dope. Drinking made her depressed. But cigarettes made Isabel more Isabel to herself in a way that the peroxide streak had failed to do. Smoking, things began to match, or at least to fall into a rough order. First, a cigarette. Second, the conversation at hand. Third, everything else: the present, the future, the past. Lottie and Isabel were in agreement that the past was a dark corridor filled with freakish or sad incidents (the door that mysteriously locked itself, the girl knocked right out of her shoes by a speeding car), the present was certain lines from certain books (*Nothing human is alien to me*), and the future was fame.

The sun slowly traversed them. Isabel and Lottie moved their chairs around the patio like the hands of a clock. Joni worried, went to Paris, went to Germany; worried, went to Paris, went to Germany. Her anxious train ran forward and backward, up and down the track of Lottie's scar, around and around the plume of Isabel's cigarette smoke. Although neither of them could see it from where they were lying on their chaise longues, they both knew that Joni's perch face was there on the inside of the album cover, the face of someone levitating. It was still their favorite record, even though it was three years old. Inside, Bettina, exiled, sullenly bounced her ball in the foyer.

Lottie said, "I'm just going to have the applesauce for dinner tonight. We've eaten so much today." Then she said, "I wrote a new poem."

"What's it about?" said Isabel.

Lottie, shining with water and baby oil, turned on her side

to talk to Isabel, low, as if there were anyone around who could hear them. "It's sort of about Ben, but not really. It starts out with a dream I had about being in this house with my mother. She was outside, screaming her head off to get in, and Ben was standing at the top of the steps, looking at me."

"Is it long or short?"

"Short. Like, maybe ten lines."

"Show it to me later."

"Okay. Before we go."

The dream was just like Ben in real life. Ben liked to set riddles. He was often cryptic. He alluded to dark depths and ironies by raising one eyebrow. He admired Lottie's poems; he respected Isabel because of her experience with death. It was Lottie and Isabel's contention that Ben's main problem lay with his father, a point they attempted to impress on him when the three of them were alone together. Ben listened patiently, said they were right, then reminded them how fucked up he was. He often wandered the neighborhood barefoot for hours at a time, dealing drugs and thinking. Sometimes he wanted to be a doctor, like his father; sometimes he wanted to be a poet, like Lottie. He said he stayed up three nights writing a play for Isabel to star in, but then he burned it before she could read it. Once Ben and Lottie started sleeping together, he would only show Lottie what he'd written; Lottie told Isabel it was really good, but disturbing. The fact that Lottie didn't tell Isabel the first time she slept with Ben wounded Isabel and made her feel unsettled when she finally found out. Lottie, twisting her opal ring around her finger, said, "I didn't want to tell anybody. It's private." As it turned out, the fact that Lottie and Ben were sleeping together did not diminish the intimacy among the three of them; if anything, it increased it. Lottie and Isabel discussed Ben; Ben and Isabel discussed Lottie; Isabel knew that Ben and Lottie discussed her. For instance, Ben also felt that Isabel should stop smoking and Lottie and Ben both thought that Isabel might be psychic. Lottie and Isabel worried about Ben's future, concerned that he would waste his IQ, a number that he refused to reveal to them, and that they often guessed at when the three of them got drunk.

Bettina reappeared at the screen door, visually faint but loud. "Lottie, you promised," she said.

"No way, José," whispered Lottie. "You lose."

"No, you lose," said Bettina, but it sounded like "Hoo hoos." Isabel started to laugh. It was like the screen door was talking.

"Isabel," said Lottie admonishingly, but then she started to laugh, too, until both of them were almost hysterical.

"Hoo hoos," said Bettina, crying now. "Hoo hoos, Lottie. I'm telling Mom."

Lottie gave Bettina the finger. Bettina slammed the inner door so they couldn't hear their record anymore.

"I think Ben wants to go tonight," said Lottie. "Should we let him?"

Isabel, the crumb-girl, knew how the night would go: the three of them in Lottie's car, Ben alternately wired and silent, Isabel flicking ashes out the window, Lottie and Isabel dancing together while Ben conducted business in the woods. In February, Lottie had kissed Isabel up in a corner of the bleachers, where they sat waiting for Ben. There was only one other couple a few risers below them; the band was bad, and the night was cold. It was a light kiss, almost the way someone might say hello. To Isabel, it felt shocking. Like someone pulling off a mask, or putting one on. Lottie's mouth was warm. Her eyelashes fluttered against Isabel's cheek. Isabel touched Lottie's hair. Neither of them moved their legs, which were flung over the bleacher in front of them.

Though they said nothing about it, the air changed between them. Two towheaded girls in their school ran away together last year; some people said they were really a couple. It was hard to tell, although they did look alike and hung around together all the time in the pottery studio, throwing lots of pots and glazing very intricate designs on them. When the girls came back, their parents sent them away to separate boarding schools. Ben was the confidant and supplier of one of them, but when asked what had happened, he just shook his head. Had Lottie told Ben about the kiss? Isabel wasn't sure. Sometimes it seemed like she had. Sometimes it seemed like she hadn't. But when Lottie asked Isabel questions like "Should we let him go?" it was, Isabel felt, a positive allusion to that kiss. They had a secret alliance, she and Lottie, forged in the dead of winter. They could call on it when necessary.

Isabel smiled. "I guess so," she said. "If he's good." But her mood was dipping. The sun had waned. The dismal, post-dope feeling settled over Isabel's sticky shoulders. She was out of cigarettes.

"I should go soon," she said.

"Okay," said Lottie, turning over to tan her back.

But when Isabel opened the back door she smelled a burnt sweetness. "Oh, shit, Lottie, get up."

They ran into the kitchen. Bettina had vanished, and applesauce had blossomed everywhere, running down the sides of the pressure cooker, on the stove, on the floor. What was left in the cooker was quickly burning to sugar. Bettina had taken off the lid—maybe for revenge, or maybe just out of curiosity. You could never tell with Bettina. She spent a lot of time on her own, often with her hearing aid off, listening to the white noise inside her head. She made mobiles. She said that their brother, Sam, was the only one who understood her; she didn't like Lottie that much.

"Christ," said Lottie, standing in the kitchen in her bare feet. She turned off the stove. Isabel uselessly picked up a wooden spoon, as if it would somehow rewind the scene, draw the applesauce back to the pot.

"I can't believe her," said Isabel.

"Fucking Bettina," said Lottie. She grabbed a sponge out of the sink and began slopping the stuff off the walls and stove. "Fucking, fucking Bettina."

Isabel pulled a great mass of paper towels out of the rack and began blotting in all directions. Lottie said, "That's a waste of paper. Use a sponge," and handed her one. As always, Lottie flowed forward, a skill she had tried to help Isabel learn. Lottie had told Isabel to stop drinking her tea with a teaspoon, to stop sugaring her cereal, and to stop saying "you know." Isabel had done all these things, but if she and Lottie were each half of Joni, Lottie was still the half that left places, and Isabel was still the half that stayed in places, waiting somehow, for something. Although they scrubbed applesauce together in the dim summer kitchen, Lottie was the one who had picked up the sponge. Isabel was the one who had picked up the wooden spoon. That was fate. In the future, they might both gaze out the window at dawn onto a foreign city, but Lottie would be the one who walked down into it. Isabel, brushing her uneven hair, would be the one who stayed at the window, waiting, always waiting, though she couldn't have said for what.

Isabel walked home, carrying her Dr. Scholl's in her hand. As she expected, everyone was in at her house, like clowns reluctant to leave the clown car. Her father was reading, as usual: *Nicholas Nickleby*. Jeannie was brushing the dog, leaving clumps of dog hair on the sofa. The dog, legs splayed, tongue out, panted in dumb ecstasy. He loved being brushed. Jeannie expertly parted his fur, brushing it forward, then back down. She paused at one of his paws, studying it, gently separating the pads. A familiar gravity began to pull Isabel down.

"The prodigal daughter has returned," said her father softly, turning a page.

"Hey," said Isabel. "Hey, Jeannie."

"Is, c'mere," said Jeannie. "Look at Howdy's paw."

"I have to get ready to go out," said Isabel, the gravity increasing by the second. Just looking at the carpet made her itch inside. Howdy, ears back, panted.

Her father said, "What's that?" Small and trim, his hair completely white, Isabel's father winced when he got irritated. He was wincing now. "Out?" he said.

Jeannie said, "You guys." A flurry of dog hair surrounded her. Howdy began to get an erection, the small pink tip of his canine penis pushing into the sofa cushion. Isabel felt her feet growing into the floor, as into a bog.

"Isabel," said her father, proceeding from wincing to leg jiggling. "Isabel—"

Isabel turned and began walking up the stairs. "Lottie's picking me up after dinner."

"I don't think so," said her father, getting up.

"Well, I do think so," said Isabel. At the top of the stairs now, she looked at her father standing at the bottom, thumb holding his place in *Nicholas Nickleby*. For the rest of her life, she knew, he would try to bar her way, wincing, irritated, outlined on all sides by the violent absence of Isabel's mother, like a man struck by lightning. The lightning was all around him still. He looked up at Isabel, wincing. "We need to talk about a few things," he said.

Jeannie and the dog went out into the yard. Through the picture window, Isabel could see them sit down together on the grass, and Jeannie resume brushing his tail with professional concentration. Though she'd been round all over as a child, only Jeannie's face was still round now, with softly backflipping scoops of light brown hair on either side. She crossed her small bare feet as she brushed; dog hair blew away, bright in the breeze.

"Leave me the fuck alone," said Isabel. "All right? Just leave me the fuck alone." She went into the bathroom and slammed the door.

Sitting on the closed toilet in her cutoffs, her bikini, and her Dr. Scholl's, Isabel felt cold all over. Rooms within rooms within rooms opened up and in the middle was Isabel, safe and quiet. Her hair had Coppertone in it; the hair on her arms was already bleached white. It was only June, but she was well on her way to being a different person: a tan person, a citizen not of Springston, but of the country of tan people, like Joni Mitchell, who lived in L.A.

Stepping out of her cutoffs and untying her bikini strings, Isabel began running a bath. Strings dangling at her waist, Isabel sat back down on the toilet and stared at the various dog breeds Jeannie had glued over the towel rack: French bulldog, German shepherd, Alsatian. The dogs' feet were already curling from the steam. Howdy, named by Jeannie when she found him at the supermarket, was of no known breed. His only talent was for fellating himself. Isabel pressed gently at the Alsatian's curly feet, trying to get them to re-adhere.

Isabel finished undressing, stepped into the tub, held her nose, and dunked her whole head. The gravity lightened a degree. The day ran off through the ends of Isabel's hair. She trailed one hand through the warm water. The way she thought about it most recently was: She took herself out.

There was some comfort in the activeness of that idea, because it often seemed that Isabel's mother had simply slid from sleeping to strange to gone. Isabel thought that her mother's hair had darkened in those last few months, thickened, like vines. She had no idea whether this had really happened. She didn't want to ask; she knew it wasn't scientifically possible. It was simply her particular image and she guarded it as jealously as if it were an explanation.

There was comfort in the numbers of her mother's age, too, little corners to stretch the story out on. Thirty. Three, zero. Like her mother: here, gone. The evening of the day it happened—an ordinary day, a school day—Isabel had looked at her Roman house sitting on the dining room table; it was elaborate and airy, each room leading squarely into the next, the doorways slightly wavy from her struggles with the little scissors. She leaned down and peered into the rooms from a Roman point of view, as if she were a tiny Roman walking through the courtyard, walking through the stables. Her tiny Roman robes billowed out behind her; her sandals echoed on the marble floors. She could hear her father on the phone, making call after call, efficiently, somberly. He said, "There's been an accident." Inside the Roman house, everything was silent, the Kleenex fountains percolating motionlessly in the ancient Roman air. In history, she thought, everything had already happened. It was already over, and long ago, not *now* but *then*. You could build a model of it, using Kleenex.

When they finally moved to Springston, Isabel's father sold a great deal of the furniture, and bought everything new. It smelled new for months. It was the kind of furniture that would always look new, too, never soften, never scratch. Lottie was right about their spending habits; her father always paid full price, and he was particularly fond of the dining room table, which came from Sweden and had chrome legs, ever shiny. Sitting at it, his hair perfectly combed, his fingernails perfectly clean, he made plans for modernizing the store. After it was modernized, he expanded it. Uncle Dave, who reverse-commuted to the store every day and tossed life back like it was a peanut, said, "Bobby, you should date."

Instead of dating, he went to night school to get his college degree; his logic books and D. H. Lawrence occupied a shelf over the register at the store so that he could read them when it was slow. He took a course in Charles Dickens, and was hooked. He read *David Copperfield*. Then he read *Great Expectations*. Then he read *Pickwick Papers*. Charles Dickens meant something to him that Isabel couldn't discern: glancing over his shoulder, she saw only that the type was small, the pages thin, the spine extremely thick. The more Dickens her father read, the more determined to get ahead he seemed to become. He got up early in the mornings to run. He often said that he did not intend for his daughters to take over the business from him; he didn't send them to Hebrew school. "This is the twentieth century," he said. Isabel's father was a great fan of the twentieth century.

Isabel's mother had not believed in the twentieth century; she was caught in some sort of endless loop in which every event turned out to prove, ironically, the persistence of the events that had preceded it. Her death had been a shock to all of them, but, in another way, not a shock. She was repeating something, proving a point. Her hair grew darker, darker, darker; Isabel imagined it darkening in the grave.

Isabel wasn't in a crying phase anymore. That was the difference between her and Jeannie, who cried on Yom Kippur, though they didn't observe it, or if she saw a dog somewhere. All dogs looked lost to Jeannie, which was annoying. Isabel was in a realistic, contemplative phase. It wasn't an accident in any sense of the word. It was a choice, obviously. She did take herself out. Like a soldier. Like one soldier shooting another when the pain got too bad. Her mother was both soldiers; she was double. She took herself out: she was both the subject and the object of the same sentence. It wasn't that Isabel didn't miss her. Isabel missed her every day. But just now she was caught up in the loops of that grammar, the grammar of someone making herself disappear. It seemed like something would always have to be left over, to keep doing the making. But nothing was left over, except the heavy immobile house, and the three of them, and the dog, and the driveway, and the terrifying new furniture, and endless Charles Dickens, and all the time before and after she took herself out somewhere they couldn't follow, a stranger to them in the end.

Isabel contemplated her body, separated by her tan lines into white continents and dark ones. The dark ones looked taut and confident; the white ones, shy and pornographic. She reminded herself that the reasons she had to be an actress were, first, because her face was so different in different lights, like the face of a lake. Second, because of her mother, who was a really good actress before she married Isabel's father and moved to Philadelphia. Third, because of Lottie. This last had a sense she couldn't articulate but that she knew was solid. It had something to do with Lottie's scar, and the silver cigarette case, and even Ben. These things made up the early Isabel. She didn't need to be famous particularly, but she did envision a succession of Isabels, some businesslike, some harrowed. Some could even be fat. Isabel did not, however, act in school plays. She had acted in her first and last one when she was eleven. It was about the underground railroad; she played Harriet Tubman. "Come along!" she had to say to the other eleven-year-old slaves, in her head rag. "Come along on this journey to freedom!"

That experience had nothing to do with acting. Acting had to do with walking out of her house in the early morning down the suburban streets, just walking, barefoot, past the sleeping houses. From each house, a different Isabel might emerge—one with a baby, one with a sword. One, like Faye Dunaway in *Bonnie and Clyde,* with a machine gun and beautiful torn underwear. Acting was not about nature. Isabel didn't care about trees. Acting was murder, theft, arson, and the more crushing forms of boredom. Acting was her father, matching tickets to receipts at night in the shop, one by one. Acting was her mother's ring on its old gold chain, which she still wore under her shirt sometimes, with its half-obvious, half-cryptic inscription: *Drama Club President 1954 Oh, Susanna!* Her mother had been sixteen then, in 1954.

Isabel acted by herself; she practiced her sense of presence. She sat quietly with her hands on her knees, exuding sadness, then joy, then the patience of a hero who was concealing a vital secret from some enemy. She attended Drama Club meetings now and then, sometimes pledging to herself to go every week, at others never to go back. One girl had the stellar complexion of a Juliet; one boy had frightening imitative capacities. They both had complicated relationships with the drama teacher, a slight man with a little Hitler-y moustache and a speech impediment that had deleted the R from his personal alphabet. Isabel despised them all. Acting, she thought, should not make you less than you already were, even if you weren't that much to begin with. Isabel dutifully read plays, trying to make sure she covered the classics, in their dull yellow covers. Secretly, they bored her, except for *No Exit,* which she found strangely compelling and read twice. It was movies that made her wild. She saw everything that came to the mall: *The Way We Were, Love and Death, The Sailor Who Fell from Grace with the Sea.* She sat through *Nashville* three times in one day, blurring her senses until by the end she was both the singer who got shot and the bullet that shot her. There was nothing at school that would let her play the bullet. And, besides, she didn't want to be a high school actress; she knew what that was. There were no close-ups in the Pierce High production of *Brigadoon.* What she had was something different, and she felt that she had to lift it up over her school days the way you'd instinctively lift a precious package up over a puddle, holding it tight just in case it should drop.

Isabel arose gracefully out of the tub like a woman in a commercial. She looked at herself in the mirror with clean, wet hair: she looked like a boy named Ray, or Roy. She could play that. Downstairs, her father and Jeannie and Howdy followed each other around, Howdy's tags jingling, Jeannie explaining his paw problem in detail, her father rattling silverware. In a movie, that would be background noise.

The candy sat in big baskets on the other side of the counter: Ghirardelli chocolate bars named after San Francisco streets, green and yellow and white foil-wrapped candy Kisses, carob-coated nut clusters. Isabel, in her blue Pier 1 smock, was supposed to guard it, which she did in the sense that she didn't allow anyone but herself to steal it. When no one else was up front, which was often, she ruled with a benevolent hand that could also, however, snap shut without warning. Isabel reached over the counter and picked up a Market Street, then called Lottie on the phone before her shift at Shakey's. She spoke very softly, knowing that the manager was listening on the intercom in the basement; John kept the intercom open all the time so he could spy on them.

"What happened after I left last night?" she said.

"It got weird. Ben was weird," said Lottie.

"Weird how?" Isabel bit into the chocolate bar, already feeling sick and bored with ruling.

Lottie said, "I don't know. Just weird. Come over tonight after work. My mom'll be out."

"Okay," said Isabel. They hung up.

The store was dead. Wicker creaked to itself here and there. Two small boys were shoplifting incense burners in the fourth aisle, stuffing the brass lids down their shirts. Isabel decided to let them go; the burners were so ugly they deserved to be stolen.

She was unwrapping a Presidio and falling into a vengeful mood when a light-skinned black man with freckles and a girl with long stringy brown hair came in together.

"It was one of those days," the man was saying, "when everyone on the bus is either insane, deformed, or just back from the dead."

The girl had a list in her hand. She did not, Isabel noticed right away, shave her legs, which made them look fat.

"Don't dawdle," said the girl.

"Bitch," said the man, and the girl laughed. She wore a plain white shirt with the sleeves rolled up, baggy shorts, and wide sandals. Her hair hung almost to her waist. Her face was wide, with long, plush lips, and her eyes tilted downward. And though her legs looked so thick, her elbows were knobby, which was confusing: was she fat or was she thin? In those clothes, it was impossible to tell. To Isabel, the girl seemed to illustrate an old song she had never exactly understood before: she had a laughing face. She also looked familiar, but Isabel couldn't place her.

"We're looking for some kind of strange items," the girl with the laughing face said, smiling in a way that made Isabel wonder if she thought Isabel was stupid.

"Sure," said Isabel, stuffing the Presidio in her smock pocket.

"All right. One bamboo screen; two sort of rattan, imperial kind of chairs, do you know what I mean? Like *The King and I.* With high backs." The girl gestured above her head. "Five Japanese fans."

"Seven," said the man. "Ray will break his." The man was wearing bell-bottoms and sneakers and a dirty T-shirt that rode up to expose his belly button. His back had a funny sway in it, like a dancer's. His mustache dipped over either side of his mouth.

"Three incense burners, but big." The girl gestured again, this time at her hairy knees. Isabel glanced at the little boys creeping out of the store.

"What kind of incense?" said Isabel.

"No incense," said the girl. "It wouldn't be safe."

The man made a face.

"What?" said the girl to the man. Isabel couldn't tell which one of them was in charge.

"Nothing," said the man, waving his hand like a king. "Drive on." He smiled at Isabel in a way that seemed to Isabel flirtatious. He leaned against the counter. "Where are we, anyway?"

"My hometown," said the girl. "Okay. Jelly. I guess you wouldn't have that."

"Fourth aisle," said Isabel.

"Oh, really? That's great." The girl smiled encouragingly, as if jelly were some sort of major accomplishment on Isabel's part. "A beaded curtain, preferably with a little color in it, ten kimonos, and then we need a really, really long purple feather." She extended her hand outward. "But with a strong—what do you call that thing at the end of the feather?"

"Darling," said the man, looking again at Isabel, who blushed.

"You know what I mean," the girl said to Isabel, as if she and Isabel were the sensible ones. "We have to affix it to this turban and it has to hold up for a while."

"Are you going to need delivery on this?" said Isabel. She wondered if the stuff was going to their house—she hoped it was, so she could find out where they lived—but that wouldn't explain the feather, unless they were going to put it on the wall as a decoration.

"No, we have a van outside," said the laughing-face girl energetically. Isabel felt vaguely sorry for the man and the girl, because they really didn't make a very attractive couple. She couldn't imagine them together in a restaurant. "And then, oh, what else? Some little things we can pick up along the way. Could you give us a hand?"

Now that the little shoplifters were gone, the store was utterly empty. Isabel came out from behind the counter, thinking, Well, this is different. The three of them began moving up and down the aisles together, finding items and stacking them by the front counter, the girl and Isabel in front, the man straggling behind them, studying all the useless objects for sale as if they were incredibly interesting, which, Isabel could have told him, they were not.

"What's your name?" he said to Isabel as the girl tore open all the kimono packages, looking for ones with flowers on the back.

"Isabel. What's yours?"

"Augie. This is Becca."

"Rebecca," said the girl, frowning at the kimonos.

"And what do you do, Isabel?" said Augie in an odd tone. Isabel thought he might be making fun of her, particularly since she was obviously standing there in her Pier 1 smock.

"I go to school," said Isabel, and then, as if to excuse the smock, "high school."

"Oh, yeah, which one?" said Rebecca, tossing her stringy hair back over her shoulder and gathering up a pile of kimonos.

"Pierce," said Isabel.

"I went to Pierce," said Rebecca, handing Isabel the pile. "Class of Seventy-four. When do you get out?"

I am not your maid, thought Isabel, the kimonos slipping silkily in her arms. "Next year," she said. "What do you guys do?"

Augie took half the kimonos. "Becca, help this girl," he said. "We're part of a theater company. The Well. Haven't you seen our full-page ads?"

"He's making a joke," said Rebecca, but Isabel already knew that. Hairiness, Isabel decided, had clearly had a bad effect on Rebecca, who then demanded, like the Red Queen, "Chairs?"

"Is that what all this stuff is for?" said Isabel, leading them to the back of the store.

"We're doing *On the Waterfront,* set in Hong Kong," said Rebecca. "Augie's idea."

This time, Isabel wasn't sure if that was a joke, though she wasn't going to ask Rebecca. She glanced covertly over her shoulder at Augie for a clue. He was strange to look at, Isabel thought, because he had a pot belly but he was so light on his feet. His body swayed gently downward from his shoulders, like an evening dress on a hanger, though his face was serious. He seemed to be moving slowly even when he was moving fast. There was also something about him, with that droopy mustache, that reminded Isabel of Deputy Dawg.

"That is a lie," said Augie. "We're doing *A Midsummer*

Night's Dream, with a kind of an Eastern twist. Becca's mad because she missed our all-black version of *The Little Foxes.*"

"Absolutely," said Rebecca, and she seemed to mean it. "Okay, Augie, those two?" She pointed at two high-backed rattan chairs with black borders.

"What do you think, Isabel?" said Augie, putting his arm around her shoulders. He smelled terribly of sweat.

"They suck," said Isabel. "Everything here sucks."

Augie and Rebecca looked at her with what seemed to Isabel a new respect. Isabel flushed; she giggled. "I act," she suddenly said, like someone jumping off a cliff. All at once, a vastness surrounded her. She hovered in the air. Then Rebecca gave Augie an amused look and Isabel plunged downward into a small bucket of embarrassment.

"Where do you act, Isabel?" said Rebecca.

Isabel felt around in her smock pocket and located a stale cigarette underneath the candy bar. "Not at school. I sort of study on my own."

Augie and Rebecca both nodded politely, as if they had choreographed it. "You know, Isabel," she said, "we use volunteers. You should come down one day."

"That would be cool," said Isabel, not at all sure whether she needed to volunteer, like a dog.

"That's how we got Miss Mary here," said Augie.

"Is that your last name?" said Isabel. "I think I remember you—"

Augie said, "Yes, is that your last name, Rebecca?" then strolled back up the aisle in his fast-slow way, waving backward over his shoulder. "Come see us, Isabel. Bec, I'll pull the van around."

"Stop calling me that," she said.

Ringing up the long purple feather that lay on the counter between them, Isabel remembered where she had seen Rebecca. It was at Talent Night two years ago. Rebecca wore a hat with a feather in it and played violin while five other girls sang a song: "Tomorrow's the day my bride is gonna come . . ." "All right!" Rebecca called out when the song was over, and all the girls on stage laughed. Isabel remembered thinking that they seemed to be out of a different era, but Isabel wasn't sure which era it was. Something before the '50s. The '30s maybe.

Now, here was the feather again, as if the one from Rebecca's hat had been growing over the last two years, although Rebecca herself seemed to have remained exactly the same. Isabel wasn't sure, but she might even have been wearing that same white shirt.

"Is Augie an actor?" asked Isabel, ringing slowly.

"He used to be. He's the director now. He's really kind of a brilliant guy when he isn't being an asshole," she said happily.

Isabel wondered if Augie was her boyfriend, but didn't want to ask. "That's it," said Isabel. "That's everything." Rebecca pulled a credit card out of the pocket of her baggy shorts and Isabel ran it through the machine; it was her own: Rebecca Fried, it said.

After Isabel helped them load everything into the van ("Bend at the knees, Isabel," Rebecca said), Augie slid over and Rebecca hopped up into the driver's seat. Leaning out the van window to check for cars behind them, she rapped the van with her knuckles, her hippie hair wisping down the van door. "The Well," she said. "Don't forget, Isabel."

"Ciao, Is," called Augie, waving backward, as they pulled away. When Isabel returned alone to her wicker domain, even finishing off the Presidio didn't lift the dust, and even smoking her last, stale cigarette with John out on the warm loading dock didn't make the rattan suck any less.

"Oh, you know who she is?" said Lottie, gently prying a plant out of a small pot and depositing it into a larger one. The greenhouse light glowed; Lottie sat with her legs folded up under her, like a child, as she worked. Her opal ring flashed among the leaves. Lottie's Earth shoes tilted in their heavy, backward way in the corner of the room. Isabel rubbed cream onto her freshly shaven legs. "She's that girl who dropped out of Juilliard. I think she's a cousin of Ben's."

"Let's call him," said Isabel, rolling off Lottie's bed, which was on the floor.

"I don't want to talk to him," called Lottie.

"She's a freak," said Ben, when Isabel got him on the phone. "The girl is like this totally talented violin player, gets into Juilliard, and leaves after the first year. Her parents flipped."

"Is she your cousin?"

"Not really," said Ben, breathing hard. He was doing reps with one arm while he talked. "She's like a second or third cousin. The smart side of the family."

"So what happened?"

"So she went to Williams instead, but I guess she didn't like that either, if she's back."

"Did she drop out of Williams, too?"

"I don't know. She's a freak. Really intense girl."

Isabel took a ring off her finger and put it on her toe. She tapped back down the hall to Lottie's room.

"Lottie, I think he wants to talk to you."

No one on the bus was insane, deformed, or back from the dead in any obvious way; they were mostly just drowsy. The sun made the bus hot, aquatic. The passengers floated along inside. Isabel sat up straight in her seat and looked at the city of Philadelphia scrolling past. The listing for The Well in the paper was so small that Isabel had almost missed it; the address was on a little street in the city. Isabel finally found it on a map. It was near the river. The bus drove and drove, sighing to a stop every two blocks. That morning, Isabel had ridden to work with her father, who'd let her off at a bus stop in Springston. She had stepped up onto the bus with the excitement of a very small girl being lifted onto an elephant. The bus left Springston. First she saw large houses, then apartment buildings, then office buildings, then rows of small houses with convenience stores on the corner. Then it was nothing but small houses for a long time. The residents darkened. Isabel wondered if she should be nervous. The white bus driver got out and a black bus driver got on. Well, thought Isabel, admiring her own reasonableness, it must be the end of his shift. She noted the house numbers; they still weren't there. The bus turned a wide corner and Isabel panicked for a minute, but then saw a sign and realized that they were still on the same street. They passed a Kentucky Fried Chicken set back to back with a gas station. They passed a hand-painted sign that read IGLESIA, tacked to the front of an ordinary building, then a big white warehouse, locked up and silent as a tomb.

Isabel was now the only person on the bus; she moved up to the front. The bus stopped. The bus driver turned around and said to Isabel, "End of the line." He was thin and old, with kind brown eyes, like a bus driver in a movie.

"Thank you," said Isabel. Through the grand curve of the front bus window, Isabel saw THE WELL, written in green letters over a set of stairs that descended to a basement level. Two stories above were the bleached remnants of a sign reading CHINA DOLL COMPANY.

"When does this bus come back?" Isabel asked the bus driver, who had begun eating a hamburger out of a paper bag.

"Hour and a half," he said.

Relieved, Isabel descended the steep bus stairs, then The Well's basement stairs. She knocked on the gray metal double doors.

No one came.

Isabel knocked again. She hadn't heard the bus pull away yet, but when she ran back up the stairs to look, the bus driver was just making a wide circle and turning the bus around. Isabel, looking down at the door, thought, Open, please.

The gray metal door opened. The bus drove away.

The close-cropped head of a plump black man appeared around the door. "Can I help you?" he said.

Isabel redescended. "Is Augie here?"

"No, Augie is not here," said the man.

"Is Rebecca here?"

"No, Rebecca is not here either. Who are you?"

"I'm Isabel—I met them at Pier 1 the other day and they said—"

"Tell me later," said the plump man. "My story's starting."

Isabel followed him through a foyer into a huge, cool, basement room ringed with theater seats. In the center of the room was a large, not quite square area laid with a dull green carpet. A few fake-looking trees dotted the carpet, bolted down into Christmas tree stands. Under one of the trees like a Christmas present was a TV, which was on, and tuned to *As the World Turns;* the cord was plugged into a wire that ran up into the ceiling. The high-backed rattan chairs from Pier 1 sat in the background of the stage; a fan had been left on one seat. The chairs looked strange here, but also oddly right. From a little distance they actually had a regal air. The incense burners were here, too, three of them scattered around like tiny brass minarets. They looked peculiarly at home as well.

The plump man lay down on the carpet and propped his head up on his hand. Isabel sat on a nearby stump that seemed to have been made out of an ottoman.

"I'm Ty," he said. "This is supposed to be the forest. Augie'll be here soon."

On the television screen, a middle-aged woman with long fingernails stood tapping an envelope in her hand in front of a fireplace.

"Oh, she is so bad," said Ty, wiggling his foot. "She is going to open it. Watch."

She opened it. Music played loudly. The woman read the letter—a little fast to read a whole letter, Isabel thought—then threw the letter into the fire. The camera focused for a long time on the letter, burning.

"Oh my," said Ty.

The forest floor needed vacuuming. A cheap-looking pink nylon dress with spaghetti straps lay under one tree like a discarded skin. Though it was summer, the room was as cold as if it were nighttime in the forest. Ty didn't appear to mind. He watched his show, one foot twitching back and forth.

During the commercial, a very, very short man walked in. He had a long, fishy face and kinky hair and wore a peace medallion around his neck.

Ty twisted his head around. "Hey, Stuart," he said. "You in this one, too?"

"Yeah, I fucked Augie and he gave me a part," said Stuart sarcastically, hopping up on Isabel's ottoman with her. His little legs stuck straight out in front of him. I am sitting with a dwarf, Isabel thought, whose name is Stuart. She regarded him with compassion. Pulling a package of E-Z Wider rolling papers and a plastic Baggie out of his pocket, he began to roll a thick joint.

"Now, that I would like to see," said Ty. "Or maybe not." The show came back on. A doctor and two nurses were standing at the bedside of a man with stiffly perfect hair.

"That is so fake," said Isabel. "Look at his hair."

"Shhh," said Ty.

"Who are you, anyway?" said Stuart the dwarf, lighting up.

"Isabel. I'm a volunteer."

"Amateurs," said Stuart.

The front door to the theater clanged open, clanged shut. A tall, curvy big-boned woman with red hair, high cheekbones, and extraordinary blue eyes came in. She was wearing hot pants and platform shoes; her toenails were painted silver. She had an air of authority about her that seemed to emanate from her long, muscular legs.

"Hey," she said. "Where's Augie?"

"Out whoring," said Stuart in a cloud of smoke. He passed the joint to Ty.

"Oh, there's my dress," said the woman, sitting down under one of the trees. "I wondered where I left it."

"Speaking of whores," said Stuart.

"Please, people," said Ty. He passed the joint back to Stuart, who inhaled deeply, then handed it to Isabel with a challenging stare.

"You lipped it," she said, puffing.

The front door opened and shut again. A girl not too much older than Isabel came in. She was curvy, like the beautiful-eyed woman, but shorter, a smaller version, with long brown hair parted in the middle and a bumpy, largish nose. She carried a big, floppy bag with a sunflower on it. "Where's Augie?" she said.

"Not here yet," said the tall one under the tree. "C'mere, I have to tell you something." Behind her, Isabel could hear them whispering.

Ty turned the volume up. Stuart leaned forward. "Turn to *All My Children*," he said. "That's the one I like."

"No," said Ty. The front door creaked open again. A slender black man with a very smooth, young face came in. He was wearing a yellow crew-neck cotton sweater and khakis, like a college boy from the fifties.

"Our show is on, Dennis," said Ty.

"Oh, I'm late," said Dennis. He sat down next to Ty, stretching his legs along the forest floor. "Did she open the letter?"

"Yes," said Ty, and the Dennis one made a clucking sound.

"*All My Children* is much better written," said Stuart, trying to push Isabel a little farther off the ottoman, but Isabel wouldn't let him.

"Stop that," she said softly, thinking meanly: Stuart Little.

"Fuck you," said Stuart.

"I was on *All My Children,*" said the bumpy-nosed one. "When I was in New York."

"I am going to turn this TV right off if you all don't shut up," said Ty.

Silence fell. The joint went around. The tree the two women were lying under shook a little as they lay back, giggling, and bumped it, releasing a rain of glitter. They all watched the television intensely. Isabel remembered how much she hated soap operas. Next to her, Stuart began to fall asleep, his head bobbing toward his peace medallion.

"Maybe you could just tell them I was here," said Isabel at the next commercial. She picked up her army knapsack.

"All right, honey," said Ty.

Isabel was leaning against the railing in the empty heat, waiting for the bus to come back, when Rebecca rounded the corner carrying a big brown paper bag with some hats riding on the top.

"Hi there," said Rebecca. Today, she was wearing a batik-print halter dress that ended at her calves, and the same wide sandals from the other day. The dress fit her in a scattered way, as if it had fallen on her in the night. When she lifted a hand to shade her eyes, Isabel could see wisps of hair extending from her armpit, like a fern. She wore no makeup, no jewelry, except for three faded wish ribbons around her left wrist: faded orange, faded red, faded blue. Rebecca did not look as if all her parts belonged together, like one of those games where you made strange-looking combination people out of different flaps of cardboard—a jaunty pirate, who was also pregnant, and wore a fisherman's gum boots.

"Hey," said Isabel. "How's it going?"

"Great," said Rebecca. "Some of the *Equus* cast is coming to start rehearsals today."

"I think they're already here," said Isabel, following Rebecca down the stairs.

"Good," said Rebecca, marching with her bag of hats into the fake basement woods, like an insane person. "Hi, everyone," she said. She put the bag down on the floor. "This is Isabel, our new volunteer. These are the hats for the third act of *Midsummer.*"

"We've met," said Ty, waving his hand in the same imperial way Augie had waved his the other day. Maybe they were brothers. "And you know how I feel about those hats."

Rebecca switched off the television, unplugging it from the ceiling and wrapping the cord into a neat figure eight. "Where's Augie?"

"God knows," said the tall woman wearily. As Rebecca glanced around the room with a measuring sort of attitude, it began to look less and less like a sweetly smoky forest and more like a basement. She went into the lighting booth and switched on some overhead lights. The trees were missing clumps of needles here and there, and all of the seats, Isabel could see, were frayed; two broken ones were detached from the others and leaned against the wall like poor people with nothing to do.

"When does Augie come?" said Isabel to Ty, helping him carry the TV to one side of the floor.

"When he's ready for his close-up," said Ty as they set it down. "And not one minute before."

Rebecca came back out from the lighting booth. "Let's move things out of the way a little," she said, "and then we can just start as soon as Augie gets here. The way it works here, Isabel, is that we begin rehearsing the new one while the old one is still up. *Midsummer* has about another month or so. Then we open *Equus*. This," she said gesturing at Ty, Dennis, Stuart, and the two women, "is our fabulous cast, plus, you know, some horses we'll pick up later."

They began moving the forest to the stage's perimeter, Ty and Isabel picking up the trees to clear a space on the forest floor; a few construction-paper-and-glitter leaves dropped on them as if a strange fall had suddenly come. The room seemed to get warmer; Rebecca went into the lighting booth and put on a tape. "Happiness," sang some women. "Happiness, happiness, happiness." The bumpy-nosed one, whose name was Sue, and the tall one, whose name was Marjorie, picked up programs from between the seats and gathered them into a little pile. Rebecca made a pot of coffee; Isabel put lots of milk and sugar in hers and began to feel happy. She pushed the vacuum cleaner around the incense-burner minarets while Rebecca on a ladder passed filmy colored squares down to Ty and he passed others back to her. Working, Rebecca had an earnest concentration; she was like an Eagle Scout in a batik halter dress.

But at the same time, sipping coffee with Rebecca and Ty in the front row after everything was neat, Isabel had to admit that there was something cool about Rebecca. Something cool and clear and strong, like glass. She probably thought she looked nice in that dress. And Isabel liked how she sat with her arms spread out on the seats on either side of her, her hair hanging loose down her back, coffee in the hand with the wish bracelets, laughing with Ty. It was almost as if she were glamorous, although everything about her was plain, and her elbows were so sharp. *Who are you?* Isabel suddenly wanted to say. *Who are you and why are you here*?

Instead, she said, "I think I have to go home soon."

Just then Augie appeared, so quietly Isabel didn't even hear the heavy front door open. He stood at the edge of the floor, his hair blown out and wild, his T-shirt dirtier than the other day, and with an inward expression, as if he were still dreaming.

"Hello," he said softly, and they all turned toward him. He walked around the room and gave everyone a very deliberate kiss.

There was something so funny about the way he moved, thought Isabel. She had never seen anyone move that way before, as if he were built on an enormous S instead of the usual grid of bone and muscle. "Isabel," he said, when he got to her. Picking up her hand, he kissed her on the wrist. "Have you met everyone?"

"I think so." Her wrist was warm where he'd kissed it. He definitely liked her.

"Okay," he said in that same soft tone. "Let's begin."

The return bus filled up and whitened in the reverse order of the trip out. The closer the bus got to Isabel's neighborhood, the more Isabel felt that she had been somewhere distant and important. She missed it already, although when she left the theater she had been glad to go, because, really, they were all a little freaky. It was just some old basement in the city where they reused the programs from the night before. But by the time she got back home, The Well was as far as Rio, as unnatural as a glitter forest, as strong as coffee. And maybe it was the coffee that kept Isabel from sleeping when she went to bed. She didn't call Lottie. She just lay there, the day revolving slowly in her mind.

Isabel and Lottie drove Bettina to the doctor. The great blue hulk of the old station wagon streamed out behind them, like the body of a prehistoric animal. They made Bettina ride in the stomach of the beast; they rode in its face. Isabel put her bare feet on the dashboard.

"So what did he say?"

"He said, 'I'm going to go downtown and join the reserves,'" said Lottie, steering with one hand, her left foot cradled against her right thigh. Her other hand was tangled in her hair; she looked tired, like a woman waiting for her husband to come home from the war. Bettina hummed loudly, in no known tune, in the back seat, trying to get their attention. They ignored her.

"That is in*sane,*" said Isabel. "That is totally insane."

"I said to him, 'Do you want to *die?* Do you want to get shot?' and you know what he said? 'Maybe.' He's such an asshole."

"Then what happened?"

"Nothing. We went to sleep. I got up at four and walked home."

Lottie was always doing that: walking places by herself at night. It made Isabel nervous. There were things, as they both knew, that could happen, although Isabel did not really see any of those things happening to Lottie. Isabel imagined her walking through the shadows, her long blond hair shining, protecting her; seen from a little distance, Lottie would make a flicker as she cut through the trees behind school to her house.

"He won't really do it," said Isabel.

"He'd better not," said Lottie. "I told him I'd break up with him if he did."

They stopped at the medical building. Lottie pulled into a parking space, then turned around and whispered to Bettina, "Go to the doctor."

Bettina hopped out of the car and ran up the steps into the building, still squeezing the little ball she carried to improve her forearm muscles.

"She loves getting her hearing tested," said Lottie. "It's like it makes her this big star—she makes all these wild faces while they do it."

"Why do they test her hearing if they know she's deaf?" Isabel asked, turning the key in the ignition so they could listen to the radio.

"My mother wants them to consider her for this implant thing. It's new."

"So she would hear then?"

"Yeah, I guess. Wouldn't that be weird? To suddenly be able to hear like that?"

"You should write a poem about it," said Isabel. She and Lottie were each leaning against their doors, car windows rolled down. Lottie pushed Isabel's elbow with her foot.

"That is so corny, Is."

"Isn't."

"Is, Is."

Isabel looked at Lottie; Lottie looked at Isabel. A sensation passed between them, then flickered out, as if Lottie had passed behind a tree, and gone down the hill on the other side. Lottie reached into her pocket and brought out her roach clip in its little woven bag. "This roach is so tiny," she said. "Bettina won't even know."

"You go ahead," said Isabel. "It'll give me the munchies."

"More for me," said Lottie. In three breaths, the roach was all gone. They went on waiting for Bettina. Lottie began braiding a long, thin braid in the front of her hair. Closing her eyes, Isabel thought she must have gotten a contact high, because she kept having the sensation that the car was moving, although when she opened her eyes she realized that it wasn't, that she and Lottie were sitting there just how they always sat, utterly and entirely parked. Lottie, quietly braiding, was humming along to the radio with a distracted look. Isabel remembered the hole in Lottie's heart, and the dry dark came down on her, and she couldn't breathe. She wanted to breathe, desperately, but it was wrapped around her, squeezing, rattling in her ear. She touched her own forehead. The dry dark drew away. *I am here,* she thought. *I am here, I am here, I am here.* Her fingertips, cool and pleasant, made a fence with five posts. She stood behind the posts and waited. Her breath returned.

Isabel, back in the world, rejoiced at how simple and bright everything was, how unfrightening. Lottie, humming, was not one bit afraid of her heart. She was probably worrying about Ben, but he wouldn't really join the reserves. That was just something he said to upset Lottie. It was so like him, Isabel thought, to get everyone all freaked out when there wasn't even a war on. And it was so unfair to Lottie, because she depended on him. Who else did Lottie have besides Isabel and Ben? They were like three strands—Isabel and Ben braided around Lottie. It was wrong of him to tease her like that. It was selfish. He knew, and Isabel knew, too, that it only looked like Lottie was the strong one. But she wasn't. Not at all. The United States didn't need Ben's protection: Lottie did. Isabel decided to tell Ben that the next time she saw him. Bettina appeared in the doorway of the clinic, making victory signs with both hands.

Isabel read all of *Equus* lying in the tub. Jeannie had added a few new breeds to her collection: Rhodesian ridgeback, Maltese, border collie. The wall was beginnning to look odd. Underneath the greyhound, Jeannie had taped a little piece of paper that said, "A very good runner."

The play was gross, but also psychological. It was about an extremely fucked-up boy who reminded Isabel a little bit of Ben: on the one hand, he acted as if he didn't want anybody to know what he was thinking, but on the other he was always calling attention to himself. He had blinded six horses for what seemed like no reason at all. A psychiatrist was trying to figure out what was wrong with the boy, but he was even more fucked-up himself, as it turned out. Actors—extras—played the horses. Isabel splashed water over her belly. The horse-people didn't have any lines, but they were crucial to the atmosphere. She could do that: be a good horse. Plus, everyone else was British and her British accent wasn't very good, Lottie had told her.

Everyone sat in a circle in the forest clearing, reading through the play. Isabel held a clipboard and a pen; whenever they came to a prop, or Augie got a new idea, Rebecca would tell her what to write down. So far she had written down "silver horse suits," "tweedy jacket for Stuart," and "large metal spike." Ty had propped the front door open with a brick, letting in daylight and the heat of the morning. Augie lay on his stomach, turning pages, looking over his glasses at Stuart, who was playing the psychiatrist. He was doing his opening speech. Rebecca sat next to Augie, writing busily in her copy of the script.

Stuart, standing up and walking around the circle, finished with, "What use is grief to a horse?" He asked this question with great sadness.

Augie said, "Dennis, you and Marjorie should sit together." Dennis was playing the troubled boy; Marjorie was his favorite horse, Nugget. Dennis was very good. At the end of the read-through, he lay on the floor in a heap of misery, as if the world were ending. Then it was time for lunch.

"Come with me," said Rebecca to Isabel. "This is a great neighborhood."

They went down the block to an Indian vegetarian takeout shop that had three orange plastic tables inside and a green bench outside. It was deserted except for a tiny, very old, bent-over white woman in a long black dress, eating slowly and staring out the window. "She's always in here," said Rebecca quietly to Isabel. "Hi, May," she said loudly to the old woman, who waved one hand in the air, at the ceiling. Rebecca ordered a complicated stewy thing that she ate with a fork and Isabel got a long roll of pancake filled with potatoes; they took their food outside to the little bench. Isabel turned her face up to the sun. Lottie would be tanning and misting now, maybe painting her toenails while she smoked a joint. Lottie would definitely get a better tan than her this year.

Rebecca was wearing a baseball cap and sunglasses and overall shorts today. She seemed like she was in a bit of a bad mood, all brim and reflective surfaces as she bent to her Indian stew.

"How do you like it so far?" Rebecca said.

Isabel took a little bite. "Well," she said, chewing, "it's really great. The play is great. I was wondering—well, if maybe I could be one of those other horses?"

"I'll ask Augie," said Rebecca. "You know, he was Nugget when they did the play in New York. I actually saw him in it, with my parents."

"Your parents?"

"Oh, yeah," said Rebecca. "They're culture vultures. They see everything."

"Wow," said Isabel. "That must be cool." Her pancake tasted awful, like paint.

"I guess. What do your parents do, Isabel?"

"My dad's a dry cleaner. My mom's dead."

"I'm sorry," said Rebecca. "Was it recent?"

"Eight years ago," said Isabel. "She killed herself." She opened her soda.

"Oh my God." Rebecca looked very straight at Isabel, studying her, Isabel thought, from behind her sunglasses. "What did you do?"

"We buried her," said Isabel, beginning to overheat in the sun.

"I'm sorry. This isn't any of my business," said Rebecca, poking at her stew. "It's really too hot to eat."

"No, it's okay—about my mother, I mean." Isabel popped a paint bubble on the bench arm. "She always had problems. And then life got more sort of orderly. So that was good. My dad's very organized." Rebecca nodded in her sunglasses. Isabel imagined her eyes behind them and they were puzzled eyes; she tried to explain. "And, you know, she had always wanted to be an actress. So I think that's where I got the acting thing."

"Well, suicide is certainly a very theatrical gesture," said Rebecca.

"What?" said Isabel.

"It's very theatrical. It commands attention."

"I don't know about that," said Isabel, frowning, but even

as she said it she saw that Rebecca might be right. Her mother, in heaven or hell, taking a bow.

"Sometimes I think she was sort of like a soldier," said Isabel. "I can't describe it."

Rebecca took off her baseball cap. "That's quite a metaphor," she said.

Isabel did not think her mother would have liked that—to be thought of as a metaphor. No, she wanted to say to Rebecca, she really thought she was a soldier. She just wasn't sure where the war was.

Isabel decided to change the subject. "What do your parents do?" she asked.

"My dad is a conductor, and my mother did play the flute, but there are five of us, so now she only plays with this women's ensemble group she has."

"Your father is a conductor?" said Isabel.

"He doesn't have his own symphony or anything," said Rebecca. "He teaches and does some festivals in the summer. My grandparents were good Communists—labor organizers—and he was the rebel artist, but even so he could never do the whole conductor star bit. That's why—well, I went to music school for a while but then I left." Rebecca's nose, Isabel noticed, was beginning to burn, but she didn't tell her because she didn't want to leave yet.

"What do you mean Communists? They were Russians?"

"What's the matter?" said Rebecca teasingly. Their conversation seemed to have put her in a better mood. "You never met a Communist before?"

"You're not a Communist," said Isabel, pulling her hair up into a ponytail and letting the breeze blow on her neck. The scent of curry came along with the breeze, mixing with her ordinary Flex shampoo and Dial soap scent.

"And what if I were?" said Rebecca.

"You're not," said Isabel. "Are you?"

Rebecca nudged her lightly in the ribs with her sharp elbow. "No," she said. "I'm something worse."

"What was that supposed to mean?" said Lottie. "She sounds weird." Lottie's seamless tan extended gently to her feet, where it shaded away into a duskiness; her hair, fine and blond, fell around her shoulders as she straddled the chaise longue, flipping up cards, playing solitaire.

"She's not weird," said Isabel, curled up, puffing into the late afternoon. "And she said she'd ask the director if I could be one of the horses."

"That's cool, Is." Lottie spilled the black and red cards fast down their little ladders. "But that girl sounds kind of melodramatic."

"Maybe. Maybe not."

Lottie swept the cards into their piles with her tan fingers, tapping each completed one as she finished it, until she had her four. "Yes, she is, Isabel."

After four Saturdays, Augie pronounced Isabel a horse. He also said she was the best volunteer he had ever seen, not that there seemed to be any others, and entrusted her with opening up the theater for rehearsal on weekend mornings. He handed her the keys, which Isabel put on an enormous key chain, so as not to lose them. She wore the key chain on her wrist, like a charm bracelet, as she rode into the city on the bus. The weekends assumed a pattern: she'd make herself a lunch at home very early, get a ride to the bus stop from her father, and have the lights on at The Well by ten, when she'd begin the first of the day's many pots of coffee. At night, she'd hand out programs, and then she was free to leave, but often she stayed to see the show anyway, and rode the bus partway back home with Sue, who was playing Puck as well as several Fairies in *Midsummer.* Or so Isabel told her father when he came to pick her up. Actually, most of the time Sue had a date, leaving Isabel to ride the bus alone the whole way, but Isabel didn't care.

Stuart was always the first one there in the morning, wanting to run lines; he really wanted to be a serious actor and Isabel admired him for his dedication. He suffered from continual back pain, something to do with his dwarfism, that only his special hybrid homegrown seemed to soothe. His girlfriend, a woman who was not a dwarf but was very short, was named Mary Jane. She knitted one-of-a-kind God's-eye afghans that apparently sold for hundreds of dollars. Stuart had run with a motorcycle gang for a while in his youth, but they were mean to him when they got drunk and one time they hoisted him into a tall tree and left him there, gunning their engines and laughing as they roared away. Stuart still hated them for that, although in every other way he seemed to still love them. "They were the real thing," he said. "You know what I mean?" Isabel, nodding, felt that she did.

Isabel was pleased that she had begun to get the jokes—for instance, the Mary joke. When Augie called her Mary, which he sometimes did, Isabel felt pleased, because that was like *tu* in French. Often he'd wrap his arms around her from behind and whisper some ordinary thing in her ear like "Don't forget Dennis's crown," his belly against her back, his lips at her neck. Isabel stood quite still at these moments, electrical, entwined in him. Augie seemed to live in a world inside the world, a place that was smaller and finer and more secret. Stuart had told her that Augie was bisexual, a distinction that evidently didn't hold much water with Stuart. "He's a candy-ass," said Stuart contemptuously, and Isabel knew what he meant but felt that Stuart was missing the point.

Augie had what Lottie called *sling,* and sling radiated wherever it was.

Isabel began to wear her hair in a different way when she went to The Well. She pulled it off her face and wrapped it into a twist at the back of her head. When her father said, "Don't you look pretty and neat," she said, "It's because it gets so hot," but that wasn't true; in fact, the theater, being in a basement, was nearly always chilly. She snipped off the peroxide streak, which left a thin spot, but you couldn't see it when her hair was wrapped in the new way. It was as if, wrapped and twined around her hair, were secrets, new words, new things she had never quite heard of before and that she thought about for a long time on the bus home at night. Such as: the elderly male twins Augie said he knew who lived together downtown and spent all their time dropping acid and going shopping. When they came to the show one night, they looked disappointingly ordinary in their short-sleeved sport shirts and Sansabelt pants, though they did wear blush. Isabel didn't relate these new things to anyone at home, not her father, not Jeannie, and not Lottie. Now she understood why Lottie hadn't told her about Ben, that first time. There were some things that you had to hold close to yourself for a while.

It wasn't long before Rebecca said, "Let's do this for real, Isabel. You be my assistant stage manager." She pulled two battered headsets out of a trunk backstage and slipped one over Isabel's precarious twist of hair, deftly shortening the earpiece. That night, standing offstage beneath the fire hose, Isabel could hear whatever Rebecca said in the lighting booth. Dennis, wearing a crown, a gray and orange sarong around his waist, and carrying a plastic rose, stood next to Isabel, concentrating, waiting for his cue.

"Light cue three ready," said Rebecca in her ear. "Light cue three warning. Light cue three go."

Marjorie, bathed in blue light, paused in the papier-mâché grove, head cocked. Her sarong was slipping. Isabel stood with her clipboard, script clipped open to the correct page, ready to whisper to Marjorie, "Come, now a roundel and a fairy song . . ."

"Light cue four coming up," said Rebecca. Marjorie pranced a bit closer to Isabel, head cocked more intently. "She forgot again, didn't she?" said Rebecca, laughing in Isabel's ear. Isabel couldn't say anything back, because the audience would hear her, but she nodded. "Lordy," said Rebecca. "Light cue four warning. Moving on. Get it together, Marge."

"Come, now a roundel and a fairy song!" cried Marjorie triumphantly, prancing around a tree and delicately hitching her sarong back into position. Sue, as a Fairy, pranced behind her, singing, and then Marjorie reclined beneath a tree to sleep.

Dennis walked onstage regally, barefoot. "What thou seest when thou dost wake," he began, gently touching Marjorie's eyelids with the plastic rose.

"Isabel," said Rebecca in her ear. "You look so serious. Smile."

Isabel smiled tentatively.

"That's better. Light cue four ready."

Dennis, in his crown, finished his speech and disappeared behind the glittery branches.

Isabel and Lottie and Ben sat in Lottie's living room. Lottie and Ben lay on the sofa. Isabel sat in the chair. Ben, one arm around Lottie, was using his other arm to separate stems and seeds from his dope on the cover of *Yes: Live.* He was wearing a pair of wrecked jeans and nothing else, the jeans falling so low on his hips that he couldn't be wearing underwear. He had substantial muscles and lovely eyes, with long eyelashes. Together, as the three of them had often said, he and Lottie, who lay atop his bare chest in her bikini, would make beautiful babies. Idly, one-handed, he undid the bikini top string, then traced little invisible patterns on her smooth, brown back with it.

"I don't get it," said Ben.

"It's experimental," said Isabel. "It's really cool. They cast people in ways you wouldn't expect. Like, dwarves and stuff."

"She's friends with your cousin now," said Lottie. "That Rebecca girl."

"We're not exactly friends yet," said Isabel. "I mean, I know her. She's nice."

Lottie pulled at one of Ben's wild curls, turning her head to look at Isabel. "Is, do you think we knew each other in a past life?"

"Probably," said Isabel.

"How many more lives do you think we have?"

"As people? Or bugs?" said Ben.

"Shut up, honey." Lottie sat up, retying her top. "Really."

"Really?" Isabel gave the question serious thought, enjoying her momentary authority. "All right. One hundred."

"Only a hundred?" Lottie looked concerned. "But how many do I have, individually?" She looked like she truly wanted to know, sitting up on the old white sofa, her scar visible; the scar never quite got tan.

Isabel hesitated; she and Ben exchanged a covert glance. Lottie had the formula wrong: it was better to have fewer lives, closer to nirvana, than to have more.

"You have a thousand lives, Lottie," said Isabel, and Ben smiled. "Thousands and thousands."

Isabel didn't have to lock up the theater at night after the show; Rebecca did that. Usually, Rebecca's friend Jasmine came by at the end of the night to walk her home. Jasmine was black, with blue eyes and a tremendous quiet to her. She wore a thin circlet of leather around her wrist and no socks with her shoes. She told Isabel that she meditated every day; to Isabel, Jasmine seemed to be meditating when she walked, meditating when she talked. Jasmine always said "Hello, Isabel" in a friendly way, but Isabel wasn't fooled. She knew that Jasmine didn't think about her when she wasn't there.

One night after the show as Isabel hung around, dawdling, practicing being horses with Sue, she saw Rebecca slip around the wall into the entryway, heard the heavy door open and close.

Sue, still in her green and black, fringed Puck outfit, was shimmying. "Let's do like this," she said.

"I don't think a horse would do that," said Isabel, but she tried anyway. There was no noise at all from the other side of the wall.

Sue said, "Give it a little more—you know."

Isabel laughed. "I can't." It was silent in the entryway for at least three minutes, and then Rebecca and Jasmine came around the side together.

"Time to lock up," said Rebecca in a strained tone. Her eyes seemed to be tilting down more than usual; her lips looked smaller. Jasmine leaned against a seat, her sockless legs crossed, as Rebecca shut down the lights one by one.

"Hey, Isabel," Jasmine said.

"Hi, Jasmine," said Isabel. She held her wrist up, shook the key chain. "I've got keys, Rebecca," she said.

"That's okay," said Rebecca. "We'll take care of it."

"Come on," said Sue to Isabel. "Let's go." She had pulled a denim skirt over the lower part of her costume but kept her stage makeup on; she looked like one dangerous sprite.

"Okay," said Isabel reluctantly, turning away from where Rebecca and Jasmine stood under the remaining set of house lights. "See you guys later."

"See you," said Rebecca, turning away.

"Lo-ver's quar-rel," said Sue, as she and Isabel pushed open the door.

"What?" said Isabel.

Sue laughed roguishly. "You," she said. "I can't believe you work here sometimes."

Isabel, abashed, didn't say anything else. Slumped in the hard bus seat alone after Sue got off in the brightest part of town, Isabel shook the keys, quelled them, shook them again. They made their tinny, familiar sound, like keys anywhere.

The next day, between rehearsal and the setup for *Midsummer,* Rebecca leaned in a tired way against the ottoman, watching something on the little television and eating Indian takeout again, the same stew, it looked like.

Isabel, headset around her neck, sat down in a front-row seat. On the screen, a redheaded woman in a ruff was standing with her hands pressed against the front of her enormous skirt. Her back was extremely straight.

Isabel watched for a few minutes. "Who is that? She's great."

"Glenda Jackson," said Rebecca.

Isabel looked at Glenda Jackson. She had tiny eyes in a white, white face. She seemed mean. "It's all in her voice," observed Isabel.

Rebecca folded her arms around her knees, rapt. She was pale from being in the theater all the time. The fraying ends of her wish bracelets fluttered over her pale knees. Isabel wondered what she had wished for.

"She's such an incredible star," said Rebecca. "She reminds me of Greta Garbo—so knowing."

"You like Greta Garbo?" said Isabel. She was surprised.

"I *love* Greta Garbo," said Rebecca. "Don't you?"

"Yeah, sure," said Isabel, although she didn't particularly. She liked Jane Fonda. She mentally compared Jasmine and Greta Garbo: it made sense, in a way.

Isabel sat outside in the backyard, in the dark, smoking. Through the picture window, she could see her father and Jeannie sitting at the table with the chrome legs, playing Scrabble. He shook the velvet bag of tiles and Jeannie stood up to reach in, eyes squeezed shut. Howdy wandered in and out of the room, lying down, then standing up again. If her mother were here and looked in the window right now, Isabel thought, she would probably feel fine about how it had all turned out. Jeannie got her dog, and the store was bigger, and their house was bigger, and Isabel did well in school. Isabel wondered what her mother had thought about Greta Garbo, tried to remember if she had ever mentioned Garbo or watched a Garbo movie on TV. Nothing came to mind. She stubbed out her cigarette in the grass. She ran her finger around the inside of the ring, the inscription a whisper of lines and curves: *Oh, Susanna!* She twirled the gold chain around her fingers, the ring wrapping last, like a tiny tetherball, then untwirled it again. Her whole life, she thought proudly. This was the beginning of her whole life.

Lottie led the way into a Thursday night, racing ahead of Isabel, her eyes bright at ten, brighter at eleven. Isabel was staying over. Lottie's mother was out on a date. First Lottie and Isabel were talking and talking in Lottie's living room, drinking vodka and grape juice in old thick plastic cups, playing *Court and Spark,* the sliding glass doors open to the warm night. The room seemed to belong not to the rest of the house anymore, but to the outside. The room seemed to be dissolving around its edges into the dark. Ben was away with his family in Maine, Lottie missed him, she was so horny—Jesus, Isabel, she said, I'm like my mother already. Can't go a week without it. Bettina was with Lottie's father; at 11:30, Lottie's mother called to say she wasn't coming home.

"Is," said Lottie, hanging up the phone, "Is." Grape juice had stained her lips, the corner of her mouth. "Let's stay out all night."

Isabel set down her cup. "I don't want to," she said. "And I'm getting tired of this record."

"Well, excuse me," said Lottie.

"You're excused," said Isabel.

"Ooh," said Lottie. "She bites." Lottie lay down on the sofa and put a throw pillow over her face. "I'm drunk!" she yelled through the pillow. She sat up, alight. "Let's take the car and go down to the creek. We haven't been once this summer."

"I don't want to die in a fiery car crash, Lottie," said Isabel. She crumpled an empty cigarette pack. "But I am out of cigarettes."

Still holding the pillow over her face, Lottie reached into her shorts pocket and pulled out a set of car keys; she dangled them over the back of the sofa, making them jingle. "As if by an invisible hand," she said through the pillow.

Isabel looked at the keys; they were to Lottie's mother's

Pacer, which had AM/FM radio and air-conditioning. "I drive," said Isabel, taking them. "And don't throw up in your mother's car."

"I'm taking this for the road!" said Lottie, waving her cup.

As they backed out of Lottie's driveway, Isabel remembered how much she hated to drive the Pacer. The car was wide and awkward; driving it was like trying to roller-skate with a bar between your legs, and the bubble of windows all around it made Lottie's vodka cup visible to everyone on the road. Driving to Springston's little strip, they were the bubble over their own heads that showed everyone what they were thinking. Lottie turned up the radio. "I love this!" she yelled. "Welcome to the Hotel California!" And then Isabel, driving down the parkway, began to love it, too. She even began to love the Pacer. The parkway cradled Lottie and Isabel on the curves, hurled them along the flat stretches. The night breathed its hot wet breath on them. Isabel raced the streetlights to the strip.

Coming out of the 7-Eleven with a carton of cigarettes, Isabel saw Lottie sitting in the Pacer looking like a scented Kiddle inside her plastic bottle, if Kiddles could fuck and roll joints, and Isabel loved Lottie with a strong, uncomplicated, acquisitive love, as if she could simply put the bottled Lottie on a string and wear it around her neck, carry Lottie with her all the days of her life.

Isabel got into the car, which already smelled of vodka; Lottie, who was still singing, must have spilled some.

"Okay," said Isabel, turning the key in the ignition. "To the creek."

But first they had to drive past Ben's house, and then they had to stop at Jordy's, who was Isabel's ex, and then Lottie got involved in a long conversation with Jordy about Ben while Isabel and Jordy played Frisbee with the same incompetent malaise with which they had conducted their brief affair. The Frisbee skidded to a stop on the grass again and again. "I'll get it," said Jordy. He was skinny and didn't really like to kiss. He preferred to play records. Lottie, oblivious, lay on the ground directing her analysis toward the stars, and then Isabel couldn't find the car keys, and by the time Jordy found them near the pool Lottie was hungry, so they had to go back into town, with Jordy, for donuts, and then Lottie did throw up for a while on the service road near school, Jordy holding back her hair, and then they had to drop Jordy at home, and by the time they got to the river the sky was already bleaching and expanding upward and the world was getting bigger all around them.

Lottie turned the radio off. She said, "You're driving too fast. It's all speed traps out here, you know that." She kicked the vodka cup under her seat and folded her tan legs up under her. She closed her eyes, ready to go to sleep.

Isabel peered through the windshield. The secret creek road was marked by a certain tree with a piece of painted wood nailed to it, which she almost always overshot.

"Two point two miles from Friendly's," said Lottie patiently, eyes still closed. "Set the odometer."

Isabel set the odometer. The edge of town slipped past, the last backyard with the rusted swing set giving way to dense green trees where all the best keg parties and intrigue were, but now, Isabel saw through the Pacer window, one vast patch had been mowed to dirt. A rough driveway led up to a house standing starkly by itself, half-built. Though there were no walls on the upper story, there was already a lantern by the front door. So that's it, she thought sadly. That's how it goes. Instead of feeling tired from not having slept, she felt wildly awake, although in a half-transparent sort of way. She wanted to sprint across the field and knock the house down, smash the lantern into bits of metal and glass. I'd rather go to hell, she suddenly thought, and the thought was very satisfying.

"Look at that," said Isabel excitedly to Lottie.

Lottie squinted. "What? It's a house, Isabel. *Casa.*"

Isabel wanted to explain, but before she got the chance, the odometer rolled over from 2.1 to 2.2 and the correct tree magically appeared, as always, like a familiar refrain. Isabel stowed the Pacer behind it and she and Lottie walked silently back through the forest to the creek, where they sat down on separate rocks.

"No one's here," said Lottie, disappointed. "Oh, man. I am already hungover."

"Me, too," said Isabel, although she wasn't. Her head felt as light and clear as ever, maybe clearer. Isabel's rock said LAYLA in shaky scratches and then, a little farther down, MAX + SANDY 1972.

"We did it," said Lottie. "We stayed out all night." She looked happy, as if this feat meant something to her.

"Yeah," said Isabel, but in her new clarity she saw that the night had run out on them. She was hungry. Her lungs hurt from smoking for so many hours straight; she really should quit. The Pacer's gas needle was on low and Isabel only had a dollar. Her rock was cold. The creek was polluted. Lottie was simply Lottie. Isabel was simply Isabel. Isabel flipped open her little cigarette case and looked at her face in the dully reflective underside of the lid. A smear of nose and eyes and lips looked back at her indistinctly, as if from a distance, or in memory. I would like to write myself a letter, thought Isabel. *Dear Isabel . . . Dear Isabel . . .* She wasn't sure what came next. She clicked the cigarette case shut.

"Hey," said Lottie from her rock. "I talked Ben out of the reserves thing before he went to Maine. I told him I'd never sleep with him again and he changed his mind, like, immediately."

"Cool," said Isabel. She didn't bother pretending that she was surprised.

"It is," said Lottie.

"That's what I said."

"Right. That's what you said." Lottie's tone was testy. She was pulling at the fringe on her shorts.

"What?"

"Nothing."

"What, Lottie?" Isabel put her hand in the creek, which was cold, and pressed her cold hand to her forehead, watching the dirty algae wave along the creek bed.

"Nothing." A little tepee of threads began to grow on the rock in front of Lottie. "It's just—Ben thought you might be mad at him."

"I'm not mad at Ben," said Isabel. But was she? She searched her mind.

"Are you mad at me?" said Lottie.

"No." Tonight didn't really count; Lottie was drunk. Nevertheless, Isabel began to feel uneasy. Were they mad at her? "Are you guys mad at me?"

Lottie added to the tepee. "No, we're not *mad* at you. We do miss you."

"Why do you miss me? You see me all the time."

Lottie, pulling threads, didn't look up as she said, "Ben could be in the army now, Isabel. You wouldn't even know."

"He's not in the fucking *army,* Lottie. He is totally full of shit." Isabel sensed that something else was afoot. She began to wonder if that had been the plan from the beginning: to keep her up all night, then pounce.

"Unlike Rebecca."

"Rebecca?" Isabel's unease increased.

"That theater girl. I mean, I hate to say this, but you're a little obsessed with her, Isabel."

"I am not."

"You talk about her all the time, all the things she does, all the stuff she says to you in that little gadget—"

"I'm the ASM. It's my job."

"You just think she's so great," continued Lottie bitterly. "I know how you are."

Isabel was stunned. This was wrong of them, it was terribly wrong. They were snatching something away from her and ruining it, laughing as they tore out the pages. She stood up. "No, you're the one who thinks you're so great, Lottie. You are such a fucking snot!" She paced frantically on her rock. "You think you're so right all the time, you think you know what everything's about, the Great Lottie, but you don't know anything. Anything!" Isabel was yelling now, red in the face, smashing at the lantern. "You're just a, just a—" Isabel searched for something horrible, something searing, something that could not be taken back. "You're just a fucking *drunk*! And you know what else? You can drive yourself home." Isabel hurled the car keys onto Lottie's rock, scattering the tepee into the creek. The threads whirled away.

"I most certainly can," said Lottie, but she was crying as she jumped over the strip of river at the point of Isabel's rock farthest away from Isabel herself, who was left alone on her rock as the night ran down the drain. She stood there, fixed to the spot. She heard the Pacer start and drive away. What did that mean: *I know how you are?* She did not know how Isabel was; she did not really know about Rebecca; she did not understand about the lantern, or the house by itself in the dirt. Lottie's family was from Ohio; they were not from Philadelphia. Isabel was the one from Philadelphia. She'd never liked Springston. Isabel, standing stiffly on her rock, took comfort from that geographical fact. It seemed like the beginning of an explanation. In the distance, the sound of hammering began.

After a while, Isabel hitched a ride home with a lady dentist who told her the whole way how dangerous hitchhiking was for girls and illustrated the point with several gruesome stories that did not, to Isabel, sound entirely plausible. Isabel almost told Lottie about it when she got home, but then, hanging up after one ring, she didn't. Lottie was the one who should call. After a week went by, Isabel understood that Lottie wasn't speaking to her.

Something new and inevitable arose in Isabel, like a fin above water. It circled her heart. It drew a line.

Nothing was as beautiful as Philadelphia, where everything was old and modern at the same time. Nothing was so fantastically loud, reverberating inside Isabel's head all week long as she idled behind the counter at Pier 1, not really there, not really anywhere as she waited, suspended in motion, to get back to Philadelphia. Isabel wore her hair in the new way all the time now. She stopped eating candy bars out of the basket. She smoked more cigarettes than ever. She began going to The Well not only on Saturdays and Sundays, but on Wednesday nights, too. Riding on the bus, she watched Philadelphia flow by: its few ornate buildings, its row houses, its peeling billboards flashing then disappearing as the bus curved through the low, hot, brick city. Once she saw a man running with a baby in his arms, dodging cars to get somewhere, frantic. That was a poem. She saved it to tell Lottie, after they made up. She thought she glimpsed the back of their old house down a side street, but then she was never sure as the bus moved on and the house whirled away. Sometimes Isabel got off the bus and walked for blocks and blocks before getting back on again farther down the line. She looked in windows; she talked to strangers. She was never afraid anymore, even when it was very late and she was the only one on the bus. She learned about transfers.

Isabel breathed in Philadelphia, its bitter, its sugar, filling herself with it, trying to get enough to last her from Monday to the next Saturday morning—Wednesday was so brief, it only whetted her appetite. She threw away all her eye shadow and bought a shiny beige kimono on her discount at Pier 1. She sewed it up the middle and wore it every weekend when she went out with everyone after the show at night. She ordered Manhattans, like Augie, and felt exhilarated after one sip: she said there should be a drink named after Philadelphia, too, and he seemed to think that was quite funny. If she called her father at midnight so he knew she was alive, she could stay out even later, so she never forgot to call; she began wearing a watch. She danced with Augie, who barely moved at all, no matter what the song was. He didn't think that disco sucked. When they went to Small's, or The Tavern, or Josie's, no one in their crowd—Stuart, Rebecca, Ty, the others—seemed to belong with anyone else in any way that people could easily figure out, and Isabel loved that. They all, Isabel included, looked like people who could get back into their caravan and disappear at any minute. Isabel disappeared every Monday to Friday, but every Saturday she reappeared, a shining creature that had no name.

◈ ◈ ◈

Rebecca and Isabel walked down South Street, past the record stores and pawn shops and sandal makers. They stopped in front of a head shop to watch a horse-drawn carriage go by. Philadelphia, trying to be the Manhattan of Pennsylvania, had initiated the Liberty Rides during the Bicentennial last year. Decked out in red, white, and blue and drawn by profoundly bored-looking horses, the carriages made a sweaty little circuit from Independence Hall to Society Hill. They were supposed to add class, but mostly they added to the traffic, although the ancient hoof-sound was pleasant to hear, particularly on the streets that were still cobblestoned.

"I've always felt like I belonged in this neighborhood," said Rebecca as they walked along, her hair in a messy braid, her long khaki shorts loose and faded. "It used to be the Jewish part, did you know that?" Rebecca looked like someone from another country, thought Isabel, some country that didn't have television. She looked—Isabel searched for the right word and came up with *thoughtful.* "My brother Danny lived in that house there before he went to Canada," said Rebecca, pointing at a blue Victorian with purple trim that now sold pottery and wind chimes. "Philadelphia Freedom" was audible from its porch.

"Do you ever hear from him?" asked Isabel, imagining a man with a long braid like Rebecca's and a beards snowshoeing along a deserted highway.

"All the time, silly," said Rebecca. "He took the amnesty. He manages a health-food store in Michigan."

"Your family," said Isabel, "is so, I don't know, brave. They all do such brave things."

"That's the funny thing about America, isn't it? You can do all these brave things and then come home and run a shop." That was the kind of phrase Rebecca was always using that seemed to Isabel not quite of this place: "run a shop." Isabel could see Rebecca running a shop, a little place that sold things made out of wool, next to a moor.

Down here, there were no moors. Mixed in with the old pawn shops and barber shops were bookstores, storefront art galleries, and pottery places, with people leaning in the doorways, talking in the sun. The trees arching over the street seemed to draw it all together, as if the whole thing were one eccentric person's backyard. Isabel spotted a pottery bowl with a ferociously intricate design on it in one store window. In another, four mannequins in bridal gowns all had the same out-of-fashion hair. Isabel and Rebecca dawdled, dragging out their lunch break. Marjorie hadn't even arrived at rehearsal yet.

"How long have you been seeing Jasmine?" asked Isabel, lighting up.

"About a year. She brought me out," said Rebecca. "She's a wicked older woman." She raised an eyebrow, but her smile was shy. "A wicked island woman."

"I didn't know she was older. She looks so young," said Isabel, wanting to ask, but not asking, what island Rebecca meant.

"Oh, yeah. She's in graduate school. Anthropology. It's really conservative, but there's one guy there who's great, so Jasmine pretty much just sticks with him."

"Oh," said Isabel, not wanting to hear one single more word about Jasmine and wondering if that made her what Rebecca would call *homophobic*. Stuart was definitely homophobic, although no one seemed to mind when he said, "You fucking fairies," or "Jesus, you fruits." Maybe they were easier on him because he was a dwarf.

"Do you ever want to go back to school?"

"To music school?" Rebecca never said "Juilliard" and Isabel never told her that she knew. They both pretended that Rebecca was like anyone else, that she had gone to a plain music school in a little town. "Um, I think of playing again sometimes, but not there." She faltered, laughed uneasily.

"Why not?" Two men in tight, colored T-shirts and mirrored sunglasses passed by, muscular and not speaking to each other.

"Because—oh, this is hard to explain. Okay, where I went to school, you have to go before this jury every year."

"A jury?"

"It's just like this test at the end of the year, you have to play for your teachers, but it feels like you're auditioning all over again."

"So you thought you were going to fail?"

Rebecca began walking more quickly. They turned onto Front Street, where the river ran by. "No, I was doing very well. My violin teacher told me, privately, which you're not supposed to do, that I would be placed in the orchestra the next year, which is usually only for grad students. She told me on the Friday before my jury, which was that next Monday. So I was walking down Broadway—this is in New York, that's where the school was—and it was spring, and everyone was outside, and I knew that this was wonderful news, but then I don't know what happened, I just started to get this terrible, terrible feeling. Like the world was ending. I didn't know what to do. I kept walking, and walking, until I was all the way downtown, and then I was too afraid to take the subway back so I took a cab and I didn't have quite enough money and he yelled at me—it was awful. I ran upstairs to my apartment and shut the door and thought about it all weekend, but I knew what I had to do, and I did it."

"What do you mean?" said Isabel.

Rebecca stopped walking. Her face was clear, determined, the downward tilt of her eyes seeming like gravity, or age. "I knew I had to leave there. I knew I was in the wrong place and that now, with the orchestra thing, it was going to be even more humiliating. Because I knew—I knew that I was going to completely blow my jury. So I left. That Monday."

"Your jury day?"

"Yes," said Rebecca seriously. "I came home."

They crossed over the highway to the river; the city stretched out behind them, its city noise blown away by the river breeze. The sun was very bright. Isabel shaded her eyes with her hand. "I get that," she said.

"What?" said Rebecca.

"I get that feeling. The end of the world."

"What do you do about it?" Rebecca said, looking as if she truly wanted to know.

"I touch my forehead," said Isabel, embarrassed, not knowing why she was telling Rebecca this, sure she would regret it.

"Where?" said Rebecca.

"Right here," said Isabel, touching Rebecca between the eyes, with two fingers, then quickly withdrawing them.

Rebecca closed her eyes, put two fingers up to her own forehead, wish bracelets fluttering in the breeze. There was marking on the orange one, but Isabel couldn't read it. "That's nice," she said. "Very soothing. Did you make that up?"

Isabel shrugged, dropping her cigarette and stubbing it out with her shoe.

"Thank you," said Rebecca.

"You'll go back somewhere," said Isabel. "You don't want to stay here your whole life."

"I like it here," said Rebecca, as they walked on.

Ben called Isabel on the phone. "Just say you're sorry," he said in his sweetest tone of voice. "That's all she wants."

Isabel twined the cord around her fingers. "I can't."

"You mean you won't."

"No."

"Yes."

Isabel remained silently aloof. She had recently come to realize that all the things Lottie liked, she, Isabel, did not like, and all the things that Lottie didn't like, she, Isabel, liked enormously, but she wasn't going to tell Ben—or Lottie—that.

"She *cries,* Isabel," said Ben.

"Yeah, well, me, too," said Isabel. That was a lie. The truth was that these days, she was trekking alone across the surface of the moon. Dust whirled up behind her.

"Call her."

"I will." But day after day, the phone remained untouched. She couldn't. She didn't really know why. Everything had fallen into awkwardness: she couldn't apologize, and she couldn't explain. She wanted to call; she would call soon. Just not yet.

Isabel cantered on her little hooves up and down, up and down the alley behind the theater. She held her hands to either side of her face, for blinders. Slivers of the Dumpster, the brick wall, a long-dead basketball flicked past again and again as she trotted up and down. Her hips felt loose and light in their sockets, like horse hips. She didn't think she was a horse—she wasn't a child—but she sensed a horse within her, slowly taking shape. The horse narrowed her legs, coarsened her hair. It didn't like the alley; it was looking for a way out. The horse kicked at the wall, shied away from the basketball. Isabel took her hands away from her face and stood quietly, breathing. How shy was the horse, and how powerful. Isabel flinched, rolled her shoulder back. She picked up one hoof, tightened the string holding her right desert boot to the little metal block. In the real show, the hooves would be attached to the costume and the blinders would fit over her head like an upside-down crown. Isabel cantered awhile, thinking, trying not to scuff her new hooves.

In one day, the forest was gone, replaced by a bare stage with a desk, a couch, four wooden side benches, and a sort of four-poster wooden platform on wheels for when Marjorie and Dennis ran away together to a field in the middle of the night. All the other horses had to twirl them around in a frenzy as Dennis leaped onto Marjorie's back, having a fit. Augie became less patient, and was never late to rehearsal anymore.

"Those tassels," he said to Rebecca, pointing at the on-set couch. He glowered from the door of the lighting booth, where she and Isabel were testing each set of lights. The center spot flickered, dimmed, came back up again, but weakly.

"We don't have another couch, Augie," said Rebecca.

"Can't we cover it with something? It looks like it belongs in a bordello." His hair, more blown out than ever, was outlined by the exterior light in all its spikiness, nearly straightened with exasperation.

"Augie," said Rebecca. She sighed. "A black sheet, maybe."

Isabel wrote it down.

"Lightbulbs," said Rebecca to Isabel, but Isabel had already written it down.

"I think the gels are too dark," said Isabel, pointing at the lights on the side of the stage, and Rebecca nodded.

"Let's go down to Consolidated and get lightbulbs and four new gels, then stop at my apartment for the reel. Augie wants to do a run-through with the music this afternoon."

Isabel was quiet in the van; she felt moody, restless. She let Rebecca go in to Consolidated Theatrical Supply without her, even though she loved the fake blood, the costumes, the plastic weaponry, the cardboard suitcases piled high, with old-fashioned stickers on them reading Paris or London; the wigs. It was as if the world had broken up in a shipwreck somewhere offshore and what was left had washed up in Consolidated. You couldn't make a real life out of it, exactly, because big chunks were missing—food, for instance, and machinery that worked. You could only make something that was like life magnified in random parts: the screen door that made a living room in Texas, the buoy that made a dock, the mirrored ball that made a discotheque. A javelin, leaning against the wall, to make a war. But she didn't care about that today, because today she had something real on her mind; she practiced how she would say it.

Rebecca got back into the van, slammed the rusty door. She handed the bag of lights and gels to Isabel. The van rattled as she backed it up, twirling the wide, round steering wheel between her hands. They rattled down a few avenues, stopped in front of a brick row house with a porch on the front. A blue balloon bobbed gently up and down against the porch roof. Rebecca jumped down out of the van, then leaned back in the window.

"You want to come in?"

Isabel nodded and got out, still holding on to the bag. She followed Rebecca up the stairs.

"I live down here," said Rebecca, turning the key in the front-door lock.

The first floor, Rebecca's floor, was wide and light: light sofa, light wooden floors, a small wooden coffee table, a bookcase off to one side, a butterfly chair with a yellow canvas seat. A music stand with sheet music on it; a violin case propped up on a chair in front of the stand. Hanging high up on one wall, above the entryway to the kitchen, was a picture of a dark-haired woman screaming; underneath her face it said, WOMEN UNITE! Rebecca's living room windows looked out onto the porch; the balloon bobbed into view, bobbed away, bobbed back.

Rebecca said, "Would you like some lemonade?"

Isabel said, "Okay," and sat down on the light, nubby sofa. She set her bag carefully on the coffee table. She took out one of the gels and looked at the balloon through it; the balloon turned a heavy, inexpressive purple. She put the gel back in the bag. "Do you think we'll get through the whole thing tonight?"

"Maybe," said Rebecca from the kitchen. "If Stuart and Dennis don't start arguing." Rebecca came back, handed Isabel her lemonade, then sat down in the butterfly chair. "Let's veg for a second. We're going to be there forever."

"Who else lives in this building?" said Isabel.

"Some old hippie friends of my brother's have the upstairs. Cherie and Dave. They smoke too much dope, but they're nice," said Rebecca. She kicked off her sandals and began rubbing a spot just above one ankle. Her legs, Isabel decided, actually were thin. Rebecca was a thin person who sometimes seemed larger because her gestures could be so wide, so assertive. The violin case on the chair was battered; it had a peace sticker and a women's symbol sticker on it as if it, like the suitcases in Consolidated, had traveled.

Marooned on the sofa with her lemonade, Isabel crossed her legs, uncrossed them, crossed them again. She looked at the poster of the screaming woman. She leaned forward. "I want to ask you something." The balloon bobbed into sight, like an eavesdropper.

"All right." Rebecca sat up straight in the butterfly chair and put both feet on the floor in her half-funny, half-serious way.

"I'm like Augie," said Isabel. "I figured it out." She pushed a bobby pin tighter into her hair, held her breath. "I'm like that."

Rebecca said quizzically, "Like what?"

"You know." Isabel felt giddy. She waved her hand back and forth in a pendulum motion. "Both. Do you think Augie's foxy?"

Rebecca seemed puzzled. "Both what? Oh. Oh. Okay. It's great to be both," she said carefully, in a distant way that made Isabel regret having brought it up. Rebecca was missing the darkness, the majesty of it. In fact, she was nodding patiently, like a doctor. "Foxy. Sure. But he's—how long have you been thinking about all this, Isabel?"

"A while, I guess. I have this friend, or I did—" Isabel paused. She didn't want to go into all that. "What about you?" That was her question.

"Me?" Rebecca seemed surprised, or maybe wary.

"Do you think you're both, or just one?"

"Oh." Rebecca looked serious again. "No, Isabel, I think I'm just one." The balloon bobbed away, leaving the window empty. "Maybe you want to talk to Augie about this? Or Dennis? Jasmine has a lot of books, I'm sure she'd be happy to lend you—although, well." She shifted uncomfortably in the butterfly chair. "We're in a little bit of a moment right now." She smiled oddly. "But I'd be glad to call her for you."

"I don't want to read any books," said Isabel, knowing she sounded sullen, like a child. This was all going wrong, not at all the way she had planned it in the backyard, when she figured it out. Because she had had some dates, but then there was this kissing thing with Lottie. Sitting in the backyard in the dark, she had admitted something privately that she wouldn't have admitted before, something she imagined she might say to Lottie when they made up: that since then, since that night in the bleachers, she had been waiting for Lottie to kiss her again. Plus, she might be in love with Augie, who was bisexual. It had all made sense to her then, and it was very interesting, but now Rebecca was standing up with a frightening cheerfulness, gathering the reel, the van keys, her jacket. "Have you seen my script?" she said. She patted Isabel on the knee reassuringly as she passed by.

Isabel felt extremely disappointed, but couldn't quite think why. She considered it, still sitting on the sofa. It was as if she had come riding up with her sentence held high, ready for the thud of it meeting the light of day, and Rebecca had simply noted it and ridden on. It was as if she had said, "That's nice, Isabel," in the distracted way second-grade teachers notice you're good at four-square. Isabel sat on the sofa with her crumpled—or, worse, uncrumpled—sentence. Her entirely manageable sentence.

"Do you need a sweater for later?" called Rebecca from the bedroom.

"No, I brought one," said Isabel in a low voice.

Rebecca came back into the room. "Are you all right?" she said.

To her horror, Isabel started to cry—hot, crumpled, frustrated tears, as if she had been misunderstood, but worse, really, it was worse. Because she had been understood, but Rebecca's serious gaze was like the balloon: it bobbed away.

It bobbed back. Rebecca, full of keys and braid and cotton jacket, had sat down on the sofa.

"Oh, God," said Rebecca. "I'm such an asshole."

Isabel sniffled.

"It's just because Jasmine and I had a fight this morning. I'm sorry. Come with us Tuesday—we're going to a concert. Okay? Isabel?"

Rebecca's shoulder was bony, but her hands were warm. Isabel nodded, slowly crying less.

Isabel put on her costume. Her jeans and T-shirt lay over the back of a chair. She could hear Marjorie in the next room, arguing with Dennis. "You have to jump better. You're going to put my back out."

"Step more forward," said Augie.

"Bend your knees," said Rebecca.

"This is bullshit," said Marjorie.

Isabel took a sip of coffee, pulled on the silver jumpsuit with its dangling silver hooves. She got up on the trunk so she could see herself in the makeup mirror, although then she could only see her bottom half. Isabel pawed the air, clip-clopped on top of the trunk. Her silver legs and silver feet were beautiful. She hung her head over so she could see her face in the mirror; it hung, upside down, next to her beautiful silver legs, like a coconut. Her hair swirled off the top of her head the way hair did in water. Being upside down made her eyes look funny. Isabel whinnied, although no one was actually allowed to whinny onstage. Everyone was going to wear ponytails, and blinders. They'd look half like creatures from outer space, the other half animal. They had to move, Augie had said, with their whole heads, the way horses did. The inquisitive way of horses. They had to move in a herd, like fish turning. They should make the audience a little bit afraid with their silent, animal presence. "Quiet faces," he'd said softly to them. "Quiet faces." When everyone was completely still, he'd stood back, as if he had just invented them and was waiting for them to dry.

Isabel, upright, tried to have a quiet face. She pawed the air again. She thought of the other horses, bumping her, pushing her, breathing against her, muttering under their breath. They moved in a herd, like fish turning.

As Rebecca and Isabel and Jasmine entered the park, Rebecca carrying the blanket, Jasmine carrying a small red plastic cooler, Isabel saw that the opening act had already started: a white woman with an Afro was playing the piano, and the crowd was fanned halfway down the field. They were late. Jasmine had picked them up late, in her boxy old car full of books and papers, but she didn't apologize. They rode to the park in silence, car windows rolled down, the hot Philadelphia air blowing in.

Rebecca walked determinedly toward the stage, Jasmine and Isabel following. Triumphantly, Rebecca spread the blanket out on a little patch up front, far to one side. The bandshell loomed above them. They were so close that Isabel could see women carrying rolls of cable and wearing headsets standing in the wings, or perched in rigging. Some of them wore overalls. Jasmine lay down and put her head in Rebecca's lap. Isabel sat a little apart from them, next to the cooler, which she wanted to open up, because she was hungry, but didn't. It was their cooler. The dusk was coming in, deep blue at the edges; the bandshell, lit up and faintly yellow, glowed benevolently. The piano woman was very smiley; watching her, Isabel thought, She looks weird. Plus, she was wearing a Hawaiian print shirt. She reminded Isabel of an art teacher. She played the piano loudly, fervently. Her songs were slow and all seemed to offer advice. They weren't rock songs; they were something else, like the solo parts at a rock concert where the spotlight was turned momentarily on the bass player, or the drummer. Isabel listened carefully, trying to catch the words. The woman had a fury, she said, pounding happily, proudly, she had a fury. Isabel could understand that.

It was a field, Isabel noticed as the night settled in, almost entirely of women, most of them older than her, but some of them clearly about her age, and here and there even a little girl, somebody's daughter. The women in the field had a tendency to drape themselves around each other. They leaned; they embraced; everywhere Isabel looked a hand was touching a shoulder, a knee was being used as a pillow, and very often one woman was leaning back into the arms of another, like a woman resting in a rowboat. The field was dotted with these little rowboats of two, momentarily anchored. Some of the women in the field looked like hippies in their baggy clothes, their strings of beads, their long hippie hair, like Rebecca's. There were women in halter tops and gauzy skirts that swept the grass, walking barefoot across the field with women who had braided flowers or beads into their hair. But more than a few of the women had short hair that flicked lightly at their shirt collars, like David Cassidy. Some of them had hair that was even shorter than that, short enough that you could see their necks. They turned their sleeves up, the way boys did. There was something embarrassing to Isabel about this crowd, something that made her blush in the dusk. And at the same time, she felt privileged: this was where Rebecca and Jasmine went, a place they believed in together. She looked over at Rebecca, who was gazing down at Jasmine. Her hair tilted over Jasmine's face, like an uneven curtain.

"What are you thinking?" said Rebecca to Jasmine.

"About Mesopotamia," said Jasmine with a smile.

Rebecca, in turn, smiled wryly at Isabel, but Isabel didn't get it exactly. She couldn't remember where Mesopotamia was, either.

Not far from their blanket a group of four was eating tacos and laughing, all of them touching each other at some not exactly personal but not exactly impersonal juncture—an elbow, a hip. One of them, wearing a bandana, was feeding a taco to another with a teasing motion: it's yours; no, it's mine. The bandana one could pull the taco away very fast, like someone who was good at thumb wrestling. She had wide hips, and curly iron-gray hair. Her friends seemed to have wide hips, too, except for the one being fed the taco, who was very skinny and sunburned and wore high-tops with her cutoff shorts. Her legs were covered with dense, soft, blond hair, like fur. After the bandana one finally let the other woman have the taco, she licked her own fingers instead of using a napkin. Isabel thought that was gross, but she kept watching covertly, curious to see what the bandana one would do next. The piano woman was still singing. This was a long opening act.

"So Jasmine," said Isabel, trying to make conversation, "are you studying about Mesopotamia? Is that—where was that?"

There was a silence.

"Tell her," said Rebecca.

"Well, Mesopotamia was the ancient place where the Tigris met the Euphrates, Isabel," said Jasmine. "It was the cradle of civilization. The work I'm trying to do is about the matriarchal cultures—cultures that handed things down through the mother line—which we know existed, but no one has really studied them." Jasmine's tone was patient, kind; she seemed happy for the first time that evening. Isabel thought she was probably a very good teacher.

"So what did they do there?" said Isabel. The old bandana one and the furry sunburned blond one were lying down now, propped up on elbows face to face, talking intensely to each other.

"Do?" Jasmine frowned and laughed at the same time. "They weren't warlike. They were hunter-gatherers. They worshiped the mother-goddess. They collectivized the land they did have, although there were these other tribes that were nomadic. Those are the ones I'm interested in, which are very hard to trace. Sometimes all you have to go on for, like, two thousand years of history is a few pottery shards."

"I see," said Isabel. "And they didn't have any wars. That's interesting."

"Isn't that amazing to think about?" said Rebecca. "That we really only know a tiny fraction of our history?"

"Uh-huh," said Isabel, feeling self-conscious suddenly. It had to be obvious that she was an interloper here.

But looking around her, Isabel realized that their threesome must look something like the other groups on the other blankets, the three of them and their red plastic cooler, the cooler that was actually Jasmine and Rebecca's, but nobody else knew that. Isabel herself, in her cutoffs and her Dr. Scholl's, did not look appreciably different from the other women in the field; she could, easily enough, be mistaken for one of them. Her unease passed. Suddenly she felt free, unknown. Leaning back, she decided that maybe she liked the music a little. She tapped her foot. She smiled at the old one in the bandana, and the woman smiled back, and then Isabel hoped she wouldn't come over or anything, and she didn't.

After a few minutes, Isabel was glad she hadn't asked Rebecca about the opening act, because she got it: there was no other act coming on. She understood that this was Rebecca's gift to her, after what Isabel had told her the other day. Isabel was grateful, but she felt awkward, too, listening to the woman who looked like an art teacher, as if she had suddenly stumbled into an art class and been handed a brush. She had no idea what she was supposed to paint, here in this field where everyone seemed to be related. The woman in the bandana stroked the calf of the furry one. Isabel looked away.

Jasmine and Rebecca had gone back to being as quiet as they had been in the car. Jasmine rolled away from Rebecca and leaned over the edge of the blanket, as if she were studying a landscape far below. She picked up a stick and began scribbling in the earth, drawing up little invisible ledgers.

Rebecca popped open the cooler. Inside were a bottle of orange juice, some sandwiches with alfalfa sprouts, three pieces of cake neatly wrapped in plastic, the cool underlying web of ice. The smiley piano woman was singing plummily in Spanish.

"I'm going for a walk," said Jasmine, and Rebecca said, "Okay," in a measured tone. Jasmine wandered into the crowd, hands in her pockets. Her legs were very thin and strong; they carried her away like stilts, moving her cleanly through the rows of evening picnickers. Head bent, she seemed like she either wasn't listening to the music at all, or was listening superintently, as she disappeared around the edge of the bandshell.

"Would you like some juice, Isabel?" said Rebecca. Isabel shook her head as Rebecca took a long swallow. "Isn't she great?" said Rebecca. "I saw her play in New York. She's such a wonderful musician."

"Do you want to move back there?" said Isabel.

"One day," said Rebecca, flipping over onto her stomach, her naked heels up in the air behind her. "It's so different from here. So much more intense." Now her face was close to Isabel's face, near her shoulder, so that she had to look up at Isabel when they spoke; Isabel could smell her faint scent—some cedar, and something darker, too, like a low tone, mixed with orange juice. Her downward-tilting eyes seemed larger in the dark.

"What are you and Jasmine fighting about?" ventured Isabel.

Rebecca looked down, picked at the blanket. Her broad forehead furrowed. "She wants to be able to see other people," she said abruptly.

"Oh," said Isabel, taken aback. "Why?"

"Because it's the way she is," said Rebecca. "She just knows herself really well. I'm having a harder time with it."

"Well, God, it doesn't exactly sound like it was your idea," said Isabel.

"This is true," said Rebecca. In the dark, Rebecca's paleness gave off a delicate light, like the bandshell, but smaller. In the dark, she was just that: a paleness, a smudge of hair, a smudge of heel, a delicacy of ankle, a wry smile. Rebecca wasn't, Isabel reflected, really that much older than her. They listened to the concert in silence for a little while. They ate the sandwiches. They ate the cake. They drank the orange juice. Rebecca put Jasmine's share back on the ice and closed the cooler lid with a little snap.

"She'll be hungry when she gets back," said Rebecca.

"Right," said Isabel, although she doubted it. Jasmine was like Ben: always brooding and walking around the woods somewhere. She was the kind of person who would threaten to go off and join the army, too. A nomad. "You know," she offered, "if I were you I wouldn't, like, wait around for Jasmine so much. I think she wants you to worry."

"That's very astute," said Rebecca, nodding.

Isabel shook out a cigarette and lit it up, blowing smoke into the air. She blew a few smoke rings. She was happy to be with Rebecca among the women in the field, totally happy in some way she hadn't expected that was peculiarly familiar but that also made her feel slightly sick to her stomach. And she was happy, ridiculously happy, to have been admitted that small distance into Rebecca's confidence. She felt that she had just climbed in a window, and was now standing in a dark room looking around, like a thief.

"Let's all come together on the chorus," said the piano woman merrily. No way, thought Isabel. Jasmine appeared around the other side of the bandshell, heading in their direction. Rebecca, singing along, grabbed Isabel's hand and squeezed it and Isabel, at first gently and then quite firmly, squeezed back, singing the words she could make out.

In the days following the concert, Isabel attempted to rise in Rebecca's mind, like a second sun, like the balloon bobbing at her window, like Mesopotamia, unearthed in shards by Jasmine. She started with little things. She stole a biography of Greta Garbo from Brentano's and signed it to Rebecca on the flyleaf: Love, Greta. Rebecca thought that was very funny and seemed to find it a little wild as well, a little bit bad. Lottie and Isabel's idea of bad was considerably further out than that, but Isabel didn't say anything. It was nice to be the bad one. Rebecca was possibly the most serious person Isabel had ever met, but instead of weighing Rebecca down, her seriousness steadied her. She walked on top of it the way a girl would walk on top of a wall, waving, glancing down now and then at the pavement, but essentially unafraid. It was a balance she must have been born with, a Communist temperament, although when Isabel made this point to Rebecca late one night at Small's, Rebecca said, "Oh, I don't think I'm more serious than you at all. You're so intense. You have all this intense energy."

"I do not," said Isabel in the disbelieving way that girls did at her school when receiving a compliment. But, just to herself, she agreed. She thought it was probably because she didn't believe in God, although when she made this point to Rebecca at The Tavern, Rebecca said, "Aren't you Jewish?"

"Not really," said Isabel. "My father doesn't do all that stuff."

"So you're godless," said Rebecca. "A godless woman."

"Yes," said Isabel, pleased. She was godless, and motherless, too, and this made her different from other people, although when she made this point to Rebecca at Josie's, Rebecca said, "No woman in America is mothered enough. Not a single one," and Isabel felt simultaneously quashed and relieved.

It was odd to know that someone as serious as Rebecca thought of herself as a revolutionary. Until meeting Rebecca, Isabel had thought of revolutionaries as hippies who took drugs and burned things, more or less. Rebecca was more like a lady pioneer. She was always lifting things, carrying things, plunging her arms into piles of props and costumes, picking up tools, hammering at things, wearing a kerchief around her head. But she was, nevertheless, entirely feminine. She was fundamentally dress-shaped, despite the fact that none of her dresses fit her very well. She drove totally like a girl, too; Lottie could have left her in the dust anytime, if Lottie had cared to try. With Rebecca, Isabel saw that real revolution was different from what she had imagined or seen on TV. Revolution was a thing that happened in conversation, a road that appeared out of nowhere.

Jasmine came to the theater much less often now; Isabel brought Rebecca a dark chocolate, pistachio-laced Golden Gate Bridge. Rebecca ate it all in one sitting, just like anyone with a broken heart, and when she was done Isabel could tell she was sorry that she didn't have another one. Isabel brought Rebecca a tape by the smiley piano woman. "Oh, thanks," said Rebecca. "I already have the record of this, actually." Isabel, undaunted, listened to it herself, at home, until she knew all the words. Rebecca, sitting with Isabel in the Indian take-out place, their headsets discarded on the table between them, said, "I feel so shut down the days you aren't here, Isabel. I miss having you to talk to." Curry wafted around Isabel in a brilliant cloud. Isabel attempted to rise in Rebecca's mind like a second sun, which wasn't quite right because if you stopped to think about it, why would the planet need another one? But Isabel was hoping that by the time Rebecca might stop to think about it, it would already be too late. She would be tumbling, off balance, off her wall, into the extra warmth.

Sue was a horse, and Marjorie was a horse, and Isabel was a horse, and Ty was a horse, and some balding friend of Augie's named Don was a horse. They huddled together in their imaginary pen upstage while Dennis rolled around on the floor. Standing in the dark between Sue and

Ty, Isabel felt the chain of their horseness tying them all together. They were all very good at it. Augie put his arms around them. "Good," he said. "You're there. Good." He didn't have to tell them. They knew they were there. They were a pack of muscular, nervous horses now, and Isabel was among them. Ty gently bumped her neck with his head, and it was the same as if he had spoken.

"Hey," said Isabel, clip-clopping up to Rebecca at the light board. "Is Jasmine coming to the party Friday?" Isabel was in costume; they were about to start dress rehearsal. Silver horses were everywhere. Dennis was standing with a profound stillness in the hallway, as if praying. Stuart was walking around the stage, stopping now and then to say lines to himself. Augie was zipping Marjorie into her suit, whispering in her ear.

Rebecca pushed one bar all the way forward, another all the way back, staring intently at the stage as it lit up and then went dark in various spots. "No. She has a meeting."

"Oh, too bad," said Isabel, galloping off.

Isabel put her silver horse suit, her hooves, her blinders, two ponytail holders (in case one broke), a hairbrush, her copy of the script, a pack of cigarettes, a roll of breath mints, and an orange into a brown paper bag with handles. She put her mother's ring on its fine gold chain around her neck. It was the afternoon of the opening Friday night. Her father would be home to take her to the bus stop soon, but right now the house was empty. He was still at work; Jeannie was probably with him, working the counter. Isabel was ready early.

She walked with Howdy out into the backyard; his gait was already arthritic and he wasn't even that old yet. He was a supermarket dog, generic and cheaply made. He sniffed at a tree, then peed, looking at her while he did it. They got Howdy, who was more or less a present to Jeannie, just after Isabel's mother died. Instead of sating Jeannie's hunger for dogs, however, Howdy only increased it. Jeannie got books; she knew the name and habits of every breed. Jeannie was haunted by dogs; it was as if each one were a ghost or a memory, appearing to her in a form a small girl could stand. To Isabel, every dog taped up on the bathroom wall was like one of those MIA bracelets with a missing soldier's name on it. Terrier. French bulldog. Irish wolfhound. They all carried her mother's name in their teeth. Cassie. The name of someone who laughed a lot and went to parties. Cassie didn't. Maybe that was the problem all along: she didn't fit her name, and it chafed her where it didn't fit, and finally she took it off, the way she'd take off her name tag in the car at the end of her shift, not even waiting to get all the way home, tossing it onto the dashboard and lighting up a cigarette.

Isabel looked at their house: it was smallish, flat-roofed, a collection of rectangles, painted beige. Her mother, Isabel was sure, would not have liked it. She liked old houses.

The phone rang. Isabel left Howdy in the yard and went back into the house to answer it, through the dining room, where her paper bag sat on the chrome-legged table, and into the kitchen. It was John, from Pier 1. He said she had to fill in the next day for Jennifer, who had run away from home to ride across the country on a motorcycle with her boyfriend. Isabel, actually, had known that Jennifer was going to do this, because she had shown Isabel her new helmet, and sworn her to secrecy.

"But—" said Isabel.

"But me no buts," said John gleefully. "Be here or be fired."

Isabel hung up. She didn't care anyway. Alone in the empty house, she could feel the presence of everything she knew about acting, which was a lot, and still not enough. But she knew that there was a door and that she was about to pass through it.

Cassie Gold: that was almost an actress's name, wasn't it? An interlocking CG on a towel, a robe; Cassie Gold written in cursive on the flyleaf of the big Shakespeare Isabel had carted off to her room; Cassie Gold punched on her name tag. Isabel kept the name tag, a cheap plastic tile with a rusty pin on the back, in her jewelry box. It was a ridiculous memento, impersonal and dull, floating in the air, pinned to nothing.

When it happened, everyone at school knew. Isabel and Jeannie were the Gold kids; they moved through the halls in a nimbus. People were afraid of them. Teachers, too.

It was a grimy, terrible time. Isabel got too thin; Jeannie refused to let anyone cut her hair. Now and then she'd get things stuck in it—a rubber band, a bit of gum—and their father would have to delicately cut it out. He went to the Rite Aid and bought a special, extra-sharp pair of scissors with blue plastic handles. Jeannie insisted that he cut the mat out without disturbing the overall length. Her fine hair got as far as her elbows before petering out. He bought them matching blue coats with stripes on one sleeve. He didn't insist that they visit the grave with him; he got thinner, too. Cassie Gold settled into the floorboards, stood before the window, sat in all the chairs, like someone who never went to work. The shivah was the worst. Isabel's Roman house was still sitting on the dining room table. Relatives and neighbors, milling through their house with coffee and cake, kept pausing to peer into the little rooms, touch the Roman fountains Isabel had so carefully fluted out of Kleenex. She hated them, blindly, passionately, for that: their big cakey hands, their stupid questions. After the first day, Isabel picked up her project and stuffed it into the trash. It barely fit, even folded and crunched up. Her teacher, sympathetic, gave her a B minus; Isabel would have preferred a D, something hard and strong and final.

Later, when they were packing to move, Isabel found two drawings in a manila folder in the bookcase. One was of her, one of Jeannie. CG was written at the bottom of each in a sure, quick hand. The drawings were good and bright and happy; both she and Jeannie looked eager, expectant. Her mother had clearly taken some time with the colors and shadings, the exact tilt of Isabel's eyes. Isabel couldn't remember ever having sat for her mother to draw her picture, couldn't remember her mother ever drawing at all. When had she looked at them so carefully? Isabel had slid the pictures back into the folder, dropped the folder into a box, closed and taped the box shut. When they got to the new house the box had gotten lost somehow, and Isabel was glad.

The pictures in the folder were like Cassie Gold herself: she had talents that surfaced unexpectedly, only to disappear again without warning. Sometimes, she seemed to be the kind of person who was good at everything she tried, but she rarely tried anything more than once. It was humiliating that in order to remember her they all had to pretend that she was somehow a finished person, a done person, a person you could remember with confidence—Cassie was a great tennis player, a great fan of the theater—when the evidence lay all around them that finished was the one thing she wasn't. Her father's line was, "Cassie had great potential," but Isabel knew the truth. Her mother hated being a nurse. She smoked too much. She hadn't played tennis, or any other game, in a long time. All she did was watch *General Hospital* in the afternoons, in a trance. If she did have potential, she died still clutching it in her hands, like unplayed cards.

Isabel intended to play them. All of them, one by one. Beginning with this beautiful silver horse.

She picked up the phone to call Lottie, then put it down.

Isabel's father and Jeannie drove up the driveway. Jeannie leaned out the window, calling Howdy into the car. Isabel grabbed her paper bag and got in the back seat, refusing to let Howdy ride in back with her. "You brought him," she said to Jeannie, pushing him over into the front seat. She watched the houses of their neighborhood go by, lawn after lawn. Tomorrow, she knew, they would look different to her.

As she got out at the bus stop, Isabel said quickly, "There's a party after, Dad." Howdy jumped in the back seat. A bus was already waiting, puffing impatiently. She got right on it before her father could say anything.

The house lights came up and there were horses in the house. They were the horses. It was wonderful to be a horse. It was also boring. The small of Isabel's back hurt after the first act; Ty, she felt, had lost his focus. When their part of the stage was dark, he just sat down on the floor. But Marjorie led them, ruled them; her hooves made her nearly six feet tall.

From her vantage point on the stage, Isabel could make out her father and Jeannie in the fourth row, just the bare outlines of Rebecca in the lighting booth, Augie way in a back row, sipping a soda. All the horses trotted forward; all the horses trotted back. They crowded into one corner, not whinnying but projecting a whinnying atmosphere. They rioted around in their stalls. Isabel knew that it wouldn't always be like this, so easy and wordless and entirely physical, so intimate without anyone even touching. Between acts, she and Sue stood in the alley and had a cigarette. "You should stick around, Isabel," said Sue. "Get Augie to put you in something else."

"What's the next one?" said Isabel, pulling off her blinders to redo her ponytail. Her temples were sweaty where the blinders had been.

"I think *Marat/Sade*," said Sue. "It's great. Augie and I did it up in New York. Everybody just goes totally fucking crazy." She flicked the butt into the alley. "Cathartic as hell."

The lights came up for the second act. Isabel stood pressed in a clump with the others, upstage, in a semiblackout. She tilted her head the way a horse would, but very slowly. Directly in her line of vision, Dennis knelt at Marjorie's hooves; gradually, in a serpentine way, he moved up along her body, his hands sliding along her silver flesh, his head pressing close to her chest, like someone in a trance. Dennis pulled on an imaginary rein and led Marjorie away, offstage.

Stuart went on talking, spreading out his small arms as he asked questions about life. Isabel knew every one of his lines from having run them with him so many times. He inhabited them now, running along them with a grace Isabel hadn't expected. She turned her head slowly the other way, subtly scratched her knee. Watching Stuart, Isabel could almost believe that, like the psychiatrist, there was a long white well inside him, a blank space that echoed with the sound of horse hooves.

The second act sped toward its sad conclusion. Isabel and Ty and Don all put on big horse-head masks for the part where Dennis, naked, pretended to put their eyes out. Isabel was glad she had her mask on for this part, because it always made her blush even though Dennis couldn't care less about them when he got to this point. He was completely inside his own performance, entirely fixed on a point within himself. It was impersonal, how naked he was, how swiftly he came at each of them with his paper spike. He never touched them—it was like a pantomime, conducted in silence—but the gesture always made Isabel feel as if she actually had been struck.

Now the three of them stood there in the spotlight in their huge, ugly masks, hot and itching and barely able to incline their heads without toppling over, and when Dennis flew by, stabbing at them, they each shuddered in turn. First Marjorie, who screamed, then, in total silence, Ty, Isabel, Don.

Standing there, hot, her mask so heavy and hard to see out of, Isabel felt momentarily blinded. Plaster from the inside of the mask dusted her eyelashes. The silver suit was itching her on the inside of her elbows, behind her knees. Everyone in the audience, she realized, was looking at her. The dry dark swept over her, and then something else, something new: she wanted to scream and scream and scream, to let loose a scream that would echo along every street of Philadelphia, flatten every lawn of Springston, a scream that would burst into every house, a scream that even Bettina would hear. Isabel wanted to scream so loud that she would wake the dogs on Jeannie's wall, wake them and set them loose on the neighborhood, an entire horde of them racing through the streets, barking. Isabel wanted to scream a single name, the first name, the name that contained all names. She wanted to scream it, and scream it, and scream it until something happened that she couldn't even imagine. "What use is grief to a horse?" Stuart had said. What use is grief to a horse? Isabel thought, wanting to scream, not screaming, standing in a line with Ty and Don like people in a chorus. Dennis was pressing himself, naked, to the ground now, his ribs opening and closing like a fan, the muscles of his thighs folded against the cold gray tarp on the floor. His forehead pressed into the floor as if he could draw the world up into his brain by sheer force of will, drink it in and obliterate all his awful thoughts. What use is grief to a horse? Isabel had no answer to this question, which was a ridiculous question, anyway, a riddle, like: What has four hands, two socks, and no feet? Grief was a horse. Grief was a dog. Grief was a table with four chrome legs, designed to always look new. They each rode something different, or maybe it rode them. Like Dennis and Marjorie, it was hard to tell who was riding whom. Grief was a paper spike that blinded you. Grief was a bullet, and the actress it shot. The scream passed away, dragging tatters of dry dark behind it, leaving Isabel exhausted and worried, poised in her place on the stage. Had she screamed, for real? Evidently not, because the play was finishing just as it should.

"There is now, in my mouth, this sharp chain," Stuart was saying, standing over Dennis where he lay, panting, on the floor. "And it never comes out."

The applause broke over them all in a warm, full wave

that picked them up and carried them along to Augie's house, where the party was.

Dennis and Ty and Marjorie were doing shots in the garden. Marjorie lined the little glasses up along the garden wall. Dennis was back to himself again, shy, in a polo shirt. He did his shot very fast, then shook his head—no more—even while Marjorie was saying, "One more round, then I'll read everyone's tarot cards." There were paper lanterns in the trees, shining red and gold among the leaves. In the kitchen, Augie had set out a buffet of quiches and salad and bread and cheese and an enormous cake in the shape of a horse's head that said *Congratulations* in green script. Isabel lingered by the buffet table, filling her plate. Augie's two-story row house was full of people, many of whom Isabel hadn't seen before, but who most everyone else seemed to know. Stuart, in cowboy boots, was talking to a little knot of them in Augie's living room. Sue, picking at the salad on her plate with her fingers, was talking to a hugely fat woman in a red caftan, both of them nodding as if in perfect agreement. Don had arrived wearing jeans with a belt made all of bullet casings, and no shirt; he had brought with him a coterie of young men, one of whom was wearing a transparent pink shirt and quite a lot of eyeliner and had teased blond hair.

"Cheap," Ty had said when the man with eyeliner came in, and Isabel had to agree. Isabel didn't know where Rebecca was; she had said she would come after she locked up the theater, but she wasn't there yet.

Isabel was still wearing her costume—minus the blinders and hooves—which looked good, she and Sue had discovered, with jeans. It wasn't even that hot, and the top part could be unzipped like a shirt. A tight shirt. Isabel liked the effect. She wandered into the garden, eating salad with her fingers, thinking about how maybe she didn't want to be an actress anymore. When she had pulled off her huge horse head to take her bow, the plaster mask dangling heavily from her fingers, she was so tired, and so frightened: what if she really had screamed? A professional couldn't do that. Isabel sat down on the lacquered spool table Augie had set out in the garden for the party, idly watching Marjorie lay out Ty's fortune on top of the stone wall.

"Uh-oh," she said. "Swords." They both leaned down and studied the cards.

Stuart, radiant in his cowboy boots, came out to the garden, too. He sat down on the spool next to Isabel.

"It was so real tonight," he said. "Could you feel it?"

"Totally," said Isabel.

"I loved your horse," said Stuart.

"Thank you," said Isabel.

She wasn't sure she liked it at all. Somehow, during all the times she had thought about acting before, and all the things she had practiced at home, and all the plays she had read, Isabel had forgotten that the audience was made up of individual people, each one endowed with the capacity to stare. It was creepy. Even when the house was dark, Isabel could easily see individual faces, particularly since she had so much time on stage to look out at the audience. Their faces were embarrassingly attentive; and then, at the end, they just left, emptying out into the street. It seemed to Isabel that there should be a parting ceremony for leaving the theater, some sort of solemn, deferential gesture. That the audience was the one that should bow.

"Hey," said Marjorie to Isabel. "Opening night." She held up one of the little glasses. "Come on."

"Okay," said Isabel, going over to the wall, and Marjorie poured golden tequila into the little glass. Isabel drank it, fast, like Dennis, and everything went warm.

"Want me to read your cards?" said Marjorie.

"No, thanks, I'm superstitious," said Isabel, although she wasn't. She just didn't trust Marjorie's sense of fate. Leaving her plate on the spool table, Isabel wandered out of the garden again and into the house, into the living room, where Augie was sitting on the sofa with Don and the fat woman in the red caftan. Isabel sat down next to Augie and he put his arm around her. "Miss Isabel," he said. Everything about him tonight was smooth and content; he obviously felt that it had gone very well. Although the summer night was warm, he was cool in his black turtleneck, his black pants. Sitting so close to him, Isabel studied his freckles once again. The man in the transparent pink shirt was sitting on the arm of the sofa, his legs crossed in a twining way, leaning on one elbow along the back of the sofa, like a large pink and blond cat. "Oh, please," he kept saying in his Spanish accent, no matter what anyone else said.

"Then what happened?" said Augie, sipping his Manhattan, to the fat woman. Her makeup was dramatic.

"I gave him a pamphlet I had in my purse," she said defiantly.

"Oh, please," said the pink-shirt man.

"You didn't," said Don.

"I did," she said. "People misunderstand it all the time. It's a science."

"What?" said Isabel. Augie put his hands over her ears.

"Dianetics," said the woman, leaning toward her. "Dianetics. It's a science."

"Oh, please," said the twining man again.

"I agree," said Augie. "Let's not corrupt this child any more than we have already."

"How old are you?" said the twining man, tapping Isabel on the head.

"She's sixteen," said Augie.

"Almost seventeen," said Isabel.

"Oh," said Augie. "Almost seventeen." He kissed her wrist. "My apologies."

"That's old enough," said the twining man.

"Old enough for what?" said Augie.

"Whatever," said the twining man.

"Where's Rebecca?" Isabel said casually.

"I don't know," he said. "Maybe she went to pick up Jasmine."

"I don't think so," said Isabel, worrying. She hadn't considered the possibility that Jasmine might change her mind. Jumping up off the sofa, she headed out to the garden, where she sat on the spool by herself for a long time, pulling at her split ends and thinking: Never mind.

By the time Rebecca finally appeared in the doorway to the garden, the party had thinned, then reconcentrated itself in the living room. Isabel had moved from the spool to one of two white webbed metal chairs sitting near the back wall. Dennis had been showing her his master gesture, the disturbed boy's trademark hand tremor, but he was gone now. In the kitchen were discarded plates, glasses; the cake had become a heap of abstract shapes. A sparkly sweater was lying dangerously close to the icing. Isabel's plate was still lying on the spool table, her napkin crumpled in the center.

"Hi," said Rebecca, sitting down in the empty chair. "The van died. I had to get a jump." They were alone in the garden.

"That's a drag," said Isabel, flipping her hair back over her shoulder.

"You did great tonight," said Rebecca.

"Thanks," said Isabel.

"Did your dad like the show?"

"He said he did." Isabel didn't mention that he had also said, "What's with the naked guy? Do you know him?" He had shaken Augie's hand enthusiastically as Isabel stood off to the side, coolly tossing her blinders and hooves into the prop box.

"But something else happened," Isabel continued.

"What?"

"I had that end-of-the-world thing."

"You did?" Rebecca tilted her head, concerned. "When?"

"In the last act, when Dennis stabs us. It was terrible. I don't think I want to be an actress anymore."

"Oh, Isabel," said Rebecca. "Don't say that." She put two fingers on Isabel's forehead, between her eyes. They were light and slender. "Just do this."

Isabel kissed her. Leaning forward out of her white

webbed metal chair with a certainty that seemed even at that moment more gravity than volition, Isabel kissed Rebecca fully, and softly, and with an expertise she had never managed with Jordy, not once.

Rebecca kissed her back. Laying her hand gently along Isabel's cheekbone, Rebecca drew Isabel to her, and then gently parted Isabel's lips with her tongue, opening her mouth to Isabel's mouth in such a way that Isabel felt the skin all along her breast wake up, and stiffen. She felt the skin along the inside of her thighs.

Isabel slid one hand up inside Rebecca's loose cotton shirt. Rebecca's skin was soft and cool. Drawing on this new ferociousness that seemed to have come from her horse suit, and the silly cake, and how long she'd been waiting in the garden, Isabel took Rebecca's surprisingly full breast in her hand and stroked the nipple with her thumb, raising it. No one had ever done exactly this to Isabel, but, doing it, she felt that it was her master gesture. And the feeling of Rebecca's breast in her hand, Rebecca's nipple against her thumb, set up a tickle in the back of Isabel's throat, an almost palpable sense of thirst. Isabel unbuttoned the top button of Rebecca's shirt. Rebecca sighed, moving closer. The party seemed to fall further and further away; no one came to the kitchen or into the garden to bother them.

"Don't stop," said Rebecca as Isabel drew a breath.

"God," said Isabel. They leaned in to kiss again, and this time Rebecca slowly unzipped Isabel's silver horse costume, sliding the zipper down just past Isabel's breasts. Isabel could feel her mother's ring, cold and clear, against her breastbone. It reminded her of where they were, how they got there. Glancing up first to make sure no one had come to the patio door, Rebecca began kissing Isabel's neck, beginning just under Isabel's ear and making her way down from there.

"You have beautiful skin," she said. Isabel felt the cool air on the skin that was exposed now, and then the warmth of Rebecca's mouth. Rebecca moved the zipper down a little farther so she could slide one hand up along Isabel's ribs, along the side of her breast. Her wish bracelets fluttered against Isabel's skin like a butterfly kiss. Rebecca ran her thumb along the chain Isabel wore, stroking the chain and the flesh together. Her touch was sure. Isabel closed her eyes.

"Little horse," said Rebecca, and then, leaning down, she took Isabel's breast in her mouth, circling the nipple with her tongue, then taking it gently between her teeth. The crown of Rebecca's head brushed against Isabel's breastbone. A current traveled from Isabel's breast down between her legs.

Isabel opened her eyes. "Hey," she said.

Rebecca sat up. Her top button was undone and her hair had come half-unbraided; strands were snaking over her shoulder. Her laughing face was serious and flushed. Her eyes tilted at their delicate downward angle. Isabel couldn't help kissing her one more time, and her mouth was warm, but then Isabel had to stop, she had to say something, although she wasn't sure what. "Rebecca—" she said.

"You're right," said Rebecca. "I mean, my God, how old are you again?" She buttoned her button.

"Old enough," said Isabel. "That isn't what I meant." It occurred to her that her suit was still unzipped; it occurred to her not to zip it back up. She rezipped it a fraction, and leaned back.

"What did you mean?"

"I don't know," said Isabel. She wound the chain and ring around her fingers, unwound it.

They looked at each other in the dark for a while and Isabel thought that Rebecca had the most beautiful, the most beautiful face she had ever seen.

It was sometime later that Isabel made her way back into the living room. Rebecca had left before her. Isabel felt much calmer in her mind, and lighter, and not nervous at all. Everything was so clear once you both talked about how you felt. The lights were off in the living room, leaving just the street lamp shining through the windows. The twining man reclined on the sofa; Don sat on the floor next to the sofa, smoking. Augie leaned over the stereo, slipping a record out of its jacket and setting it into place.

"Where have you been?" he said, straightening up. He pulled her close to him and rested his head against her head, in a subtle dance. A woman was singing about a skylark.

"In the garden," said Isabel.

Augie swayed, swaying Isabel with him. Isabel wrapped her hand around his hand. The light from the street filtered in blue.

"When are we going?" said the twining man.

"Soon," said Augie, lost in some thought of his own. Isabel wondered, just for a moment, if Rebecca knew how she was. Holding Isabel's thin hand in his plush one, Augie turned the two of them around in the blue light. Isabel smiled. She wouldn't be going with them, wherever it was they all went at night: Berlin, Paris, the river. Somewhere not too far away, the sound of horse hooves echoed on the street.

Isabel stood behind the counter at Pier 1. It was a half-busy day. Over the intercom, Isabel could hear the scuffling of boxes as John unpacked a shipment in the basement. Metal clanged, distantly. Although she hadn't had much sleep, she wasn't tired or lonely; the warm curve of her skin kept her company. She had pulled her hair back into a ponytail. Her face felt clean and planed as she stood there, ringing things up efficiently.

It was all new. The taste, the scent, the feel, the tumble of nerves in her stomach, the memory of the night before. She wouldn't call Rebecca, because they would see each other at the theater that night, but she wanted to call Rebecca. Ringing up bits of brass and rattan and sugar, she summoned the feeling of Rebecca's teeth pulling gently at her nipple; the sensation went all the way down to her heels. And she could summon Rebecca's voice, too, her carefully interrogative way of speaking as she said, "Is this too weird for you?"

What was too weird? Isabel leaned her elbows on the counter, realizing as she did so that she was, actually, a bit light-headed with fatigue, and wishing for a cup of coffee. What was too weird? Her father didn't even ask why she didn't call; he didn't ask how she got home, so she didn't have to tell him that she walked the mile from the bus stop, fast and silent in her silver suit, passing by each dark house like a wayward star. Isabel's father drove her to work in silence—not an angry silence, more an uncomfortable one. As if he wanted to ask her a question, but wasn't sure how to ask it. Shutting the car door, Isabel understood that he thought she had been with a boy. Heart sinking, Isabel knew that he would gather his courage to talk to her about it that night.

She reddened, imagining it. He probably thought it was the naked one.

Isabel was leaning under the counter, putting the bags of different sizes in order, when she heard a voice that was unmistakably Lottie's. When Isabel stood up, the first thing she saw was Ben's wild curly hair, silhouetted against the storefront window. He was turned away from Isabel, barefoot, wearing a white T-shirt, and holding up a straw sandal.

"Ah, Kung Fu," he said. "Break this shoe with your mind."

Lottie, standing in the aisle, was laughing. Her hair was shorter, shoulder length. It made her look older. Seeing Isabel, Lottie turned right around and walked away, toward the back of the store. Isabel could see one hand fluttering behind her, her elbow hyperextended in that funny way it did when she walked, pushing the air aside.

Ben swiveled. "Oh, it's you," he said. Just past him, Bettina was browsing in the flip-flops.

"Yeah," said Isabel. She tried to smile casually. Ben didn't smile back.

"You girls," he said. "You say you like each other so much." He shook his head, and made a sound like air going out of a tire.

Lottie came back up the aisle, fast, carrying a little fern.

"This one," she said loudly, banging it down on the counter. Its fronds shook.

Bettina looked up from the flip-flops. "What's going on?" she said in her strange melody of tones, and then, seeing Isabel, "Hiya."

Isabel stared at Bettina. "Did she hear you?" she said to Lottie.

"They did the implant thing," said Lottie. "She can hear." She said this as if it had been Isabel's fault in the first place that Bettina couldn't hear.

"Wow," said Isabel. "That's really great."

"It's okay," said Lottie, looking away. "I want to buy this plant," she said firmly. That was so like her, to insist on her right to the fern as if to say: *This is just a store now.*

Bettina took off one of her sneakers to try on a flip-flop with a bright yellow toehold. She was wearing a chain of little bells around her ankle, and they jingled as she flip-flopped unevenly up and down the aisle.

Isabel held up one pale green branch so that Lottie could see the brown spots. "This one has bugs," she said. "Don't buy it."

Lottie eyed the little fern suspiciously. "Fucking rip-off store," she said, clearly including the people who worked there among the inventory.

"Yeah," said Isabel. There she was: Lottie. Her blue-green eyes, her opal ring, her scar, the sealed-over place. Me, too, Isabel wanted to say, touching her own chest. Always, Lottie.

The innocent plant sat between them, awaiting a decision.

"So do you want it?" said Isabel.

Lottie flicked at the frond, pushed the plant away. "Bettina!" she said. "Come on." Bettina slid the flip-flop off, slid her sneaker back on, jingling. The three of them walked out of the store together, Lottie and Ben with Bettina between them, all three so tan. Isabel saw them pause in front of the window. Ben was tall and barefoot in the light, his jeans riding low as ever. Lottie's blond hair blew back gently in the breeze. Their mouths were moving, but Isabel couldn't hear them. Then they walked away.

EVENING

Isabel sat on the stoop, smoking. The sun was going down, although Isabel couldn't see it from where she sat; she wondered for a moment which way was west. Was it really toward the West Village? Or was that west in relation to something else? In her five-year-old down jacket from high school and a series of mismatched earrings—a silver hoop, a red star, a cross, a larger silver hoop, and on the other side, a feather—Isabel smoked three Trues, slowly, because she was trying to quit. She really should quit. The November cold bit at her. Her stoop was not at all romantic or inspiring; the metal railing was worn away unevenly, as if it had been burned once, and was still scabbing. Down the street, kids shouted on the playground. At night, their older brothers and sisters pounded the equipment—the enormous faded-green fiberglass turtle, the metal roundabout, the big battered seesaw—making it echo.

Isabel retied her boot laces. She ran her hands through her short, short hair, which was a bit scraggly at the moment; she and Thea usually cut each other's hair, in the kitchen, with the kitchen scissors. Thea, actually, was fairly good at it. Isabel was not, although Thea didn't seem to mind. Thea stood in the kitchen in her overalls, one strap undone, a cigarette dangling from one side of her mouth, her own coal-black hair standing up here and there (Isabel's handiwork), ample and warm, singing along to the Pretenders as she carefully snipped away at Isabel's hair while Isabel sat on the wooden bathtub cover. They liked to make the lentil stew that came, dry, in a plastic bag at the bodega on the corner while they were cutting hair, adding their own carrots and things, so the stew would be simmering, very pleasant, and there were their two glasses of red wine on the scuffed Formica kitchen table they had found—a treasure!—right in front of their building on Avenue A. Then, for some reason, they always had sex.

That was what they might have done on this late afternoon. Instead, Thea was upstairs with Cricket and Isabel just did not feel comfortable there, she didn't know why—well, she did know why, but Thea swore there was nothing going on, Cricket was just an intense person. A committed person: Cricket had been to El Salvador twice. She was a small, slender, dark-haired woman, kind of on the boyish side, which was not really Thea's type, but Cricket had the look of someone who was willing to try anything once. And, apparently, had. According to Thea, who seemed to admire Cricket's reckless streak. Also, they did a lot of coke together, Cricket cutting up the lines, holding the razor in her stained, stubby fingers, her tiny, braless breasts clearly visible in her carelessly buttoned shirt. Cricket, over a few extra-generous lines she had cut for Thea, had recently let on that she wanted to work on their film with them; she had asked to read the script. So that's what Thea and Cricket were doing upstairs right now, papers scattered all around them on the bed.

Isabel lit another True, feeling unworried. The crisp sound of the match against the flint strip seemed to indicate that quitting was a simple matter of will. Like many things. When she and Thea had graduated and left the small college town they both disdained back in July, the most precious thing they carried with them to New York was their script. They knew it wouldn't be easy. Their film was experimental; it incorporated all the theories they both knew about film, but, they both felt certain, went beyond those theories. As Thea often said, "We're in completely new territory here. We're inventing a language." It didn't have a title yet; they couldn't find the phrase that encompassed, or referenced, all the myriad things their film was. It was political. It was nonlinear. It was diffuse. It made use of film *as film:* the celluloid itself was to be scratched, bitten, torn, painted on, and generally roughed up. Thea was planning to do the biting herself. Isabel would do the painting, although she couldn't really paint, but that was part of the point. Isabel had written most of the dialogue; Thea was going to do most of the filming, although Isabel would do some, too. They shared a deep sense of ethics about women and equipment.

But unlike Thea, who would remain entirely off-camera, Isabel had a pivotal onscreen role as Diana, goddess of the hunt. Diana was also the goddess of the moon, the virgin goddess, twin sister to Apollo, and an avenging deity: the protector of women. She carried a bow and arrow. Thea and Isabel planned to use Diana ironically, as a witness to the modern degradation of women and the planet: sitting in her robes with her bow and arrow next to tired female office workers on the subway, attending rallies, listening in at Pentagon meetings. Isabel had practiced raising her eyebrow in a knowing, vengeful way. At the climactic moment, Diana was going to kill anti-abortion protestors with her bow and arrow, outside an embattled abortion clinic. Isabel and Thea had already made Diana's papier-mâché bow and arrow, which was leaning against a corner of their bedroom. They had worked very hard getting the bow right, making sure it wasn't too heavy, gluing iridescent feathers to the arrow; Thea, as a surprise, had made Isabel an earring with one of the leftovers.

Isabel eschewed the idea of "stardom," but she did have a special fondness for her bow. She liked to practice holding it when she came home from work at night, striking poses around the apartment in a mythic and empowered, yet ironic, manner. When Isabel grasped the chalky bow, she felt a vengeful strength flow up and down her arm. Her construction-paper crown of laurel leaves rested lightly, benevolently, in her hair. She bent her knees, clasping the stringless bow in one hand, the papier-mâché arrow in the other. She believed in Diana, not as a deity, but as a principle. She knew she could play that principle. When she thought about the things that happened to women, the violence, all the large and small deaths of the spirit—look at what had happened to her mother, for instance—she felt she had been born to play this very part.

Now all they needed was some money. Thea, whose family was Greek, and rich, and thoroughly scandalized by her, had money, but she couldn't touch it until she was thirty. So they lived on Isabel's paychecks from her lowly office job at the Van Zandt Foundation for the Arts and Thea's paychecks from driving a newspaper delivery truck. They tried to save. Thea wrote an impassioned letter to the maiden Greek aunt she was sure was a lesbian, but so far there had been no reply. They had to start shooting soon, because in the summer they wanted to take their film to a women's film festival in Mexico. They were already practicing their Spanish. So Isabel didn't really care what Cricket thought of the script; she had other, larger matters to consider. And then there was her birthday, which was tomorrow. Thea was working on a surprise; she'd been whispering into the phone at night. Isabel wanted whatever the surprise was, but the impending occasion also felt troubling in a way she hadn't expected. To be twenty-two. What was that, being twenty-two? What did it mean?

Isabel had noticed, during recent birthdays, that a melancholy tended to settle over her for a few days before and after, and that her dreams became darkly vivid. Subways going into the ocean. Huge animals in their bedroom closet. And with each birthday it increased, subtly. In the last few days, she'd felt a thick weight on her shoulders and a fatigue no amount of coffee could unseat. Truth be told, she was almost glad when Cricket showed up in her black watch cap and quasi-devilish expression so that Isabel could say, "Oh, I think I'll go outside and have a cigarette." Having to smoke outside was the new rule to help her quit; by wintertime she should be either nicotine-free or frozen to death.

And so there she was, on the stoop alone. Nearly twenty-two, but no closer to knowing something she couldn't quite make out, but wanted to know, something important. Something that, on her birthday especially, tried to get into, or perhaps out of, a part of herself she secretly called her soul. Isabel stubbed out her cigarette on the stoop. She would write about it in her journal, later. A single star appeared in the sky. Evening had arrived.

Upstairs, the heat was clanging. They balanced tin pie plates of water on each radiator, but it was still dry as a bone and hot enough to melt wax in their low-ceilinged, railroad apartment. They kept all the windows open a crack, so that as Isabel walked from one room into another a little draft of air tapped her, combined with the increasingly intense scent of Thea's hand-rolled cigarettes. (Thea had no intention of quitting smoking, so she smoked wherever she wanted.) Isabel could always find Thea by that scent, the lightly sweet scent of Drum loose tobacco. Isabel stepped extra heavily in her heavy boots, so Cricket and Thea could hear her coming, just in case. She'd rather not have to deal with anything unpleasant the day before her birthday. However, in the furthermost room, the bedroom, what she found was Thea on the futon bed surrounded by papers, Cricket tilting back in a wooden chair, reading. Thea, smoking, was watching intently as Cricket read. The dark blue Drum tobacco package lay beside Thea on the bed. On the wall over her head hung a poster from Fellini's *City of Women.*

"Hey," said Isabel, tossing off her coat and climbing, in her boots, onto the futon with Thea.

"Cricket's up to the Pentagon scene," said Thea quietly. She had on the look of unswerving concentration that made it seem possible that she would, in fact, be as famous as she planned to be. And she had been famous, in a way, at school for precisely that forceful look. It was a look that made Isabel feel safe and calm. They would be famous, or at least well-known.

Cricket decisively shuffled the papers. Her boyish, freckled face was serious. "You guys are so brilliant," she said. "I'm learning so much. But it isn't the way these military types think. They think in *numbers,* they think in statistical curves, with grids and shit. They're all about grids. You have to get that in here."

"Huh," said Thea, laying back against the pillows and blowing smoke toward the ceiling. "Interesting. Grids. What do you think, Isabel?"

Cricket looked at Isabel intently. Isabel couldn't decide if the look was hostile or lascivious. There was something sexy about Cricket, she had to admit it. Sexy like an urchin. Isabel glanced surreptitiously at the dresser. Their wallets were still there. She glanced back at Cricket, who was looking at her just as intently as before, as if Isabel's answer were going to settle a bet or put out a fire.

"Go ahead," said Cricket, biting her lip. "You won't hurt my feelings."

"Part of our idea, Cricket," said Isabel in a patient tone of voice, "was not to be constrained by those kinds of representational boundaries. I mean, when I play Diana, I'm not thinking about, like, the right way to hunt a deer. It's not about that."

Cricket nodded avidly, then cried, "But it's important! I'm sorry. I'm sure you're right, in one way, but you *have* to think about what's going on on the planet. People are being killed *every day* over just this kind of shit." She was fervent suddenly, where two minutes ago, reading, she had seemed cool and critical. Cricket jumped up. "I have to go," she said, then, to Thea, "Call me. Bye, Isabel." She gave Isabel another intent look.

Thea walked through the rooms and let Cricket out, then came back to the bed. Little bits of loose tobacco flecked the sheets. "She just broke up with her girlfriend," said Thea.

"I didn't know she had a girlfriend," said Isabel.

"This married woman. Very complicated."

"I bet," said Isabel.

Thea kissed her. Thea's kisses were always simultaneously meditative and passionate, as if she had just realized, just that moment, how important kissing was. "Are you hungry?"

"No."

"Then take off your boots."

Isabel lay on top of Thea in the dark in the manner they privately called *surfing*. Isabel bent her knees, gently waving her heels in the air. She buried her face in Thea's neck. Thea put her arms around Isabel, enfolded Isabel's ass in her hands and stroked it, slowly. Above and below them, the building echoed with the noises of conversation, TV, laughing, opening and closing doors. It occurred to Isabel to have sex again, or maybe dinner—she was hungry now—but Thea was talking.

"You know what's wild to think about? All the layers of people that have occupied this space. Their accumulated energy. A farm family, maybe, when this was land, and then all the immigrants, Italian people or Chinese people or Eastern European Jews, all crammed in here, and someone got old here, someone died here, I'm sure, someone gave birth here." Thea's hands, absently stroking, were large and warm. The November wind blew against the window, rattling it. "I think I see them sometimes."

"For real?" Isabel was getting sleepy, lulled by the sound of

Thea's voice. It was nice to think of herself and Thea as the latest in many waves of immigrants building the city face by face, like coral.

"Kind of. I don't know. Do you?"

"I don't like ghosts," said Isabel.

Thea pulled the blanket up over both of them. "Tigerlily. Shhh."

Sitting in the common room at the Van Zandt Foundation for the Arts, Isabel alphabetized files, a task she found absurdly pleasurable. She sang along to Sheena Easton on the radio and popped one file behind or in front of the next. The pile slowly grew heavier in her lap. Next to her at the table, Patrick, her boss, was carefully clipping out a picture from the newspaper of Ronald and Nancy Reagan laughing together under an umbrella in Paris. As Isabel slid *Fatina* in front of *Fattorusso*, Patrick expertly snipped out first Ronald's, then Nancy's head. Then, using a glue stick, he glued Ronald's head onto Nancy's body, and vice versa, and pasted the newly constructed image onto a piece of typing paper.

"What are you doing?" said Isabel.

"New Year's invitations," said Patrick, a small and snappy man. "My annual event. It's a costume party. You'll have to come—in your Diana outfit!" In his black jeans, pointy black boots, black shirt, and goatee, he looked slightly like the devil. Patrick took the piece of paper over to the Xerox machine and keyed in one hundred copies. While the copies were being made, he leaned against the machine and regarded Isabel, smiling.

"You look like Prince today," said Isabel.

"I am a prince," said Patrick. "When I'm not a princess."

"And when are you a princess?"

"Sometimes."

"Like during lunch?" During lunch, Patrick sometimes slipped away to the men's room of the subway station nearby. He always came back with a little styrofoam cup of coffee, as if that was what he'd gone out for, and drank it down with relish.

"No, Diana, darling. Speaking of princesses. During *lunch* I'm the queen of Manhattan." He laughed. "That was too easy." He cocked his head. "Isn't today your birthday?"

"Yeah."

"How old? Tell the truth."

"Twenty-two," said Isabel. "I don't know. I hate Lady Diana, don't even joke."

"Oh, I adore her. I got up at four A.M. to watch the wedding. Plus, I think she's a dyke—have you seen those pictures of her as a teenager in her field hockey uniform?" The Xerox machine glowed behind Patrick, a stack of Ronald

Reagan in a belted dress, Nancy in a suit, growing on the plastic output tray. "You don't know what?"

Isabel stacked the alphabetized files on the desk. "I guess I don't like birthdays. But it's not like I fetishize age or anything."

Patrick frowned at his stack. "We need toner."

Isabel grabbed the box from under the table. "Here. I can't quite explain it. I feel—vaguely unsettled. Maybe I'm just impatient to get started on the film."

Patrick flipped open the machine, emptied a flurry of black toner into the chamber. "This shit is so radioactive," he said, closing the machine back up again. "Okay. Well. Two modern solutions. One, therapy."

"Can't afford it."

"Or two, sex." Ron and Nancy, considerably brightened, smiled once again, over and over, from the output tray.

"I have sex," said Isabel. "Maybe not quite as much as you."

"Oh, that's just lunchtime trade," said Patrick. He collected his stack. "Do you want a cake later? I'll make Faith buy you a cake."

"I don't want a cake," said Isabel. "I think Thea's planning something for tonight."

"Oh, really?" said Patrick in a meaningful way. "I wonder what *that* could be."

"Don't tell me," said Isabel. "I want to be surprised."

"That's very twenty-two," said Patrick, and left the room.

Isabel turned up the radio. *McLeod. McGough.* In her short time there she had grown fond of Patrick, and he, it seemed, of her. He had a veneer of snideness, but he was actually very loyal to the foundation. He had been there ten years already; Faith Van Zandt, the founder, relied on him entirely and said so often. They were like brother and sister, those two, which, now and then, made Isabel jealous. She tried to imagine herself and Jeannie as that close, but the image never quite held.

Isabel took herself out to lunch at a Cuban-Chinese diner she had discovered just a few blocks from the office, and what an amazing combination that was, Cuban and Chinese. How had that happened? She sat at the counter eating a plate of beans and avocado and yellow rice, which smelled fantastically good in the cold. The windows of the restaurant were steamed up on the inside so that the daylight coming in was both diffuse and glowing. Isabel pulled her journal out of her knapsack along with a birthday card from her father and sister that had come the day before. The birthday card was red, with a raised illustration of a bouquet of flowers on it; above the flowers, in gold cursive, it said, "Happy Birthday to a Wonderful Daughter." Inside, there was a check for fifty dollars, and her father had written, "What are you up to in the Big Apple? Jeannie and I can't wait to see you at Hanukkah! Love and kisses." Then they had both signed their names, her father's firm and swift, Jeannie's a bit childish-looking, even now, when she was no longer a child, and worked in the store with their father. Isabel still thought Jeannie should have gone to college, but Jeannie was determined. She liked the business.

Isabel folded the card and drank some lukewarm tap water out of a dull red plastic cup. Her journal was a black-and-white composition book, reassuringly schoolgirlish, with wide lines. She opened it, wrote the date. Wrote, *Today is my birthday!,* reread the sentence, found it lacking somehow, and closed her journal again. Isabel ate her beans and rice and avocado, knapsack on her lap, with suitable lunch-rush dispatch, while imagining, slowly, what her mother would have given her on this birthday.

Isabel had done this on every birthday since her mother died. At nine, the imaginary gifts were meeting the Monkees and white go-go boots and every single Nancy Drew. At twelve, a record player, a trip to California, just the two of them. At eighteen, a dalmation and a long red silk scarf, and at twenty-one, a piece of property in the woods no one knew about. It had white paper birches, and a lake, and a little house. Isabel didn't tell anyone that she did this, not even Thea. It was her private birthday ritual, a ritual she almost forgot until her birthday came around again and then, like an animal, she would find herself going off alone for a moment or two, sometimes longer, and a vision of the gift would appear to her, floating up from the depths of her mind with great lightness and inevitability, as if it were truly a gift from without and not from within. Sometimes the gifts were lavish. Sometimes they were elegantly astute, the thing Isabel needed most without even knowing it herself. Sometimes they were intensely useful. But they were always serious.

As the lunchtime din rose and fell around her, what came to Isabel as the gift on this, her twenty-second birthday, was a luminescent strand of pearls. A long, luxurious strand of pearls, cool to the touch, with the tiny imperfections of the real thing. In her mind, she ran the pearls through her fingers, held them to her cheek. She didn't put them around her neck, not yet. She imagined rolling them in her palm and hearing them click with a subtle and beautiful sound. Ordering a *café con leche,* Isabel thought how absurd a notion it was, herself in pearls. She didn't wear pearls. She cut her hair with the kitchen scissors, lived on Avenue A, and wore black work boots. She hadn't shaved her legs in years. And it seemed mocking, such a delicate gift from one who had been in so much pain.

But there they were, hanging luminously in her mind. They were the day's gift, and it was Isabel's private rule that once the gift appeared—a very specific phenomenon that

ticality: a large, cumbersome video camera, with its web of wires and cables, that Thea had bought from the college media center with a bond from her grandmother, an elderly, deaf Greek lady who had never left the island where she'd been born. They kept the camera locked in a special cabinet; Thea wore the key on a piece of string around her neck. The images on videotape, which they could play back only on the television after a laborious hooking-up procedure, were strange: grainy, tinny, with sharp echoes. On videotape, everything looked like shadows. There wasn't much you could do on video, but Thea, in one of her energetic moods, had had to have the thing. So far, they had used it to take memorial pictures of the old station wagon that had gotten them to New York and then, belching green smoke, promptly died the second they parked it on Avenue A.

The apartment was a great deal. Although, as Isabel rushed past the playground, nodding in a friendly way at the boys who stared at her as she passed, she wondered if maybe what Cricket maintained was right, that, tragically, their very presence in the neighborhood couldn't help being anything but gentrification. "So what's the solution?" Isabel had said, tapping an ash into her empty beer bottle. "Move out?" This was at the Duchess, in the summer, where they had met Cricket, who was avidly pumping quarters into the jukebox to play all Donna Summer. Spotting them, Cricket had asked if she could draw their picture because she found them so incredibly beautiful.

"Solution!" yelled Cricket over "Hot Stuff," sketching rapidly and sniffing from time to time. "There isn't one!"

"Sure there is," said Thea loudly, leaning in. "Become a part of the community. Organize."

"It's too big!" said Cricket. "It's bigger than all of us! The city is *dying*!"

Isabel tried to exchange a look of exasperation with Thea, but Thea was staring curiously at Cricket. "The city isn't dying," said Thea. "I love the energy here. You need to have a little faith."

"I have no faith!" yelled Cricket wildly. "Jesus. I am a Puerto Rican *orphan* raised by Orthodox Jews! How could I have any faith?"

Thea squinted thoughtfully. "We have to talk more about this," she said. It occurred to Isabel at that moment that Thea had a thing for orphans—wasn't she, Isabel, half an orphan?—but that Cricket out-orphaned her. She had felt nervous about Cricket ever since. When Cricket finally turned the sketch around, Isabel and Thea looked consumptive, which was especially strange considering that they were both quite tan at the time.

At any rate, Isabel thought, climbing the steps of their building, Cricket might be slightly crazy but she was also, in a way, right. Avenue A, like a small town, didn't consider you a true citizen until you had lived and died a little there. Shed some blood.

Isabel sat in the La-Z-Boy recliner, surrounded by presents. All their friends, plus several people she didn't know, stood around and fanned out through the rooms, drinking, smoking, talking, watching Thea, who was wearing a heavy battery belt, make a video of Isabel on her twenty-second birthday. "What kind of camera is that?" said a woman with a platinum ruff of hair and one long pinky nail.

"Look here!" said Thea to Isabel. "Speak up!"

"Oh my," said Isabel, opening a box wrapped in Playboy centerfolds. Inside the box were garters, crotchless underwear, a rather spectacular red bustier. "Who is this from? Celia! You pig!"

Patrick, perched next to her on the arm of the La-Z-Boy, said, "She'll never wear it."

"I will too," said Isabel.

A box with a blizzard of crepe paper on it, full of good-luck candles. A basketball; there was a hoop on the playground. A picture postcard of a painting of Diana in billowing white robes that hung in the Met. From Thea, a box of bubble gum, to help her quit smoking. Isabel put a few pieces in her mouth and began blowing bubbles as she opened more presents: a pretty little paper envelope of cocaine. A teapot and a box of Long Life Tea. An entire box of Mao caps for the generals in the movie to wear (there was a lengthy Chinese interlude). From Patrick, tomato seeds and dirt and three perfect, cobalt-blue pots. "It's always good to farm a little in the city," he said. From Thea—her main gifts—a book about Mexico, a light meter, a woodcut print of the phases of the moon, and an old book about the sport of archery with a hilarious 1950s bobby-soxer in a short gym skirt on the front, pulling back the bow.

Isabel, opening boxes, blew a big pink bubble, popped it. People drifted in and out; Cricket was in the kitchen, mixing drinks. Isabel could hear the blender going: piña coladas were her specialty. There was a slender, string-of-pearls-sized box balanced on a box covered in newspaper, but when she opened it there was only a nice pen inside. From one of their more unimaginative friends. "Thanks," said Isabel.

Around three in the morning, sitting on Thea's lap in the La-Z-Boy amid a sea of wrapping paper and bows and open boxes, Isabel picked up one of the cobalt-blue pots from the floor, pulled open the bag of dirt, and awkwardly dipped the pot into it. She tore open the bag of tomato seeds, shook a few into the dirt. "Look," she said, holding it out to Thea. "Nature."

Thea, still wearing the wide battery belt, laughed, bouncing the basketball. The woman with the platinum ruff of hair and one long pinky nail was sitting on the floor, reading the archery book. "How old is he?" Thea said.

"Patrick?" Isabel read the tomato seed package. Strong sunlight required. Maybe in the bathroom. "I don't know. Mid-forties, maybe."

"Wow," said Thea. "Do you think he was always so conventional?"

"He was a stage actor for a long time. He said he burned out on it."

"Yeah," said Thea, then, wryly, "theater kills."

"But I think," said Isabel, shaking a bit of earth over the seeds with a forefinger, "that he had the potential for more than that, you know what I mean? There's something subversive there, even though he's also such a conscientious—"

"Bureaucrat," finished Thea. "He made his choices." She palmed the ball, held it aloft, as if about to shoot. "But he's a nice guy."

Isabel set the pot on the floor and picked up the bustier, held it against her chest. "What happened to Celia?" she said. "I didn't see her leave." She wondered if the bustier would actually fit her; it seemed somewhat small and it was scratchy, cheap. The kind of thing Celia would wear with attitude and hairy armpits at her bartending job, but would Isabel? Really? Maybe Patrick was right, though she hated to think so.

"She's passed out in the other room," said the platinum-haired woman. "Can you get any cabs out here?"

"Cricket goes a little heavy on the rum," said Isabel.

"A woman of extremes," said Thea. "Never anything halfway." She bounced the basketball against the wall, which caused a crumbling, shifting sound, as of plaster falling within. The platinum-haired woman got up and wandered away, taking the archery book with her.

Isabel felt a twinge of loneliness. She sighed, longing for the pearls. Had her mother ever even worn pearls? She couldn't remember, but maybe she had. "Let's light one of these good-luck candles," Isabel said, leaning over Thea and grabbing one from the floor. "Here: For True Love. Give me a match."

Over the next few days, the pearls continued to haunt Isabel, like a puzzle she couldn't figure out. She liked her basketball, she loved her framed postcard of Diana, she and Thea had enjoyed the pretty little paper envelope of cocaine, but the pearls came to her bathed in yearning; she thought about them at stray, defenseless moments: in the tub, just before falling asleep. Thea got bronchitis, her annual winter occurrence. Sitting by the vaporizer, smearing VapoRub on Thea's chest, Isabel imagined the pearls' creamy, opalescent weight. If she had them, she thought, she would keep them in a special box. She would do whatever it is you're supposed to do to pearls, polish them or air them or wrap them in silk. As Thea slept one afternoon, the bold *City of Women* poster watching over her, Isabel opened the dresser and unwrapped the bit of jewelry she did have wrapped in silk: her mother's old high school ring on its fine gold chain, the chain that had once seemed so elegantly long but was actually, for an adult, just barely medium-length. Isabel put it on under her shirt, next to her skin. The vaporizer exhaled damply. The odd purposeless pipe began collecting moisture. Thea coughed, turned over. The old ring lightly, awkwardly, thumped Isabel's breastbone. It didn't quite fit either under or over her shirt button. Isabel looked at Thea, wondering what she was dreaming.

Isabel and Thea sat on the stoop, working on their script. Isabel read carefully, making little notations in pencil. Thea leafed through the *International Herald Tribune,* which she regularly stole off the truck she drove. It was a Saturday morning; their laundry was piled in pillowcases in the red laundry cart upstairs, but the day was bright, they had slept in, the coffee was good, and then Thea had said, "I made some interesting changes, sit down and let me show you, just for a minute."

To which Isabel had replied, "Only if I can smoke."

So now Thea sat on the top step and Isabel sat one step below her, between Thea's legs, as the pages ruffled brightly in the breeze and the smoke from their two cigarettes—Isabel's light True, Thea's heavier hand-rolled one—wafted away from them into the Saturday street. Both their pockets were full of quarters. People carried home grocery bags, walked dogs; Ukrainian Catholic schoolgirls, released for the weekend from their uniforms, sashayed past in tight Jordache jeans and swatches of plum-colored eyeshadow. Their blocks' drug dealers—the two skinny Juniors—were engaged in earnest conversation with each other on the corner. Isabel saw it all out of the corner of her eye as she read, in the pleasurable way one continually glimpses the waves when reading at the beach.

"I don't know about this chorus business," she said. "I think it's heavy-handed."

"We have to get in the idea about global capital," said Thea, "so I thought, why not just have them say it? Or sing it."

"I think it's too much. Let's just go from the shot of Teresa and Sue on the road to the meeting of the generals. Then we'd have that contrast—"

"Cricket liked it," said Thea.

"Really?" said Isabel. "I'm surprised. She seems like such a literal person."

"I wouldn't say she's literal. I think, because of her experiences in South America, and her background, she likes to keep it real. Did you know she can put together an M-16 blindfolded?"

Isabel craned her neck around to look up at Thea, who had an innocently impressed expression on her face, as if the value of Cricket's skill were self-evident. "Have we agreed that Cricket is working on this project?" said Isabel. "Have you already made that commitment to her?"

"Not exactly," said Thea. "I told her you and I had to talk about it. You know, she really respects you. I think you scare her a little bit." She playfully pulled a strand of Isabel's hair. "Tigerlily."

Isabel pulled her head away. "I'm serious. This is serious, Thea. You know, it is *our* project, and I'm not convinced her sensibility—"

"Is it?" said Thea.

"What?"

"Is it still our project? Are you still into it?"

Isabel looked up at Thea again. Thea's look was cautious. "Of course," said Isabel. "What are you talking about?"

"I don't know." Thea dropped her gaze, closing the newspaper. "Sometimes you just seem a little—less interested."

Isabel stared at Thea. "I am totally committed to this, Thea. It's been my birthday thing. My mother or whatever. You know. I always get that way."

"Okay," said Thea slowly.

"My job is nine to five," said Isabel. "It's not like yours. I'm not home in the middle of the day to work on the film, and then at night you fall asleep so early—"

Thea nodded. "We should make a specific time to work on it every night," she said. "We haven't even looked at locations yet."

"Right," said Isabel. "That's just what I mean. Do you want to be nonmonogamous?"

Thea glanced down the street as a car backfired. "No," she said offhandedly. "Do you?"

"Not right this second."

They sat in silence for a few minutes. Thea leaned down and put her arms around Isabel, kissed her head. Thea smelled like sweet coffee and strong Drum tobacco. She was all wide, dark strokes and broad beams, held together by the magnetism of her forceful look. Isabel reflected that you can never really know what's going on inside someone else's mind; she wondered how difficult it could be, really, to put together a gun.

"But listen," said Isabel.

"What," said Thea. "My ass is getting cold."

"Maybe I should go back to school."

"Why? We just got out of school."

Isabel shrugged. "Maybe I should go to film school."

"You already know so much more than those jerks," said Thea passionately. "See, this is what I meant before. This is what I've been feeling from you recently."

"What?" Isabel moved up to sit beside Thea on her step, her legs stiff from the coolness. It was almost time for lunch already.

"That you've been looking *outside* for your sense of vocation, that you're not centered in your art. You seem all restless and perturbed. But the art—" She tapped Isabel's chest lightly with her forefinger. "The art is there. And I know it's there in you. It's why you're Diana, Isabel, don't you know that? She's the goddess of the hunt, she's chaste. I'm so in love with that in you." Her eyes were alight, and sure.

"With what? Since when am I so fucking chaste?"

"No. That purity of spirit."

As they unloaded their laundry into the big metal washers, Isabel silently admired Thea's casual strength, the way she could heft and empty the laundry bag in one smooth gesture, pulling quarters out of her overalls pocket with the other hand and tipping them quickly into the little metal slots. Despite her patrician roots, Thea had the sort of strength usually attributed to peasants. Although she seemed entirely unaware of it, she had natural physical grace, even in overalls, even with the few extra pounds she always carried. Her black hair stuck up, uncombed, all around her head. She had dark circles under her eyes. But she was beautiful, even more beautiful, possibly, undone like that in the Laundromat, with bad Saturday-morning hair. She smiled brightly at Isabel over the washing machine, clearly reassured by their conversation on the stoop, and Isabel, in turn, felt reassured by Thea's smile. They were back to being famous together, and free; somehow the two were connected. When she walked down the street with Thea, Isabel felt like they were sailors on leave together, loose in the world, hands in their pockets. Isabel poured soap powder into the machine. Thea pushed the coin slot in. They sat down, the red cart between them, watching the wash go around. You couldn't leave your wash untended here; junkies would steal it. Thea took the folded *International Herald Tribune* out of her back overalls pocket and went back to reading it. Isabel saw through the washing machine's glass window that her new maroon shirt was bleeding pink into the soapy water. Too late now. A wisp of doubt floated across her mind. Thea was right: she was restless and perturbed, had been ever since her birthday. *Was* she losing her sense of vocation? She worried, watching the water pinken. Maybe she didn't have the pure spirit of an artist. Maybe she was one of the ones who wasn't going to make it. The thought was unbearable; she tapped her boot heels on the linoleum floor, summoning her will.

On Sunday afternoon, it rained. Isabel painted Diana's bow in the middle of the living room floor while Thea, in the recliner, worked on the storyboard, drawing little frames with stick figures in them, and drank a beer.

"It's so hard to fit in everything we want to do here," said Thea with frustration. "I have all these ideas and not enough space to put them in. And we still need to write the end. Let's stay up all night tonight and do it. I got these great pills from Cricket."

"Mmmm," said Isabel. "I don't know. I don't think Cricket is a pharmacist. Besides, I have to go to work tomorrow." The bow's tip gleamed with black. "I think I want a purple stripe down the center." She left open space for the stripe as she continued painting.

"Fuck," said Thea. She wadded up a piece of paper. "And fuck the job, Isabel. This is more important."

"Did you hear from your aunt yet?" said Isabel.

Thea scowled at the paper. She wasn't really listening. Isabel feathered in black paint on the craggy papier-mâché surface. The *International Herald Tribune* under the bow, smeared with black, was full of international news: NATO something. Japanese Automakers Decline something. Isabel finished the bow and spent a long time making a black swirl over the headlines with the paint left in the brush. The bow looked beautiful, she thought, strong and supple as a tree limb. Diana was such a benevolent goddess, without fear. But she had another quality, too, Isabel thought, a subtly sorrowful quality that Isabel planned to bring out when she played her in the movie. Diana was a witness. She understood it all: women in childbirth, women in war, Cassie in a hospital supply closet, pills clattering to the floor from her sleeves.

"Maybe Diana's robes should be black," said Isabel.

Thea abruptly tossed the entire storyboard to the floor and stood up, looking around wonderingly as if she'd just dropped into the apartment from the sky. The empty beer bottle fell over and rolled under the recliner. "I can't think in this room," she said, and left it.

A few days later, Thea fell into what Isabel had come to call her Greek mood; she pretended to work on the script, but didn't really. She gloomily took on an extra shift on the truck, getting up early in the morning, then sleeping all afternoon, grimy from the bundles of newsprint tied with twine. In the evenings, she constantly talked about the script to various people, sitting in the La-Z-Boy with the phone in her lap; she left tobacco in the seams of every piece of furniture; she ate too much. She said she was raising money, on the phone all the time; she did manage to raise a thousand dollars from their former women's studies professor. Her aunt sent $250, and an evil eye. Thea said her mood was because of the winter. "I always get bummed in the winter. I don't like to be cold," she told Isabel, snipping slowly at Isabel's hair. Chinese take-out cartons littered the bathtub cover. "Maybe we should move to California."

"Maybe," said Isabel. "After we're done with the movie." She felt the back of her head; it felt choppy. "That's okay. It's short enough now."

Thea put down the scissors and wandered into the living room. Isabel heard her turn on *Hill Street Blues*, the creak of the recliner tilting back. Thea's own hair was beginning to curl up at the ends. She said she was growing it out. There was no obvious reason for Thea's malaise; it was just something that happened to her, like weather. She tended to emerge from these times strikingly renewed. She and Isabel had met, in fact, when Thea was in a Greek mood. Thea sat in the last row of their Third World Women class, up on the back of her chair, her sweatshirt hood on, speaking up rarely, but with great conviction. Isabel thought she looked exotic and strong; she seemed to know a lot about international politics, the governments of distant countries. She seemed to know a lot about oppression. They went out for beers and talked about dualities. Thea said somberly, "I have such fierce inner contradictions I almost get ripped apart by them sometimes," lighting Isabel's cigarette off the end of her own. Her face in the dim bar light was like a face etched on an ancient wall. The next day, she jumped up and finished two overdue term papers. Her Greek moods were always, Thea reminded Isabel now, transformative. She was moving to a deeper level.

Isabel walked to the foundation through the cold November mornings, crossing First Avenue, Second Avenue, Third Avenue. She took St. Marks across to Broadway, then headed down into SoHo, which was vast and hushed, so unlike their own cluttered, crowded neighborhood. There never seemed to be anyone on the street in SoHo, only traces of people on the walls: a spray-painted black shadow of a walking man in a fedora, a ragged mural of a surreally melting Three Mile Island with a motto on a painted ribbon underneath that read WHY? Trucks pulled up on the cobblestoned streets and men carrying large, flat wooden crates disappeared into gloomy warehouses. Once, Isabel turned down a street and discovered that it was full of plaster high-heeled shoes, some painted, some left raw. They were scattered there, Pompeilike, their wearers vanished; Isabel picked up one high-heeled shoe and brought it home to show Thea. The next day all the plaster shoes were gone.

When Isabel told Patrick about the shoes, he was unimpressed. He didn't care about SoHo; he was always dashing back and forth with armloads of files or tossing on his coat, with Faith, and heading off to the theater. They got invited to every show in the city.

"Here," he said to Isabel one day on his way out to lunch. "Look through these five and tell me how much money you'd give them."

"Is this a test?" said Isabel.

"Yes," said Patrick, pulling the elevator gate closed and disappearing downward. Patrick, Isabel noticed, had a widow's peak.

By the time Patrick's widow's peak ascended once again several hours later, Isabel had laid the files in a neat stack on his desk. To each file was paper-clipped a typewritten evaluation of the project along with a suggested grant amount. On one of the files, however, was a pink piece of paper on which Isabel had written by hand, *Suggest we re-evaluate.*

Patrick, still in his coat, appeared in the doorway of the common room, where Isabel was trying to make sense of a chaotic assortment of rejected grant applications from years past. What had happened to them all? she wondered. Did they simply give up from lack of money, or find a way to go on? Patrick held up the file with the pink note. "Why?" he said.

Isabel looked up. "Spitting on the audience is not that interesting. I think we might want to look back through some of the other applications before just handing these guys a check. Plus, if you look, they've already had two NEAs. There's a *much* better performance artist who did a thing I saw this summer with beheaded dolls that was just so brilliant. I don't even know if she applied—"

"She did," said Patrick. He tapped the file, considering.

"Well, you know, no one can live on these things, but at the very least we're keeping people from that extra, totally exhausting waitressing shift. These guys—" she gestured toward the pink-noted file—"are not waitressing."

"Okay," said Patrick. "Miranda quit this morning. You can help me screen. We're already getting flooded." The deadline for grant applications was January 1.

"Do I get a raise?" said Isabel.

"No," said Patrick, rushing off again.

Isabel set down her dusty stack of applications with *Rejected* scrawled in pen across the front of each one and walked out into the open loft. There were plans on Faith and Patrick's part to subdivide it one day, but at present there were simply plasterboard walls demarcating Faith's office and Patrick's office, and then an open cluster of desks and activity nearish to the elevator, like a space station. Isabel walked down to a far end of the loft, where a few mismatched desks and chairs had been left. She got a chair and carried it over to a spot underneath a high window where the sun came in every afternoon. The metal bottom of the chair fell off as she was carrying it. She paused to thread it back on. Then she went back and, after looking over two or three variously wounded strays, picked a metal desk whose only flaw was that one of its drawers didn't open. With some effort she pushed it, squeaking loudly, to join the chair. She sat down at the desk. The chair was a bit too high, and unnaturally springy. Isabel found that she didn't mind. She glanced down at the wall beside her. There, as if it had been waiting for her arrival, was a phone jack. Going back to the assemblage of office furniture leftovers, Isabel discovered a black phone lying on the floor. She brought it back to her desk and plugged it into the jack. She picked up the receiver; a dial tone sounded immediately.

Isabel, seated at her new/old desk, suppressed a laugh. Here was a funny turn of events, but why not? She could be Robin Hood for a few months, until they finished their movie. She would learn about how power really worked: inside information for the future. She picked up the receiver again to call Thea and tell her the news. She dialed. The line was busy. Isabel opened a desk drawer. Inside, there was one bent paperclip, a takeout-size plastic package of ketchup, and an old lottery ticket that obviously hadn't won.

⟡ ⟡ ⟡

With Thea working the extra shifts, Isabel, eating breakfast alone, wrote in her journal every morning before work. (*It's inherently corrupt, this whole business of grants and patronage, like Medicis—New York is the least modern of all cities, I think.*) It gave her a meditative feeling that stayed with her during the walk to the office. She casually scouted locations as she walked: a wall with a peeling Nina Hagen poster, a cavernous Ukrainian church. On St. Marks Place, the pita shop hung a silver lamé wreath in the window. The Van Zandt Foundation itself seemed like a location, with a recurring role for Isabel as an office worker. She played it empathetically, thinking of female office workers everywhere and how hard their lives were. Maybe she could organize the foundation before she left to make her film.

Isabel's personal interest, of course, ran to the performing arts, but the foundation also gave out writing grants, dance grants, visual arts grants, and, for some reason, architecture grants. Isabel wasn't entirely clear on what the architects were supposed to do with their grants—what could they do, build their own buildings?—but it was important to Faith, a small, unlined woman of fifty-three with an air of being both fey and canny, who slipped silently around the loft all day in her flat little Chinese slippers. "We are an *eclectic* institution," she liked to say. She had a peculiar, nibbling way of eating and, blooming in dry patches here and there on her face, eczema.

Isabel didn't mind her temporary role, because she found that she liked Patrick and Faith. She liked Patrick's goatee and his faint Bronx accent. She liked Faith's little slippers. She even liked Faith's scaly eczema, for its mystery. She did get a tiny raise, at Patrick's insistence. She bought a brown skirt with it, which she wore with her work boots as a kind of sartorial critique on the whole enterprise, though no one seemed to notice. She heaped files on her desk, panning for gold. She empathetically noted the poor working conditions: the uneven heat, the frequent lack of toilet paper. The loft was quiet during the day, except for low conversation and the occasional tip-tap of a typewriter. Isabel particularly liked that sound: tip-tap. Tip-tap.

Isabel stood on top of the playground's enormous faded-green fiberglass turtle, the wind blowing her makeshift sheet-robes against her legs, holding up the bow. "Thea, my arm is getting tired," she said.

Thea, her face half-woman, half-machine, fiddled with a knob on the video camera. She hitched up the battery belt. "One more minute."

Isabel sighed. "It's almost dark." Even with socks on, her feet in sandals were freezing, but Thea had taken one of the Cricket pills and now she was all energetic again. But maybe it meant her Greek mood would be over soon.

"No, it isn't," said Thea. "Come on. Two seconds. For art."

"Fuck art," said Isabel.

Thea laughed. "You look great. You're a goddess. You're a star."

"I have to pee."

Thea raised her head above the camera. "Be patient, Isabel. This is helping. I needed to *see* it. I couldn't draw the other way."

"I could have stood on a chair."

"A chair isn't high enough." She bent down again.

One of the drug-dealing Juniors appeared at the fence, wearing a sweatshirt from Disneyland. He had a cut over one eye that appeared to be still bleeding. "Hey," he said, "you girls making a movie?"

"*Si,*" said Thea. "A great, great movie."

"Cool," he said, then unzipped his pants, and peed. Isabel envied him. "You let me in free, all right?"

"*Sin duda,*" said Thea.

He walked away, zipping up. Isabel shifted the bow to the other arm. "We're going to get mugged."

"Don't be so paranoid."

Isabel looked over Thea's head at the letters and ornaments graffitied on the wall. A cat sat washing itself in the remnants of the afternoon sun in front of an elaborately spray-painted red rose. Under the rose, it said, MI CORAZON

MAGDA, 2-GETHER 4-EVER, LUV JULIO. It must have taken Julio hours, thought Isabel, crouched down by the wall to make the stem and thorns, the many delicate petals, all those letters. Maybe Magda helped him. She tried to concentrate on her Diana-ness, holding the bow aloft. But she was distracted by the shout of aqua bubble letters outlined in black, written higher up from Julio's labor of love: SHAZ40! The letters seemed to pop, brief but forceful. The same thing had been written somewhere on the wall before, Isabel remembered, in orange. Julio must have written over the orange one. The new one stood out on the much-written-on wall, like an aqua handprint. What was SHAZ40: name, place, beloved? The mark was mysterious, defiant, and irrefutable: Shaz40 was there, end of sentence. And who had made it? Probably a boy, Isabel thought, but why not a girl? A girl out with a can of spray paint in the middle of the night. Did she have to sit on someone's shoulders to reach that high or did she have a ladder? However she had done it, the word, whether name or place or beloved, proved the truth of what it asserted: she was there because she said so, because this was her mark. She could be written over, but not erased.

"Your arm's dipping," said Thea.

Isabel raised the bow again. It wasn't that interesting, just standing there while Thea excitedly fiddled with knobs. It was cold, and she couldn't see whatever Thea was seeing. It felt like being a prop.

"Lift your chin," said Thea. "Look mad."

Isabel grimaced.

Isabel, Cricket, and Cricket's friend Hector lay around the living room amid the remains of their Cuban-Chinese Thanksgiving dinner. Hector had brought a paper Thanksgiving turkey centerpiece with a foldout orange and yellow tail; since they didn't have a table, the paper turkey perched in the middle of the floor. Thea was standing and sweating in her long-john shirt by the open window and saying to Hector, "You cannot *act*. Do not *act* for me, Hector. You already know everything, that's what I'm trying to tell you, acting would only get in the way of what we're trying to do, it has to do with film—"

Hector looked confused. "I brought my head shots," he said. He was a small, muscular man with a mustache. "I prepared a scene from *The Effect of Gamma Rays on Man-in-the-Moon Marigolds.*" He stood up. "Listen—"

Thea waved him back down. "No scenes," she said.

Hector, looking disappointed, sat down again.

Cricket, ensconced in the recliner, poured Hector, then herself, a consoling glass of red wine. "We should all go out tonight," she said.

"Where?" said Isabel. She was feeling dreamily full, reclining on pillows on the floor. Maybe she would call home later, or maybe not. In New York, she was a sailor on leave who did what she wanted.

"Somewhere we can dance all night," said Cricket.

"I did that last night," said Hector, yawning. "I'm tired."

"I'm going to work on the script all night," said Thea. "I can feel that energy coming on. Isabel?"

"I don't know," said Isabel. "It might be fun to go out." The candles had burned down to puddles on the plates; she chipped at one stiff puddle until it looked like a Hershey's Kiss.

"Besides," said Hector. "I'm on duty tonight." Hector was a cop.

"Hey," said Cricket, "how hard was that test?"

"Police academy? Hard. And the physical part—very hard."

Cricket rolled up her sleeve and made a muscle. "Feel," she said to Hector, then, "Ha! See? I could do it."

"Lots of girls on the force," said Hector equably.

Isabel didn't bother to point out the absurdity of this latest professional ambition from Cricket, who was, as her name suggested, always leaping lightly from thing to thing. Isabel considered having another piece of flan.

Thea looked uncharacteristically angry. "Don't talk that fascist shit in our house, Cricket," she said. Isabel felt her dreamy mood stall, then shift downward. Why, she wondered, did it matter to Thea?

"It's not fascist," said Cricket. "Just because it's blue-collar doesn't mean—"

Thea snorted. "Don't make this about class—"

"Well, we didn't have our own *stables*, Thea—" Cricket looked truly upset.

"Cut it out, Cricket," said Thea. She stepped around Isabel and Hector on the floor. The wind blew in. "You can just get out of here if you're going to run your mouth all night," Thea said as she left the room. A minute later there was the sound of a door closing.

"Oh shit," said Hector.

Cricket, drinking her wine, had tears in her eyes. Now she looked small and punished in the big green recliner, as if she had been banished there.

Isabel lit a cigarette. She felt a little bit sorry for Cricket, but not sorry enough to say anything comforting. Cricket deserved to discover Thea's moods for herself.

A cold breeze knocked over the paper turkey. Hector stood up and shut the window.

⊕ ⊕ ⊕

TEA

The coffee at the foundation was so bleak and bitter that Isabel switched to tea, which at least had the advantage that she could make it fresh herself each time. Reading through applications, she slowly dipped the bag in and out of the hot water.

The plebeian applications were like lonely-hearts letters. The applicants had to describe their projects and provide a sample budget. "I would most desire to stage *Othello* on the Staten Island Ferry, throwing Desdemona, dressed as a homeless woman, overboard. . . . Cost of life preserver: $25 . . ." "My one-man show is about the loss of both my legs during the Vietnam War . . . It's called *My Legs* . . ." "Sorcery has been a time-honored art since time immemorial. In my act, a common egg mysteriously becomes transfigured into a dove . . ." "It's a musical for our time, about a young man and his dream of becoming a pilot . . . Cost of fake airplane (I would build myself, as I am a skilled mechanic): $250. . . ."

The patrician ones were somehow worse. "I received a Guggenheim in 1973, an NEA grant in 1976, a Prix de Rome in 1980, my work has been lavishly praised by. . . . Cost, including libretto by Gore Vidal: $95,000." So few people, Isabel lamented to Thea when she went home at night, were doing anything really innovative. Thea wasn't surprised. And yet Isabel felt a profound sense of obligation to her pool of applicants; she read each application several times, taking notes. Her *Possibles* folder remained empty. She wished that she and Thea could apply, but that was against the rules.

At the end of a day of well-intentioned but hopeless plebeians and polished but corrupt patricians, Isabel opened a battered manila envelope with far too much postage, from an address in upstate New York. "Dear Patron," a typed letter inside began. They were, the letter explained, a summer theater for high school students in a town called Friedrichsville. Their award-winning director (the award remained unspecified) had staged sold-out productions of *Cat on a Hot Tin Roof, A Streetcar Named Desire,* and *Godspell,* using high school students. Reviews from the local paper—all glowing—were enclosed in a thick sheaf, one with a picture of Mr. Singer, a balding man with a wide smile, standing in front of a *Godspell* poster, his cast, in costume, arrayed around him. This summer, the letter explained, they wanted to stage *The Miracle Worker* and had a verbal agreement from Miss Joanne Woodward, whose daughter had coincidentally been at riding camp with one of the players, to play Annie Sullivan! But Miss Woodward was Equity, and an actress of her caliber . . . and for such a special production . . . they anticipated a long run . . .

The letter was signed by all the students, and Mr. Singer. It was encased in a clear plastic binder with a red spine. The budget, down to the cost of xeroxing the programs, was laid out in painstaking detail in a separate binder with a blue spine: $20,000, total.

Isabel tried to recall if she had ever seen *The Miracle Worker.* Helen Keller, wasn't it? And her teacher? She looked at Mr. Singer's picture, his hand resting on the head of a girl with wavy high school–girl hair and a serious expression, wearing a boa. Probably Mary Magdalene. Probably his favorite, the one who he already had in mind to play Helen Keller. Probably, thought Isabel affectionately, Mr. Singer longed to play Annie Sullivan himself, but didn't dare. She looked more closely at the girl. Her eyebrows were thick and unplucked; they almost met in the middle. She wore the boa not tossed around her neck in the standard coquettish, face-framing frill, but slung diagonally across her chest, military style. She had a defiant air, even in striped tights. Isabel wondered what her name was, but the caption read only, *Director William L. Singer, and cast.*

She heard the foundation elevator clattering downstairs. The space-station area was dark. It was getting late. Isabel put the application for William L. Singer's high school summer-theater production of *The Miracle Worker* in Friedrichsville, New York, into the *Possibles* folder, feeling a sense of accomplishment.

❧❧❧

Christmas, like a giant, was looming large over the city now. Tinsel hung from some of the lampposts. On the playground near their apartment, someone had put a Santa hat on the head of the enormous fiberglass turtle. Thea's Greek mood lifted somewhat, boosted now and then by a Cricket pill. When Isabel came home from work, Thea was often bent over the desk in the study, working away on the script or making lists of props and locations, calculating costs. She tacked the growing storyboard to the wall. Isabel studied it. The storyboard looked official, each square tied neatly to the next. Thea drew in quick, short, firm lines that made everything look small and telegraphic, like a cartoon. Diana looked like a superhero, descending from the top of a frame with her bow and arrow. Thea had made little sparkle points around her that seemed to Isabel a touch mocking. Of course, Diana was terribly ironic, but as sketched in these quick, firm, little squares, she seemed only that. When they had written the script, Diana had seemed central, a presiding spirit. But now—Isabel counted the squares with the goddess in them—well, it was going to be hard for her to preside in so few squares.

Maybe she should have drawn the storyboard instead of letting Thea do it, but it had seemed such a straightforward, almost mindless task, like taking dictation. Now she saw that

that might not be the case. And there was something else, too, that was disappointing, subtly. Graphically laid out this way, their film looked—ever so slightly—dull. Could that be true? Isabel stepped back, trying to get the arc of the whole thing. It was hard to believe, considering how excited they had been about it, how more than once it had kept them up all night in entrancing conversation, but today the conclusion was difficult to avoid. It looked boring. It lacked, first of all, a plot.

Isabel felt troubled. Later, she sat on Thea's lap in the La-Z-Boy recliner, feeling troubled, as they watched the news. Carly Simon and James Taylor were handing out leaflets at a military installation.

"I was thinking maybe we should shoot the dream sequence in here," said Thea.

"Oh, God," said Isabel. "That would be such an enormous drag. It would be a mess. I don't want to do that."

"It would be cheap," said Thea. Carly Simon explained nuclear power to a newswoman. "Dilettantes."

"So I was looking at the storyboard," said Isabel.

"It's really rough," said Thea quickly. "And so much is going to happen *during* filming, it will probably be a completely different thing. I didn't want to overplan."

"Yeah," said Isabel hesitantly, "that's cool, but I guess I was a little surprised—" She paused.

"What?" said Thea, tilting the recliner back until they were nearly horizontal.

Isabel remained uncomfortably upright. "I think something else might need to happen."

"Right," said Thea. "That's what I just said. *Lots* of other things are going to happen, once we get on set."

"No, I mean, I think we need to plan some things."

"But what would be the point of planning spontaneous things?" said Thea, looking annoyed against the green vinyl. "Then how will they be spontaneous?"

"It just looked so different," said Isabel. "It looked different than what I had imagined."

"I don't know what you mean," said Thea warily. "What did you imagine?"

"Something—oh, something beautiful and meaningful, I guess, but, I don't know, Thea, instead it seems all jumbly and kind of, a little, on the dull side."

Thea's expression was saturnine. "I don't think it's dull," she said.

Isabel got off Thea's lap and paced restlessly. "Maybe we should redo the script," she said.

"Isabel," said Thea, "we don't have time to do that. We *have* to start shooting, like, *now*, if we're going to make the festival. Don't you get a few days off around the holidays?"

"Yes, but I promised to go down to Pennsylvania for the first night of Hanukkah," said Isabel. "Remember?"

Thea fell silent.

"I have to," said Isabel.

"You don't," she said.

"What about your family? Don't you have to see them?" said Isabel.

"Athens is such a pit," said Thea. "And anyway, I'm not sure I can see anyone this year. I want to work on the film. I wanted to work on it with you, try some stuff out in here." She looked away, casually. "Maybe Cricket and Hector can help me."

"*Hector?*"

Thea sighed. "He's a sweet guy," she said regretfully.

"Well, maybe he can be Diana then," burst out Isabel sarcastically. "Since you've made her part so tiny and ridiculous."

"I did not," said Thea, "although if you would sit down with me once in a while and work on it instead of just thinking about your costume—"

"I do *not* just think about my costume, Thea, and that is *my* part, which should not be fucked with. She's the key to the whole thing."

"Right, so if she's so key, how could you let *Hanukkah* get in the way, you know we don't have that much time, there's so much to do, Isabel, you—I mean, where is your commitment to this project? Which you now tell me is boring."

"You're being really anti-Semitic," said Isabel coldly. The picture on the old television began to roll.

Thea made an exasperated sound. "You don't even *believe* in Hanukkah, and you know perfectly well that it isn't even that important a Jewish holiday, it's just because of the proximity to Christmas, it's completely manufactured—"

"Yeah, well, my *family* is not manufactured, Thea, all right? The holidays are a weird time. They need me." Isabel paced back and forth.

"So is that what this is about?" demanded Thea. "Or is it about your part, or what? What is it that you *want*?"

Isabel, staring miserably at the rolling image on the television, said nothing.

Finally, Thea said quietly, "It's been so long already, Isabel. You really need to stop being so consumed by your history."

"You don't understand," said Isabel.

"Maybe not," said Thea determinedly. "But I'm making this movie, on time. You may have decided it's boring, Isabel. But I think it's important." She leaned over and turned a knob at the base of the television. The picture stabilized.

"I didn't say it wasn't important," mumbled Isabel. "Of course it's important."

Thea, her face impassive but not entirely unforgiving, focused her attention on the little television. She lit a cigarette. A segment about nuclear war was on. Tiny fake missiles were heading from the United States to Russia; other tiny fake missiles headed back the other way. A flash of light exploded over New York. Though not admitting defeat, Isabel got back onto the recliner. Thea wreathed them both in smoke. After so many weeks of pale Trues, Thea's tobacco seemed almost unbearably dense; Isabel's head began to ache. Through her headache, she had the thought that she didn't want them to be apart if that flash of light happened; she didn't want to be running through the streets without Thea. And what were they arguing about, anyway?

Later, Isabel curled into Thea so that Thea, already deeply asleep, was curled around her. She picked up Thea's muscular arm and pulled it around her own belly, rested Thea's hand between her breasts. There were calluses on Thea's hands, cuts from the newspaper twine. Her skin was very sensitive. She bruised easily; the cold tore at her. In the winter, Thea never grew exactly pale, she remained olive-brown, but it was as if the light inside her went out. In the summer, she shone. Isabel ran her fingers over Thea's calluses, clasped Thea's hand in hers. It would be all right. The missiles were fake; there would be no flash of light. Summer wasn't so far away.

Isabel took the subway uptown to the Thalia, saying she had a doctor's appointment. She felt guilty lying, it was so busy, but it was the last day they were showing *The Miracle Worker,* at four o'clock. When she saw it in the newspaper, she knew she had to go. Two trains later, she bought her ticket with a keen sense of anticipation and then sat in the faded and squashy red seat in the nearly empty movie house, drinking take-out tea in a paper cup. The floor curved strangely beneath her feet; it was higher on the sides, lower in the middle, as if the theater had been built inside an abandoned swimming pool. A few rows away in the deep part, a bag man slept beside his ominous pile of plastic garbage bags, his head tilted back.

She sipped her tea in the dark as *The Miracle Worker* began. The lemon bobbed against her lip. The theater was drafty and cold; Isabel kept her coat on. The black-and-white movie began, she thought, rather melodramatically: Gothic angles, the mother screaming as she discovered her daughter Helen's blindness and deafness, pounding music. The light on the screen was strange and pearly. The marks of its having been a play were so clear. Too many words, thought Isabel. The screenplay should have been cut in half. The bag man began to snore. But then Anne Bancroft stepped out of the carriage with her big suitcase. A very young Patty Duke waited on the porch, a small, smudgy, suspicious figure with nearly transparent eyes. Their white hands met for the first time, like a fumbling conversation.

Patty Duke was almost bestial in her inability to communicate; she had no language at all, even though she seemed to be at least ten. Coddled by her family, she could do nothing for herself, not even eat with silverware. Anne Bancroft spelled words into her hand over and over. Patty Duke threw spools of thread, dolls, food, forks. She grabbed food from plates and ate with her hands. Anne Bancroft spelled words into her hand. Patty Duke threw herself onto the floor in a fit. Anne Bancroft spelled words into her hand. Isabel set her cup on the floor. This, she thought, was the real thing. The acting was incredible. No wonder William L. Singer had been saving this one, no wonder he wanted to do this one right. It was the saddest, most compelling story imaginable. Patty Duke didn't have one word, not *hot* or *cold* or even her name. She didn't know what a house was, or a barn, or a tree. She didn't know there was a sky.

Isabel leaned forward, absorbed. Patty Duke, playing, blew a veil off her face. She touched Anne Bancroft's face, over and over, with her white fingers. How had Isabel not seen this movie before? Maybe, she thought madly for a moment, she should go to Friedrichsville and audition: she could play Patty Duke's role or maybe, better, Anne Bancroft's role. She was the right age. And the wavy-haired girl with the unplucked eyebrows! Helen would be the role of her life. She was too old, but that wouldn't matter to the appreciative audiences of Friedrichsville. They would put her in a pinafore, and it would be the role that would change her life, the role that would turn her into a serious, and seriously devoted, actress. How could it not? It was that sort of part. Isabel's pulse quickened. She did have the pure spirit of an artist, after all. Here it was, come to meet her unexpectedly, like an angel, at the Thalia on a Tuesday afternoon: her vocation. She imagined herself, fresh from playing Diana, descending on Friedrichsville to be Annie Sullivan, spelling words into the hand of the wavy-haired girl.

Anne Bancroft's long hair came undone as she wrestled language into her charge. William L. Singer, that genial and half-closeted man, would be so proud. They all would be, the whole town, and perhaps even slightly afraid, although they didn't know why. They would be afraid of the raw power of *The Miracle Worker,* of the woman and the girl wrestling, wrestling, over language. They would be afraid of that much love. The water from the pump flowed over Patty Duke's outstretched hands. Anne Bancroft grabbed them, spelling. Finally—it was the end of the movie, and the choice to end there was brilliant in and of itself, Isabel thought; who wrote this movie?—Patty Duke understood one word: *water*. From that word, all the rest would flow. Isabel grabbed her coat and headed up the sticky curve of the aisle. The bag man did not wake up.

Outside, it was snowing. Isabel was crying, whether from sadness or happiness she wasn't sure. She had found what she had feared was lost forever—of course it was at a movie, just as it had always been. The snowflakes were large and soft and wet and they were just beginning to whiten the cars parked on West Ninety-fifth Street. The snow was cold as rain, but much slower, on Isabel's wet face as she walked up Ninety-fifth Street, then down Broadway to the subway. She wasn't wearing a hat; the snow dampened her hair. A packed rush-hour train entirely covered by graffiti pulled into the station. When the doors opened, an enormous spray-painted orange gangsterlike man split in half, his blasting guns going in opposite directions. Isabel walked between his momentarily divided figure, still crying a little. The train was warm and bright, full of breath and scattered talk. As the train lurched into motion, a young white man carrying a briefcase conversed, over Isabel's head, with an older, Hispanic-looking woman. She had a streak of white hair exactly down the center of her head, where her hair, which she wore in a tight chignon, parted.

The young man, whose elbow was pressing into Isabel's shoulder blade and who smelled sharply of cheap aftershave, was saying eagerly, "If we get them into position before the holiday, I think he will—"

"He won't," said the woman.

"But he has to, if the other three come in—"

"He won't," said the woman, shaking her head. "I'm telling you the truth now."

No one even glanced at Isabel's teary face as she looked around the subway car, suddenly astonished by its beauty. Here was the world, she thought. Her vision felt washed clean by *The Miracle Worker*. A little Asian girl in glasses and flowered plastic barrettes, her hand firmly gripped by her standing mother, stepped on Isabel's toe with her white galosh. She did not apologize. The row of people lucky enough to have gotten seats were all, it seemed, middle-aged women in cloth coats with shopping bags on their laps. Their coats were brown, red, black, blue, of very similar cut, but their faces were various: brown, copper, doughy white, bright lipstick on the short Puerto Rican women, brightly aerodynamic earpieces on the bifocals of the Eastern European women. The train hurtled along the track, rocking all the passengers from side to side: the careless little girl, the ambitious young man and the pragmatic Hispanic woman, the acquisitive row of middle-aged office workers. Isabel in her old down jacket, with snow in her chopped hair, felt sure that she could play them all. She stopped crying entirely.

When she got off at Times Square to change for an East

Side train downtown, Isabel saw, as the train pulled out of the station, SHAZ40! spray-painted in green and silver on the end of the last car. She watched the graffiti disappear into the tunnel, then plunged into the crowd, enthralled by the splendor of people racing around her in all directions. It was a chaotic rush-hour scene, office workers, schoolkids, nervous tourists, released and scattering everywhere. Every platform was full of people talking, waiting, craning their heads up the empty track to see if the train was coming. The station smelled of piss and cold. Although the transfer point was underground, the snow was already blowing down the stairs and through the sidewalk grates in the ceiling of the old station, pooling in its corners and declivities, melting on the tracks. As Isabel raced along with one stream of people toward her connection, the bells of the Salvation Army collectors resounded loudly against the grimy tiled walls and damp concrete floors. The bell ringers were everywhere in New York, ringing on every street corner.

Isabel labored over her memo, the newspaper photo of William L. Singer and cast propped up against her desk lamp. The typewriter was a manual with halting keys and a neurasthenic ribbon. Isabel didn't care. She applied correction fluid vigorously. Then she paper-clipped the two-page memo to the file and dropped it on Patrick's desk.

Some hours later, Patrick came over and sat lightly on one corner of Isabel's desk. His hair was slicked back into a DA at the nape of his neck and he was wearing a battered black leather jacket, like a little mafioso. "Honey," he said, gently laying down the file in front of her, "people like this have bake sales."

"It's a community-based, youth-oriented, rural program—"

"It's high school."

"But Joanne Woodward—"

"Joanne Woodward," said Patrick, "if it's even true, could not possibly expect the Friedrichsville Players, or whoever they are, to pony up a salary. It's probably just something she said over the tuna salad on Parents' Day, hoping they'd forget about it. Your enthusiasm is sweet, but honey, really. This isn't what we do."

"What happened to *eclectic*?" argued Isabel. "What happened to outreach? Did you read the part I wrote about the way language gets inscribed—"

"I read it," said Patrick. "They're in high school."

Isabel glanced into the newspaper-photo eyes of the girl with the wavy hair. "So what?"

Patrick looked at Isabel with a curious expression. "Are you all right, Diana? You seem a little agitated."

"I'm fine," said Isabel stubbornly, swiveling in her squeaky chair. "I think we just disagree."

❧ ❧ ❧

Isabel walked quickly past the empty playground. Old snow lay on the back of the enormous faded-green fiberglass turtle. The Santa hat, full of ice, was twisted on the ground. Isabel turned the key in the dirty lock, ascended the stair. When she opened the apartment door, she heard her Talking Heads record playing loudly. "Hello?" she called. "Thea?"

"We're in here," said Thea from the kitchen.

Isabel dropped her knapsack and paused in the kitchen doorway. Thea, standing, in the battery belt, was cutting the hair of Cricket, who was topless, with a hand towel around her shoulders. Scraps of hair littered the floor. Cricket's small nipples, like two little arrows, pointed just beneath the hem of the towel.

"Hey," said Cricket, her head bent forward as Thea snipped at the nape of her neck. Her back was freckled. "Thea said I needed a haircut."

"Oh, really," said Isabel.

"Hey," said Thea casually, not looking up. "We'll be done in a minute."

Isabel went into the central room, intending to turn down the Talking Heads, which might as well have been playing live. But when she got there she saw that Diana's bow was leaning against the wall by the record player. Lying next to it was her arrow, from which one feather was missing. And tossed on the open recliner, in a heedless fashion very unlike Thea, was the video camera. In the kitchen, Cricket laughed.

Picking up the arrow, Isabel went back into the kitchen. "Thea," she said, waving the arrow, "what the hell is going on here?"

Cricket lifted her head. Her nipples were hard from the cold in the drafty kitchen. "Whoa," she said.

Thea continued to snip lazily at Cricket's hair. "What's your problem?" she said to Isabel. "I told you we wanted to try some stuff while you were gone."

Anger laced through Isabel, constricting her heart. She waved the arrow again. "Look at this," she said. "What happened to it?"

Thea glanced at the arrow. "I don't know," she said, dusting off Cricket's freckled shoulders. "I guess when we were practicing a feather fell off. What's the big deal?"

Cricket's gaze was riveted on the floor. Isabel wondered how hard it would be to push her out the window. "Well, I'm not gone, Thea. And *you*," she said, pointing the arrow at Cricket, "are not on this movie."

Cricket, open-mouthed, grew red first in the face, then in the neck and shoulders. "Since when is that all your decision?" she said defiantly, holding back tears. "Thea?"

"Isabel," said Thea, "do you think you own this? Because you don't. It's art. It's not your personal property."

"The hell it isn't," said Isabel. "You can't go off and steal it all and give it to some idiot—"

"Don't call me an idiot," said Cricket, her head still bent, "just because I never went to college like you guys—"

Thea closed the scissors with an exasperated snap. "How am I *stealing*, Isabel? I'm not stealing from you. Cricket isn't stealing from you. We're all in this together, and Cricket has some really great ideas—"

"She's not on it," said Isabel curtly. "Period."

Cricket pulled her shirt on, bits of wet hair dropping to the floor. She sniffled. "I don't need this shit from either of you," she said. "I thought you were my friends." She ran out of the room; Thea followed. Alone in the kitchen holding her arrow, Isabel could hear muffled, soothing sounds from the hallway, then the definitive lock of the front door.

Thea came back to the kitchen, scissors in hand. "You are so fucked up!" she said angrily. "Who do you think you are, she didn't do anything—"

"Bull*shit,* she didn't do anything," countered Isabel, "that conniving little asshole, coming into *my* house, going through *my* stuff, and you, there you are, you're such a fucking sucker for her bullshit, Thea, if you want to fuck her so bad, just *do* it already. But you never get it. You never get when people are using you. She doesn't even know how to handle a camera and she is *not* on this movie."

"I don't exactly think that's your call to make, Isabel," said Thea, in a dangerous tone. She was large with anger, like a bear.

Isabel, holding the arrow, and Thea, holding the scissors, stared at each other in the kitchen littered with Cricket's hair. Isabel had the sudden, terrible image of the arrow going right through Thea's heart, the scissors going right through her own. They could die like that, over a movie, in a drafty kitchen on Avenue A. Isabel held tight to the arrow, watching a vein pulse in Thea's olive-brown neck.

"Forget it," said Isabel, and dropped the arrow. The Talking Heads record ended and the needle bumped, bumped against the label.

Thea very carefully laid the scissors on the bathtub cover. She turned her face away. "Leave me alone for a minute," she said.

Isabel went into the other room and set the record arm back in its cradle. She stood there, breathing hard. How were they even going to do this? she thought. They didn't know anything about making a movie. They had no equipment, hardly any money, just a million ideas that they didn't really know how to execute. She hefted the video camera onto her shoulder; it was heavy. She peered through the lens. There was Thea's clipboard on the windowsill, with its top page of closely written notes. The green vinyl La-Z-Boy recliner, which took up half the floor space. The Talking Heads album cover lying on the floor. The record player with the volume knob missing; they had to turn it up and down with a pair of pliers. The pliers. A subway token. Through the camera lens, it all looked small and faraway and the recliner looked freakishly huge; their life together seemed little more than a miniature diorama inside a sugar Easter egg: *Isabel and Thea, East Village, 1982.* Isabel slowly turned around. Diana's upright bow bisected the frame, arching up and up, the purple stripe like the plumage of an exotic bird. It ennobled the battered plaster wall it leaned against. It was grand and irrational, and wasn't that, Isabel thought, what a movie was, anyway? A grand and irrational undertaking? Wasn't that why they came to New York in the first place? If they had wanted safety, they could have stayed in the little college town they disdained and gone to work in admissions. It couldn't have been easy to make *The Miracle Worker,* either, but someone did, take after take. You had to be persistent. She set the heavy camera down.

Isabel, feeling more optimistic, returned to the kitchen. Thea was sitting in the chair Cricket had vacated, a folded hand towel on her knee. She had a stunned, thoughtful look

standing that when she said she was a lesbian, she meant that to the exclusion of marriage and five Iranian-Greek children. Thea circled Isabel's breast with her tongue, with a forefinger, then sucked it. Isabel and Thea liked to have Mustafa to dinner; the three of them sat around listening to Iranian records, which were full of songs about the wind, songs about the desert. Mustafa translated the lyrics, singing along in a high, off-key voice. Isabel leaning into the chair, Thea reaching forward, Isabel's arm resting on Thea's neck—it was awkward, and they had no kitchen curtain. Anyone could see. Anyone could have seen through the window then, too, could have seen the three of them, laughing into the evening as the strange music played. Thea bent her head, craning to get at Isabel's clit with her tongue. Isabel felt it begin, just the very beginning, the outer circle. At the same time, an inexplicable jealousy rose up in her, a jealousy of the scene of the three of them back in that little town, as if she were the one watching it through the long-ago window—although in reality, of course, Mustafa was a stockbroker in New York now. They hadn't seen him since they moved. Thea, with unusual efficiency, quickly pushed forward with her tongue. Isabel would have liked to lie down, but she felt that they were poised on the thinnest of threads together, there in the drafty kitchen, that if they stumbled to the bed the moment would pass away altogether. And so she stayed balanced on the tip of Thea's tongue, unable to move her legs very far apart because of the pants, beginning to sweat in the thick sweater. Thea ran her thumb up inside Isabel, ran her other hand over one of Isabel's breasts. Isabel passed by the window, passed from the outer circle to the next one in. They were both, she thought, her hand tangled in Thea's dark hair, just trying to get somewhere. They were just trying to get there.

The train down to Philadelphia rattled into the tunnel under Penn Station. Manhattan disappeared in an instant. Watery meadow took its place. Then red-brick buildings with broken windows, light slanting through, a plane flying overhead.

Isabel opened her journal and began writing. *Thea and I have been having some aesthetic differences. She's more Eisenstein, while I (I've just discovered!) am more some dark American like Ford, but I'm hoping we can meet somewhere in the middle, maybe at Truffaut.* The train shook and smelled of rubbery smoke. Graffiti echoed in the underpasses. She would call Thea as soon as she got in.

Isabel waited at the Springston train station for Jeannie to pick her up. She drew her scarf more closely around her neck. It always seemed colder outside the city. Maybe the buildings dissipated the winter winds. Two nights, she thought. It was only two nights. And it was probably better Thea wasn't coming with her, because Isabel's father plainly found Thea offensive, not only for being a woman, but for her inherent messiness, her bits of tobacco, her abundance of opinions, her overalls. He blamed her, silently, for Isabel's hair. When Thea came home with Isabel, the house seemed to shrink; they were always tripping over one another: Thea, Isabel's father, Jeannie, Isabel, Jeannie's three dogs. Isabel's father was wary of Thea's ongoing proliferation of ideas and projects. His lips tightened when she went on about this or that film or demonstration or movement, as if she somehow had more than her share of enthusiasms and must have stolen some. He once asked Thea with some suspicion if she was really Greek.

Jeannie's much-dinged car came into view. Along with Jeannie's head, two dog heads were visible through the windshield and another dog—Misty, the black-and-white one—hung her head out a back-seat window. Jeannie tooted the horn. Isabel waved. Jeannie pulled up to the curb, got out of the car, quickly hugged Isabel, and opened the hatch. Isabel put her duffel bag and brown paper bag inside, on a Navajo blanket covered with dog hair, next to a fifty-pound bag of dry dog food, hangers from the dry-cleaning store, and an assortment of odds and ends that included jumper cables and fishing tackle. All three dogs turned around to watch Isabel; Misty half-climbed over the back seat toward her.

Isabel stroked her soft head. "Hello, pooch. Hey. What's this?" Misty was shaved on one hind flank. Stitches crossed the shaved area in a painful-looking line of black thread.

"The puppy bit her," said Jeannie, getting into the car. Her long, dark hair was in braids and she had on a thick red plaid shirt. She looked like a farmer, square and practical, wearing the kind of plastic hexagonal glasses that could be bought in drugstores and probably, knowing Jeannie, were.

Isabel got into the passenger seat, shut the door. "What puppy?"

Jeannie smiled beatifically as they drove away from the station. "Jonas. He's so cute, Isabel. I think he's a lab-chow mix. From the A." That was what Jeannie called the ASPCA, where she volunteered.

"Wow," said Isabel. "Four. Is Dad cool with that?"

"Six, actually. You haven't been here in a while."

"Six?"

Jeannie shrugged. "It's my house, too." Something was making a chinking sound as they drove. Jeannie wasn't big on car maintenance, Isabel thought. A lucky rabbit's foot hung from the rearview mirror; maps and newspapers and a T-shirt or two littered the floor; in the back seat, the dogs reclined on glossy piles of ASPCA pamphlets on How to Pick the Right Dog for You. The dogs panted in unison.

Isabel and her father embraced. He was trim and bony as always; embracing him was like embracing a hanger. In his neat button-down shirt, ski sweater, and creased pants, he stepped away to look at Isabel.

"You're pale," he said worriedly. "Why are you so pale?"

"It's winter," said Isabel, trying not to sound annoyed. The three dogs from the car swirled around them in the entryway. Through the doorway of the kitchen down the hall, sheets of newspaper were visible on the floor and there was the faint scent of urine. From somewhere else in the house, a puppy-ish yip sounded and then, as if in answer, a deeper adult bark. Then another.

"Jonas!" yelled Jeannie, dropping the bag of dog food she had carted in on her shoulder and running down the hall. "Jonas! Cherry! Monster!" Scuffles, barks, and the clink of dog tags ensued.

"You should take up skiing, Isabel," said her father. "There are no pale skiers."

"There isn't a lot of skiing on the Lower East Side," said Isabel.

"Well. I guess you have me there." Isabel's father winced. "Can't argue with you there."

They stood in the hall, a few feet apart, both unsure of what to say next. Jeannie snapped a baby gate open in the kitchen doorway. "I have to make a call," said Isabel.

Jeannie, inside the kitchen, handed Isabel the phone over the gate. "He's too excited to meet anyone new yet," she said. The round brown puppy skittered across the newspaper covering the floor.

Isabel dialed. Misty stood with Isabel outside the gate, wagging her long black-and-white tail. She was a friendly, knee-high dog, ever happy to help. The line was busy.

Isabel took her things upstairs. Lying on her old bed, still in her coat, she thought, It's only three days, two if you don't count today. But just as it always had, her room felt like a sanctuary, especially with the door closed. Her father had, of course, kept it very neat. It wasn't dusty. Her row of Little House books and yellow Drama Classics sat on the bookshelf next to her high school yearbooks and a framed picture of Isabel looking slightly perplexed outside the Coliseum in Rome; her Joni Mitchell records, ending at *Don Juan's Reckless Daughter,* stood straight on the shelf. Her single bed felt narrow, but not necessarily in an unpleasant way. The sheets were fresh. The little six-paned window beside the bed was what felt too small, and the view outside, of the house with fake gables across the street, felt too small as well. Only a child could have thought that this was any sort of view at all;

Isabel remembered hating that view as a teenager. Today, however, there was something endearing about its very too-smallness, like a picture postcard from a seaside town: fake gables, taffy people, round orange sun. Things had been so intense in New York. Isabel was almost, slightly, glad of the temporary reduction of scale. It was like being in a doll's house.

On the dresser was her mirror with the shells glued around the frame, clean and ready to reflect her once again. The only thing that gave the room a lonely air were the hangers and hangers full of clothes in their thin, transparent, plastic dry-cleaning bags hanging in the closet: summer things, fancy things, things of Isabel's and Jeannie's they didn't wear any-more. Filling the dresser, Isabel discovered, were extra sheets, tablecloths, Hanukkah candles, beach towels, and a set of phone books. She would not be able to unpack. She unzipped the duffel bag where it lay on the floor next to the desk.

Misty curled up on the round carpet with a sigh, stitched flank up. "Poor pooch," said Isabel. Downstairs, dogs barked and there was the patter of her father and Jeannie talking. The salty-winey smell of tomorrow night's brisket wandered up the stair. If only she had a little TV in her room, and a phone. She took off her down jacket and hung it on the back of her old desk chair.

❧ ❧ ❧

Isabel and Misty sat on the sofa, which was covered with a sheet. Jeannie sat on the living room floor holding a glass of wine in one hand, a leash and a paper towel in the other. At the other end of the leash was the puppy. On another chair covered with a sheet sat a scruffy yellow dog named Monster, who, standing up on the seat and barking, was making sure that Cherry, a pointy and gently beseeching German shepherd, could not get into the chair with him.

Jeannie pushed on Jonas's bottom. "Sit, Jonas," she said. "Sit." Jonas lay down and turned over on his back, peeing a little. "Damn," said Jeannie, blotting the pee with the paper towel. "Don't tell Dad. Jonas. *Sit.*"

The other two dogs—a grayish, ghosty, lanky thing named Mouse, and a raggedly spotted chunky one named Smurf—were tugging on opposite ends of a rubber bone. Isabel rested a hand on Misty's head, which made her feel more secure, as if she had entered some foreign land, dog country, and Misty were her translator and guide. "Jeannie," said Isabel, "are they all in the house with you guys all the time?"

Jeannie tugged on her end of the leash. "Look at me, Jonas." Then, to Isabel: "There's a pen outside. But I wanted you to meet the whole gang, and, you know, it's a holiday. They take turns sleeping with me at night. And to*night,*" she said, reaching over to rub Smurf's wiry-haired ears, "it's Smurfy."

"What about Dad?"

"He doesn't mind," said Jeannie quickly.

Isabel looked around at the sheet-covered furniture, punctuated by dogs. She snuck Misty a cracker off the platter of cheese and crackers her father had set on a high table. She felt protective of old Misty; did Misty even get enough to eat with all this competition? "Are you still taking those classes at the community college?"

"Stop hassling me about that, Isabel," said Jeannie. "I don't have time right now. It's been *wild* at the A, and I'm starting dry-cleaning school next month—I want Dad to add leather and suede." Jonas yipped experimentally, and sat. "*Good* boy!" said Jeannie. "*Good* boy!" She petted him and smiled encouragingly. Isabel noted the canine gathering: Jonas, Smurf, Mouse, Cherry, Monster, Misty, barking, tugging, scratching themselves. They were not, en masse like this, cute. Isabel had the unpleasant sensation of being surrounded.

Isabel, Jeannie, and their father ate dinner in the company of all the dogs except Jonas, who was re-gated in the kitchen. The dogs did not actively beg, but they were vigilant. Isabel found that she was eating faster and faster, and made an effort to slow down.

Their father cut his meat precisely and slowly, nearly ceremoniously, as he always had. The chrome legs of the dining room table, polished as ever, shone. He seemed to be unperturbed by the considerable animal presence in the room. "So, Isabel," he said, "since we know you're not a skier, what have you been doing for fun up there in the big city?"

"Thea and I have been working on our film, Dad. The one I told you about."

"Ah," he said, "it sounded complicated. But is that fun? What do you do for fun?" He delicately salted his meat. His hair, which had been white for years, was now somewhat thinner as well. His customarily trim form was almost engulfed by the ski sweater. He was not yet old, but he was becoming, Isabel realized, a thin old man. Yet at the same time, his coloring was very good. There were roses in his cheeks. He was what was said of old men in old books: he was hale.

Isabel wasn't sure how to reply. Her father had never openly discussed fun before. She glanced at Jeannie for a clue, but Jeannie was making faces at Mouse. "Go to the movies, I guess," Isabel said. "But it's not really that complicated, Dad, I explained—"

"I remember. Some kind of women's lib thing." A shadow crossed his face. "Jeannie, what happened with the presser? Did Pete come down?"

"I fixed it," she said. "I told you I would. Pete doesn't get the old machines at all, though he'll still charge a fortune to pretend he does."

"And it didn't choke?" said their father. "Not even once?"

"Not even once. They said it might snow tonight," Jeannie said. "I think the babies should stay inside."

"All right," said their father. "Hey, Isabel, you should come down and see the new dry-cleaning machine. The filtration system is state of the art."

"It's pretty cool," agreed Jeannie.

"Great," said Isabel. She sipped her wine. He wasn't listening, as usual, but for the moment it beat arguing with Thea, whom she would not call again, yet.

They finished their meal as the dogs looked on proprietarily.

Down in the den by the fire, it was peaceful. Isabel's father, wearing glasses, jotted down a list on a pad. Jeannie read a thick tome called *Introduction to Canine Breeding.* Isabel watched the local news, which seemed to her to have a charmingly flawed, handmade quality. There was the soft sound of panting.

"Dad," said Isabel, "I wanted to find something in the attic, that box of things, is it still there?"

"Things," said her father. "What things?"

"You know. Of Mom's."

Jeannie looked up from her book.

"I don't know," he said slowly. "I don't know what's up

there anymore. Probably lots of mice." He shuddered comically.

"Is that what you've done with her things?" said Isabel. "Left them to the mice?"

Her father, making his list, said, "What are you eating in the morning these days, Isabel?"

"Toast, I guess."

He wrote it down.

Isabel tried Thea again, standing outside the kitchen in the dark hallway. Dogs passed by her in the dark. Still busy. She went upstairs, undressed, slid gratefully into her single bed, and turned out the little bedside light. From Jeannie's room, she could hear dog tags and the movements of Jeannie getting ready for bed. She could hear dog tags downstairs, too, as the four unfavored dogs made themselves comfortable inside for the night. Isabel felt irritated, but also lonely. Misty was curled up on the rug again. Isabel considered inviting her onto the bed, then thought better of it. She would not succumb. She didn't know what to make of the situation—not only Jeannie's roving kennel, but also her father's peculiarly cheerful passivity. Didn't he care that the house was overrun? He had always been so meticulous, to the point where the house had sometimes seemed like an exceedingly well-vacuumed fortress, but now he had left open a rather wide gate, through which all this animal life had entered, and made itself at home. It made Isabel uneasy. How healthy could it be to live with six dogs, day in, day out? She plumped a cool pillow under her head. Then she leaned over, reached under the bed in the dark, and felt around. It was still there.

With an ease born of years of adolescent practice, Isabel plugged in the radio in the dark. Velvety, abstract horn sounds murmured in her ear. That was her father's subtle sort of kindness, to leave the radio under there and not even change the station. She lay awake for a long time, listening.

In the morning, Jeannie, standing at the kitchen counter with a vat of crunchy dog food, said to Isabel, "Rachel's coming tonight."

"Who?" said Isabel. There was the sound of the shower running upstairs.

"Dad's girlfriend," said Jeannie. She quickly braided her hair and snapped a rubber band to the end of each braid. "And get this. She knows all the prayers."

"What?" said Isabel. The shower turned off.

"She's nice," said Jeannie, adding various powders to the vat and stirring vigorously. "Dad really likes her. She's wicked Jewish."

It had indeed snowed during the night, a light dusting of such overall regularity it seemed artificial, like something out of a can. Isabel sat in the back seat; Jeannie drove the company car, a Volvo with GOLD CLEANERS : GOOD AS GOLD! written on the side; their father sat in the front, reading the stock page, the newspaper folded into a neat rectangle.

"My God," he said. "The money that's being made! You girls should buy some bonds. Nana always had bonds."

Jeannie shifted up. "Dad, we have to stagger Thuc and Charlie. The tailoring is a disaster. We're totally behind."

"Jeannie, if you'd learn to sew a seam—"

"Not going to happen. I'll always hire out."

Isabel watched the neighborhood go by: the impenetrable private school for boys, the reservoir, the houses with Christmas lights or Hanukkah candles in the windows, a roof with a big red-and-white plastic Santa and sleigh and smiling brown plastic reindeer affixed to it, the road where she had always turned to go to Lottie's house. Isabel thought of calling Lottie, thought better of it. What was there to say? The houses went by, practically unchanged. Their suburb was like thousands of others, Isabel thought. Hundreds of thousands. It all felt like such a long time ago: she had thought she was straight then.

"Let's take Northern," said Isabel's father. Jeannie flicked on the turn signal. "Look at this, Isabel," said her father, tapping the window with a knuckle. "Incredible, isn't it?" Where the small strip shopping center and Esso gas station had been there was now an overflowing putty-colored structure called Northern Mall, anchored by an enormous Wal-Mart. It dominated the modest boulevard. And there, part of it, was a big, dark blue Pier 1 sign. Was that, Isabel tried to remember, where Pier 1 had been? Or was it down past the boulevard? Her spatial sense of the town was confused by the mall, which had erased several streets.

"God," said Isabel. "Do you go there?"

"That's where Rachel works," said Jeannie. "At the Allstate."

"Take the right," said their father. "And—here we are."

Jeannie paused the car in front of the store. There was a new sign, white on forest green, over the entrance. Every other store on the block—the butcher, the bakery, the record store—had the same white-on-forest-green signage. It looked like a pileup of highway exit signs on an extremely abbreviated highway.

"Jesus," said Isabel, "what's with the signs?"

"Town council," said her father proudly. "Everyone voted."

"Don't they look nice?" said Jeannie, driving past the store and around the block.

"No," said Isabel. "Dad," she asked, as they parked behind the store, "so who is this Rachel? Jeannie says—"

"You'll meet her tonight," he said. "She's a terrific lady. Doesn't read much, though." He laughed to himself, as if at some private joke.

They went into the store through the back. Jeannie put her brown-bagged lunch in the half-refrigerator; Isabel's father put his in, too. They hung up their coats on the coat pegs. Isabel kept hers on, following them past the machinery through a thicket of finished dry cleaning to the front, where a slender Vietnamese man stood behind the counter. Isabel's father discreetly handed him a bag filled with rolled quarters and dimes for the change drawer.

"I've got the front now, Thuc," said Jeannie. She tossed her copy of *Introduction to Canine Breeding* on the shelf over the counter, sat down on the tall stool, and began expertly cracking quarter rolls, two at a time. "Has it been busy?"

"Oh, yes," said Thuc. "Everyone picking up for the holiday." He left the counter and sat down at a low linoleum table to one side, covered with spools of thread and measuring tapes. He licked a thread end, threaded a needle, and began hemming a flowered dress.

"Come take a look back here," said Isabel's father to her. He held aside a row of clothes so Isabel could pass through again to the back of the store. "Look at this, honey," he said, pointing to the new dry-cleaning machine: huge and white and spotless, with almost no chemical haze hanging over it. "You could eat off this thing, it's so airtight. All the fumes go right out the back." A sleek black hose snaked gracefully away. There were large, new silver fans, strategically hung; several rectangular windows and a skylight were all open to let in the air. "Dave got exactly the same one for his store," said Isabel's father. "Maybe we should go over there later and I'll show you."

"That's okay, Dad," said Isabel. "Is he coming tonight?"

"I doubt it," said her father. "It's his barbershop quartet rehearsal night. They have a little group."

"Oh," said Isabel, disappointed. Against one wall was a stack of folded, empty dry-cleaning boxes, but no Louise to snap them open. Instead of the picture of Louise's son in his military uniform, an Allstate calendar hung on the wall. Where once Dave's Slim Jim wrappers and soda cans had been scattered around the countertops, there were now screwdrivers and dog collars and presser parts. At least the old insulated presser was the same, because the old manual ones were still the best. Its padded arms lay open, worn cream on the outside, bright blue on the inside. And the Suzy stood where she always had, headless but graceful in her white nylon shift. Up front, a bell rang as the door opened. The finished-clothes conveyor whirred. Isabel's father put on his glasses, picked up a pair of pants from a cloth bin and began examining them at the spotting station under a strong light. Bottles of chemicals, neatly labeled, stood in the tray next to him.

"We'll be done here by three," said Isabel's father. "Take the car if you'd like." He handed her the keys. He studied the pants again, his gold bracelet gleaming, his pale hand and arm delicately crooked. He looked like a scientist, or a jeweler. He picked up the acetic acid, then set it down again, choosing the peroxide instead.

How many pairs of pants in a lifetime? Isabel thought, imagining them laid end to end like a time line.

"I'll be back," she said. She dropped the keys in her coat pocket and headed out the door, but did not take the car right away. Instead, she walked around to the front of the block, thinking of a second breakfast. She waved to Jeannie through the window of the store; Jeannie, waiting on a woman in a crisp suit, didn't see her. Jeannie's braids and ASPCA sweatshirt jarred with the strict green-and-white signage. But on her face was the practiced, impersonally attentive look of people behind counters everywhere, nodding as the woman in the suit pointed to various spots on some sort of magenta garment. Isabel walked on, past the Christian Science Reading Room, past the Hallmark store, all marked out in white and forest green.

This, she thought, was exactly why she lived in New York,

like a sailor. Soon she would sail out again, back to the wide world from this narrow archipelago of small-time consumerism. "Happy Holidays!" it said in fake-snow letters on the record store window, topped by a white-and-forest-green sign. And who was this Rachel of the Northern Mall? Isabel paused in front of the window and studied her own faint reflection: dark, booted, puffy-coated, pale-faced (her father was right), and with her shorn hair, all cheekbones. The fake-snow letters crowned her glass image oddly. How nice it would be, she thought, to throw a rock, hear the glass shatter on the pavement; but the thought also disturbed her: the sharpness of the glass, the hardness of the pavement.

She walked on, away from that violent idea. And there, reassuringly, was the Two O'Clock Diner, still with the black-and-white clock eternally and ambiguously poised at two—A.M.? P.M.?—over the door. Isabel went inside and sat at the counter. There was hardly anyone inside: an old couple with a little girl, probably a grandchild; a man in corduroys at the end of the counter, smoking, bent over a book. Isabel ordered eggs and bacon and coffee, then began glancing idly through the *Springston Crier.* "Property Assessment Debate Rages On," was the lead piece.

"Isabel?"

Isabel looked up. It was the man with the book: it was Ben. "Oh my God," she said. "What are you doing here?"

"I'm on break," he said. "Grad school. Philosophy. How about you?"

"I came down from New York for the holiday," she said. "Just the first night."

"Right," he nodded earnestly. "Same here. Well—a few nights for me." His eyes were as beautiful and long-lashed as ever, but his curls were gone, shorn to waves. He wore a shapeless tan crew-neck sweater and a thick silver ring on a forefinger. He was thinner than Isabel remembered him, and more sincere looking, as if he had gotten not older but younger in the intervening years. His face had an open, boyish quality. "Can I sit down?" he said, closing his volume of Hegel.

"Sure," said Isabel. She found that she was surprisingly glad to see Ben and he, apparently, to see her, as he hopped up onto a stool and ordered a cup of coffee.

"This town makes me afraid," said Ben. "What is with the fucking Stepford signs?"

"I know," said Isabel. "Bacon?"

Ben laughed. "It's good to see you, Isabel."

"Where are you in school?" said Isabel, crunching.

"Michigan. I'm freezing my balls off, but the faculty is fantastic. I feel like I've found my home planet."

"Cool," said Isabel.

They smiled at each other in a comradely way. Ben's smile was as conspiratorial as ever. "Actually," he said, "I piss my professors off about every other day, but they love me for it. And you?"

"I live on the Lower East Side. I'm working on a film with my girlfriend."

"Starring you, I bet," said Ben.

"Kind of. But there aren't any stars—it's experimental."

"Great," said Ben. "That's great. Wow." He nodded appreciatively; Isabel wasn't sure if he heard her when she said *girlfriend,* or maybe he was just fine with it. Or maybe he thought she meant it generically, as in a *girl* who was a *friend.* She let it go for now. There was something so unexpectedly nice about seeing him again. "Hey," he said, opening his book, "I just read the most amazing passage—can I read you a little bit of it? Like four sentences. Listen." He read the sentences aloud; they seemed to have to do with perception, although it was hard to tell. ". . . the gulf that apparently separates us from *things in themselves,*" he finished. "Things in themselves. That's so cool."

"Interesting," said Isabel. On an impulse, she said, "You want to take a ride?"

"Love to," said Ben.

Isabel drove the Volvo with GOLD CLEANERS: GOOD AS GOLD! on the side. Ben tapped his silver ring against the paperback volume of Hegel in a syncopated rhythm that had nothing to do with the song on the radio. Every radio station in town seemed to be oldies. "I'm as free as a bird now," sang Ben softly. They passed the Northern Mall.

"This town," said Ben, shaking his head as they drove through it. "America. Every place is the same place and no place at all. We could be anywhere."

"I know exactly what you mean," said Isabel. "We could just as easily be in Texas." She turned at the yellow bubble letters of the Meineke muffler place and headed out of town, weaving down the flat suburban streets.

"We are in Texas," intoned Ben in a Southern accent. "Deep in the heart of Texas."

Isabel stopped the car. It was just a brown-and-black ranch house, no different than the ranch houses that occupied most of the neighborhood. There was the patio where she and Lottie used to sunbathe. An Indian child sat on a tricycle on the patio; the screen door opened and a woman in Indian dress came out and scooped up the child, closed the door behind them.

"She's married now," said Ben.

"Is she?" said Isabel. "I didn't know."

"This guy who made a fortune on the pipeline. He does contracting. Here. He's from here."

"Our school?"

"No. He went to Lincoln." It was the high school in the next town. "She does some kind of thing with gift baskets."

"Oh," said Isabel. She and Ben looked through the windshield at the silent house.

Ben tapped, tapped his volume of Hegel. "What are gift baskets?" he said in an unidentifiable tone.

"I don't know," said Isabel.

The sun came out, illuminated the lawn for an instant, then went back behind a cloud. The Indian child pressed his face to the window, pointed, saying something. His mother came to the window.

Isabel started the car. They drove out of the neighborhood in silence, out the back way, toward the river. Ben turned up the radio.

Isabel ran a hand through her hair. She almost squeezed Ben's arm sympathetically, then didn't. She didn't know what to say. Somehow, it had never occurred to her that Lottie and Ben would break up, although that was so foolish: of course they broke up, eventually. But in her mind, she realized, the two of them were still back there together, listening to Yes. She looked at Ben's soft profile. Only his eyes were sharp, and she could see today that they were what would mark him, had marked him probably, all his life: those lovely, long-lashed, sharp eyes. When Ben got to be an old man, an old philosophy professor, they would remain stubbornly beautiful. They would always make his philosophy lessons seem sweeter than they were; that was his personal curse, that prettiness. So now he had shorn off his curls and he lived in Michigan, where the winters were long and hard.

They passed the Deer Run Townhouses, the big supermarket, the car dealership, but finally found a small wooded spot where the river ran close to the road. Downstream behind Deer Run, Isabel knew, was the rock with the shaky scratches that spelled out LAYLA, 1972, where Isabel had thrown Lottie's car keys at her and Lottie had left Isabel to find her way home alone. Isabel turned off the car, but left the radio on. She and Ben watched the modest river flow through uneven corridors of ice.

"You guys never made up," said Ben.

"No," said Isabel.

Ben nodded. "And then it just got too long, too weird."

"Right," said Isabel. Oh, it was sad. Lottie and her gift baskets.

Ben wrapped his arms around himself. "I don't think I knew her very well," he said.

"Really?" said Isabel. "But you two were so close."

"Just in a way. Underneath, she held herself apart, kind of. I always thought it was because of her heart thing. She must be way happy now."

"Why?" said Isabel.

"Because she's past twenty-one. She was very superstitious about it—she thought if she made it past twenty-one, when all those other ones died, that she would be okay. She was so afraid that she wouldn't. I bet that's why she got married so soon. I bet she's already pregnant."

"She never told me she thought that," said Isabel.

"See," said Ben.

"Pregnant," said Isabel. "God."

"Well, I'm just guessing," said Ben. "Actually, I thought you would know by, like, telepathy or something. The way you two were." He looked up at Isabel questioningly with his sharp, beautiful eyes.

"We didn't have any telepathy," said Isabel. "We were just friends, you know?" She leaned against her window, patting her pockets for cigarettes. "Damn."

Ben suddenly leaned forward and kissed her. It was a boy's kiss; his tongue was thick, aggressive, and there was something desperate to it, a kind of seeking. Isabel was surprised, but in another way not surprised; it made sense, in its way. The radio was playing the Allman Brothers. She held his face in her hands, touched the shorn curls, the smooth jawline. She touched his chest. Even slender as Ben was, it was a boy's chest, hard and muscled. It was not displeasing, touching Ben; it had a languid, nostalgic feeling, as if they had already touched long ago. His clean and boyish smell was so familiar to her; Isabel realized that it was because it had been part of Lottie's smell, and for just a moment it seemed that Lottie was in the car with them. Then she faded away. Isabel pulled Ben toward her; now she was the desperate one, seeking, searching through his clothes and over what little skin of his was exposed: the tips of his ears, the warm curve of his collarbone. She could feel, as he half-lay on top of her in the car, kissing her, that he was hard in his corduroys. The door handle was jamming into Isabel's back from their combined weight. If they did this, she thought, that would really be the end of it all, the circle closed.

"Wait," she said, struggling up.

Ben sat up on his side of the car, hair disordered, coat open. "Sorry," he said, to the dashboard.

"It's okay," said Isabel.

It was getting cold in the car. Ben closed his coat. The Allman Brothers played on.

"You girls," said Ben, leaning his head against his window.

Isabel didn't say anything. She felt abashed. And yet—a part of her wanted to embrace him again, like a brother this time. But Ben was hunched up on his side of the car, ruffling the pages of Hegel, staring out the window. Isabel finally found a cigarette, lit up. It tasted divine. She passed it to Ben. "Without Melissa," twanged the radio. "Sweet Melissa." They watched the river flow past the ice for a few minutes more, then Isabel started the engine.

Isabel dialed New York, leaning over the gate to pat Jonas's soft head. The phone rang fifteen times before she finally hung up. A slight panic, a faint queasiness, came over her. What was happening to her? Making out with boys in her father's car to music no one listened to anymore. She touched her fingers to her forehead in the hallway, breathed deeply a few times. It would be okay, she thought. It would be okay. The panic passed. She would be so glad to get back to New York, where her real life was. Meanwhile, her father's brisket warmed and crumbled sweetly in a big pot on the stove, giving off an umber, starchy scent. Jonas pointed his small black nose into the air, trying to find the source.

Jeannie herded the five adult dogs past Isabel, through the hallway. The back door opened and shut. Isabel went up to her room and discovered her father there, pulling a menorah out of the dresser drawer. He was wearing a different ski sweater today, a dark green one with a deer pattern at the neck.

He looked at Isabel and tapped his watch. "The clock is ticking, honey," he said. "Rachel will be here soon, if you want to maybe change for dinner."

"I wasn't planning to change," said Isabel.

"Well," her father said, wincing. "All right." He walked out of the room with the menorah, shutting Isabel's door behind him in what seemed to Isabel a pointed manner.

I am not changing, thought Isabel. She reopened her door and went into the upstairs hallway. With some effort and several jumps, she managed to grab the flat ring on the ceiling hatchway that led to the attic. She pulled, and a set of wooden stairs descended from the ceiling. Isabel stomped up them. She was not changing.

She pulled the string on the attic bulb, crouching low under the beams as she made her way back toward the small attic window. Boxes were heaped up at that end. Dave's ukelele was there, its hula girl still smiling, though more dubiously, her face cracked with age. The shadow box, reflecting Jeannie's roller skates. A half-open box of the old clothes Isabel had called her "costumes." A glint of gold lamé in that box. Isabel pushed it to one side. The attic smelled of mothballs and dust and some other inchoate knot of stuff, the accumulated scents that had risen there over the years and not quite made it out. The odor of burning wood rose now, as her father lit the fire downstairs.

Isabel sat down on a stool before the window. She didn't know what she was looking for, maybe a picture of her mother in pearls, a letter, a family tree, a dress, a gesture, a promise, an omen of a future goddess. Something that might say, *I knew. I knew you would come for me.* Something she could take back with her to New York. She opened a box labeled CASSIE. There were layers and layers of things in there; Isabel carefully lifted out the long dresses and coats, separated by tissue paper once pink, now faded to almost brown. Cassie's nursing degree. A tennis racket forever zipped into its leather case. A framed photo of mountains; Isabel remembered that from her parents' bedroom, but what were those mountains? There was no way to tell; they were green, generic. Maybe a place they had honeymooned. Maybe the mountain where they met, her father on skis, her mother as Cleopatra.

Isabel dug deeper into the box. Some of her father's choices of what to save were inscrutable. A paint-by-numbers painting of a bouquet of flowers. A patchwork doll. Hadn't that been Jeannie's? A pair of Keds with a hole at the little toe. He was so weird. These odd, illegible things were only understandable as fragments of her father's memories; like the framed photo of the unidentified mountains, they had meaning only to the two who had looked on them. And there were no pearls; no picture of her mother in pearls, dressed for the evening.

But then she came upon her own exercise from grade school. *My mother's face is as pretty as snow.* Her childish handwriting scrawled, huge and round, from one end of the page to the other. The sentence took up almost an entire piece of paper. Just below it, some adult had sketched a snowflake in the fat red pencil teachers used. Isabel ran her hand over the oaktag. Who had saved this? Her mother or her father? But it was in the box labeled CASSIE, so it must have been her mother. Although, she thought, it could have been an accident, her father in his grief gathering up a pile of things and putting them into a box, taping the box shut, labeling it in block letters, leaving it all to turn to dust in the attic. He was not, Isabel thought bitterly, a man who wanted to remember much.

My mother's face is as pretty as snow. Isabel held the fragile paper in her hands, as fragile as the tissue paper that was now faded to brown the way flowers faded, browned, dried to stiff replicas of themselves. That wasn't what she was looking for. She excavated further. Finally she discovered something she hadn't seen before: a blue leather album, like a photo album, with happy dancing figures on the front. *Things N Stuff!* it said in raised orange letters. Isabel opened it. Taped inside, one to a page, were playbills: *Guys and Dolls, My Fair Lady.* Underneath each one, in her mother's handwriting, the date. Sometimes the ticket stubs were taped together in a fan shape in the corner, like a crossed pair of gloves. Most of the shows were in New York; on the opposite page from the playbills were menus from the restaurants where they had eaten. She must, Isabel thought, have stolen or wheedled them. There were two from Joe Allen.

The collection ended at *I Can Get it for You Wholesale,* 1962. The Scotch tape at the edges of the playbill was brittle and sepiaed. The rest of the thick, rough manila pages were blank. Isabel turned them over one by one, touching each one as if by doing so she might force it to yield up some secret written in invisible ink. All the playbill covers were so cheery, like the cover of the album itself. All those happy endings.

Isabel ran her fingers over the raised orange letters of the album: *Things N Stuff!* This was the book she made, a book full of happy endings. Taping it all down so she would be sure to remember. Poor Cassie, like Madame Bovary. Trapped with a man who thought only about new stains, and new ways to remove them. It was strange to think that her mother had been in New York so many times, perhaps walked the streets Isabel walked now, her head full of sugary musicals that dissolved almost before the train left the station. She had gone all that way into the city. How bleak it must have been when it evaporated each time, the evening's bright notes falling and disappearing, like melted snow, into the sound of the train on the tracks. Isabel's gaze fell on a blue coat with a double row of gold buttons, couched in paper that had once been pink but was now brown. A scrap of memory teased at her—something about her mother's coat pocket. What was in there. A quarter. A nickel. A crumpled bit of

Kleenex. And that tumbledown hippie house, way out in the country, with the water stain on the wall; that was in her mother's pocket somehow as well. And then what she had said to Isabel, seated at the little desk: it was wrong, Isabel suddenly thought, and as quickly tried to push the thought away.

But the thought returned, more loudly this time. It was wrong; it was the wrong thing to say to a child, that you wanted to die. Isabel shifted uncomfortably on the stool. Had her mother's head been so full of musicals that she wouldn't know that? Isabel knew that didn't make sense; musicals had nothing to do with it. By then she wasn't going to the theater anymore, anyway. And what had her mother saved of Isabel's? *My mother's face is as pretty as snow.* Isabel began to grow nervous. This would all look different in New York.

"Cassie," whispered Isabel, but there was no answer.

The scent of burning wood rose into the attic. Outside the attic window, the sun had already slipped below the horizon, leaving smears of orange and pink and black in the sky. Items from the box labeled CASSIE were scattered around Isabel. They were random to an almost unbearable degree. Why save the Keds? Why the paint-by-numbers painting? But, of course, it wasn't her mother who had saved these things. She hadn't saved anything of mundane real life, except, perhaps, the poem of Isabel's about her that didn't quite make sense.

Cassie liked shows. Everything else, she had simply dropped behind her for someone else to carry, for someone else to dig up and try to make sense of later. She had crept—or maybe simply walked, or maybe run, or maybe stumbled—into a hospital supply closet, pills shaken into her pockets, bottles of pills up her sleeves. Then she'd shut the door behind her. But even unwrapped after so many years and laid out around the attic, the things she left behind didn't explain anything, not really, the way the pearls hadn't explained anything. The pearls were just something Isabel had made up. *My mother's face is as pretty as snow.* She had made that up, too. Cassie liked shows. She smoked and brooded in her nurse's uniform, sipping her cold tea. On at least one afternoon she was capable of cruelty. Most of the rest, Isabel had made up, bit by bit, stroke by stroke. White go-go boots. Every single Nancy Drew. A house with white paper birches and a lake. Taken together, they were, Isabel realized, a kind of movie that she had made, by herself, starring her mother: a woman she had imagined, a woman made of tea and smoke and the air in empty rooms. And it wasn't even really tea.

Isabel sat with the album on her lap, watching as the light outside slowly dimmed, the colors fading first almost imperceptibly, then with surprising speed.

"We've been waiting for you," said Isabel's father when Isabel entered the living room. "It's time to light the candles." He was standing in the center of the room, rocking back and forth on his heels. "What were you doing? I thought you were changing."

Rachel and Jeannie, on the sofa, were turned expectantly in Isabel's direction.

"I told you I wasn't changing," said Isabel unapologetically. She sneezed. The smell of brisket filled the air, which Isabel secretly found comforting. She had run back down the wooden stair as if a fury were after her, quickly pushing the stair skyward until the hatch snapped closed. But the second she stepped into the living room she felt annoyed.

"Hello, Isabel," said Rachel, getting up and holding out her arms. "I've heard so much about you." Rachel was a small, thin, dark-eyed woman. Like Isabel's father, she was also wearing a green ski sweater with a deer pattern, although hers had a slender red ribbon threaded through the neckline. She had on nylons with her pants and her shoes were pointy, shiny pumps, with rosettes at the toes. She embraced Isabel warmly. Isabel, at least a head taller than the older woman, bent down; Rachel was bony under the ski sweater—another hanger. Jeannie sat with the scruffy little yellow dog on her lap. The menorah ornamented the center of the coffee table, its eight empty arms punctuated by one red candle at the far left and one yellow candle in the middle; the box of candles lay beside it, along with a small display of presents.

"I like the blue candles," said Isabel to Jeannie.

"Rachel and I already picked the yellow ones," said Jeannie. "Come *on*, the sun is down already."

"Girls," said their father, laughing nervously and glancing at Rachel.

Rachel laughed. "Oy! Such a fuss. Here." She shook a blue candle out of the box and handed it to Isabel. "Go ahead, honey." She laughed again. "My kids are the same way."

Isabel plucked the yellow candle out of the center spot, breaking it. She stuffed the blue one in its place. "Mom liked the blue ones," she said. "Give me the matches."

"I don't remember that," said Jeannie.

Rachel handed her the matches. "Do you know all the prayers, honey?"

"Of course," said Isabel's father.

Isabel said, "No, not really," and struck the match.

Rachel had a quick, nervous gaze, eyes darting here and there as her body remained absolutely still, with a ladylike crossing of her nyloned ankles. "So," she said to Isabel. "The budding actress."

"Filmmaker," said Isabel, from her stiff position in an armchair. Her annoyance was giving way to a sense of attenuation, as if she were looking at the living room through the wrong end of a telescope. She tried to rally. "My lover, Thea, and I are making an experimental film about the goddess Diana that references current geopolitical conditions and the oppression of women throughout history but that also sort of interrogates, you know, filmmaking itself."

"Oh," said Rachel, glancing toward Isabel's father, who was busily straining to pull the cork out of a bottle of wine.

"Isabel's an artist," said Jeannie helpfully.

"Wine?" said Isabel's father. The candles on the menorah were quickly burning to nubs.

Jeannie held out her glass. "Look at the babies!" she said, glancing woefully out at the backyard pen, where the four dogs sat by the gate.

"We can give them a treat later," said Rachel in an understanding but no-nonsense tone. "I have an artistic daughter myself," she said to Isabel, smiling. "She's an interior designer."

"She just finished a stadium," said Isabel's father, sitting down next to Rachel and putting his arm around her. Both lightly built people, together they barely took up an entire sofa cushion. Jeannie and the little yellow dog took up the rest of the sofa. "Every single skybox was Cindy's."

"Cindy lives in Arizona," said Jeannie, crunching on a

cracker with one hand and scratching the dog's ears with the other. Crumbs fell on the dog's head. "I'm going to visit her there."

"She has two gorgeous little boys," said Rachel.

"Of course she does," said Isabel.

"Well, yes," said Rachel, smiling. "That's right. She's married."

"Isabel," said her father, wincing, "Isabel."

"What?" said Isabel coolly.

There was a pause in the conversation. Isabel held tight to her meanness, hoping for some rescue from the waves of anxiety that were beginning to crest, but her meanness drifted away. As unobtrusively as possible, she brushed her fingers over her forehead.

Rachel's gaze flicked around the room several times, as around a familiar course. After three or so laps, she said, "Bobby, let's open some presents." She picked up one in frolicking puppy wrapping paper and handed it to Jeannie. "Guess what this is," she said.

Isabel's father, in his green ski sweater, stopped wincing and smiled at Rachel rapturously. Isabel regarded the pile of presents, the Peruvian slipper socks wrapped in black-and-white striped paper she had brought for Jeannie, a small square box for Isabel from her father that looked like it might contain jewelry or a watch, several oblong things in shiny pink paper from Rachel to Isabel and Jeannie. Isabel knew, without a doubt, that they were bath salts. She felt certain that if she opened the shiny pink paper and found the bath salts she knew were there, she would shatter. They would find leaves of her skin on the walls.

Jeannie carefully undid the tape on the frolicking puppy paper. "Where did you get this paper?" she said. "They'd love this at the A. Isabel, what are you doing?"

"I have to smoke," said Isabel, on her feet. Rachel and Jeannie gazed up at her. Isabel's father frowned. "I—I have to go outside. I smoke outside now." She grabbed her pack of cigarettes and lighter from the table, raced down the hall, bolted through the front door, and halted at the end of the driveway. Her hand shook as she tapped out a cigarette, then drew its inky comfort deep into her lungs. The air was cold and sharp and impressionable; she could see nearly every molecule of her breath when she exhaled, or so it seemed. The stars were numerous and close. The end of the cigarette glowed among them in the dark. Isabel's pulse beat madly. She wasn't sure she could ever go back inside. Bath salts. She shut her eyes. She wasn't going to be able to make it on bath salts.

Isabel felt that she had fallen down a well. Up at the top of the well, her father and Jeannie and Rachel were eating brisket, spooning potatoes, and talking away about whether or not there would really be a Saks at the Northern Mall. Rachel was for, because of the excellent sales. Jeannie was against, because their clothes were so impractical. Isabel's father was haplessly, masculinely neutral, which was evidently screamingly funny. She could see all their hands, the flash of Rachel's wrist bangles, as things passed back and forth across the table. She could see the brisket in the center of the table, fallen into a ropy, tender, orange-tinted splendor. It made her want to weep and explain everything, except for the fact that she couldn't. Down at the bottom of the well, Isabel lay in cold water, and calculated the hours until she went back to New York. She picked at her brisket, which was delicious. After dinner, she could call Thea again. She needed to be reminded of who she really was, where she really lived. She wanted to tell Thea about Ben, about his shorn curls, and about what she had found in the attic. She was beginning to feel unmoored; she had a floating sensation, and at the same time something in her was aching, perhaps her stomach.

"Well, what is love anyway?" Rachel was saying, spooning potatoes onto Isabel's father's plate. "Sex?" She waved her hand in the air dismissively. "Everyone talks about sex, sex all the time, they still don't know what love is. Love—this brisket is very tender, Bobby, you didn't dry it out—is *communication.*" She tapped a hoof on the ski sweater with a painted nail. "Of the heart."

Isabel's father ate his broccoli. "That is one hundred percent true," he said.

"Still," said Jeannie. "He has those big ears, even if he is practically the king of England. I don't see how she could love him."

"The British are very different," said Rachel decisively. "They have a different mentality there. But didn't you say that's what your movie's about, Isabel? Charles and Diana?"

"No," said Isabel firmly. "It's about Diana, the *goddess* of the *hunt.*"

"Oh?" said Rachel, looking confused.

"She's an ancient goddess," sighed Isabel. "It's about—you should ask my father. I've explained it to him several times."

Her father, however, was unconcernedly helping himself to more brisket. "I couldn't follow it entirely, honey," he said.

"Mmm," said Rachel in a disappointed tone. She made a little moue with her face, a *tsk* sound. "I thought it was about Charles and Diana. They're such a beautiful couple."

"They're a *spectacle,*" said Isabel. "They're not real. But Dad. Dad. All those times you and Mom went down to New York together—"

"What are you talking about?" her father said, looking at her quizzically. The skin around his eyes was delicate and very pale; it made his eyes seem wide and unprotected. "Why are you talking about this now?"

Rachel patted his hand. "Bobby," she said consolingly.

Isabel felt that she might be losing control. Her heart was pounding. "I'm just trying to ask you, because I found all that theater stuff she had, and it made me wonder—"

"What is there to wonder?" her father said angrily, shaking his head. "That she was a little stagestruck once upon a time? The thing she cared most about was you two." He gestured with his fork. "You and your sister."

Rachel patted, patted his hand. "She was a mother first," she said sagely.

"How would I know that?" said Isabel, her voice rising, and cracking.

Her father speared up a piece of potato. "She was just an unhappy woman, Isabel," he said, chewing. "She never found what she wanted in life."

"Hey," said Jeannie, gathering brisket scraps, "let's go give the dogs a treat, Isabel. Come on. Isabel."

Isabel and Jeannie stood at the gate of the dog pen with the platter of brisket scraps. The dogs ran back and forth in the moonlight, jumping and whining. It was a full moon, round and white and high in the winter night sky.

"What were you looking for up there?" said Jeannie, tossing the scraps with beneficent equality. Her breath was visible in the cold; it smelled sweetly of wine.

"I didn't really know," said Isabel miserably. "I thought maybe there was a picture I hadn't seen before or something. Do you ever remember her wearing pearls?"

"I still dream about her," said Jeannie. The dogs wiggled in place, wagged their tails. "They always know when I do, too, especially Mouse."

"I dream about her, too," said Isabel. "Sort of. Maybe not dream exactly. Think, I guess. I still think about her a lot." She gave her entire handful of scraps to Misty, in a clump.

"But the dreams don't help, you know?" said Jeannie. "I'd rather remember more real things."

"I know," said Isabel. She felt very tired all of a sudden.

Jeannie set the empty platter on the ground and the dogs crowded to it, trying to lick it through the fence. "Rachel's husband died of cancer," she said.

"Is that supposed to make me like her better?"

"I'm just saying she's a person, too. She's been through things."

"Yeah, okay, but I think Dad could be a little more considerate of our feelings. On Hanukkah and all." But even as she said it, Isabel couldn't quite bring herself to believe it. There were some years they had skipped Hanukkah altogether and gone straight to Christmas. They often had a tree; this Hanukkah, she saw now, was probably more for Rachel's benefit than anything else. It was a wooing. This was her father, wooing with brisket.

"What difference does it make?" said Jeannie. "He's going to marry her, Isabel. They communicate, like they said." Jeannie stretched out her hands in the moonlight so the dogs could lick her fingers. "It's all about who understands you."

In the living room, they ate the kugel Rachel had brought, off little scalloped plates with flowers around the edges that Isabel had never seen before. Isabel, mouth full, said to Rachel, "I'm sorry. I guess I'm a little emotional tonight."

"Forget about it," said Rachel, and she waved it all away with a motion like sweeping onions off a chopping block into soup. "It's Hanukkah. A happy time."

Isabel ate all the kugel on her plate, along with five pieces of Hanukkah gelt. The chocolate was cheap and thin, warmly pliable in its gold foil. Isabel felt ill almost immediately. Jeannie, next to her on the sofa, was glassy-eyed. Rachel was talking. "A low heel," she was saying to Jeannie, "a woman can always do with a low heel, even on the job."

"That's what Nana used to say," said Jeannie.

Rachel paused, looked at Isabel, and smiled her determined smile. "Who does your hair, honey?" she said.

"My girlfriend," said Isabel.

Rachel's gaze did a few laps, settled again on Isabel, then did a few more.

"She's a Greek gal," offered Isabel's father from his standing position in the center of the room. "Tall." He held his hand up in the air to indicate the absent Thea's tallness. She was evidently as tall as the lamp.

"I have to make a phone call," said Isabel. She headed back down the hallway to the kitchen. This time she let the phone ring twenty times. Maybe she could get on a train tonight; maybe it wasn't too late. While she was wasting time acting like a teenager, her real life was unspooling back in New York, all the bright threads of it unwinding and falling to the floor. Reluctantly, she hung up the phone. It occurred to her that Ben was probably as miserable as she was right now, and that was strange to think of, that she might have more in common with Ben than with Lottie. Maybe it was because Lottie wasn't Jewish.

Back in the living room, Jeannie had stretched out to take up the entire sofa. At her stocking feet lay the scruffy little yellow dog, one eye open, as if guarding her. Her wineglass sat beside her on the floor. She wasn't quite asleep, but she wasn't quite awake, either; her eyelids fluttered. Isabel's father and Rachel turned in unison when Isabel entered the room. "Everything okay?" said Isabel's father.

"Fine," said Isabel. "Jeannie?" She shook her sister's arm.

"She's resting," said Isabel's father.

"No—" Isabel began, but Rachel interrupted her.

"She's had a long day," she said. "She and your father are just alike: working all the time."

Isabel's unopened presents loomed in the center of the table; she felt sorry for them, so determined to be festive. "I'm sorry, I didn't know you'd be here," said Isabel to Rachel. "I didn't get you anything."

"That's all right," said Rachel, winking and tapping Isabel on the knee. "You can get me next time." With a snap of her wrist, she unfolded the afghan from the back of the sofa and laid it over Jeannie, whisked away the wineglass. "Don't want anyone tripping over this in the night," she said. She briskly rubbed the ears of the little yellow dog, who woke up and yawned. The dog glanced from face to face: Isabel, Rachel, Isabel's father, who was brushing nonexistent dust off his creased pants. Jeannie, mouth open, slept in earnest now. The yellow dog put his head down, apparently satisfied that everyone was there.

Isabel helped Rachel on with her coat in the hallway as Isabel's father made up a bundle of leftovers in the kitchen. Rachel smoothed her hair into formation, embraced Isabel again, and kissed her on the cheek, surely leaving a mark with her bright red lipstick. She smelled of perfume and brisket. "Your father," she said, "is such a wonderful man.

He's been through so much in his life." She patted Isabel on the cheek. "You take care, Isabel."

Isabel's father brought out a paper bag full of a quantity of leftovers, transformed via aluminum foil into a flock of silver swans, and went out the door with Rachel. Isabel watched through the front door. Her father held Rachel's elbow in one hand, the bag in the other, as the two of them made their way to her car. It was, Isabel noted with surprise, a sports car. A silver two-seater, which matched the swans. He helped Rachel into her low car, then handed the bag of brisket-swans through the window to her. She smiled up at him. Isabel turned away from the door, blushing, whether for him or herself she wasn't sure.

Isabel lay in her single bed, listening to the radio. She had to get back up to New York, and soon. What was going on up there? *Tweet,* said the radio. *Beep.* The sounds were abstractly soothing, but Isabel felt discomfited. The floating sensation was still with her, the feeling of floating over an unquiet sea. Misty—whom Isabel, silently apologizing to the other cold dogs, had rescued from the pen for the night—exhaled profoundly on the carpet. Isabel turned out the light. The moonlight lit the face of the mirror with the shells glued around the edge and faintly illuminated the sheaths of plastic in the closet, visible through the half-open closet door. The shapes of the abandoned clothes inside appeared, disappeared. She really had to get back up to New York. *Bop,* said the radio. *Zip zip.*

In the morning, Isabel and Jeannie let the dogs out of the pen. The dogs raced around them, nipping at the air, their furry bodies bumping into Isabel and Jeannie's legs. The German shepherd knocked Isabel's elbow with his nose, almost causing her to spill her tea.

"Damn it!" said Isabel. "Diana is supposed to have dogs, but I don't know. They bug me."

Jeannie sipped her coffee, still in her clothes from the night before, her braids messy. "Diana is a myth, Isabel," she said. She patted the rump of the gray dog as he passed by. "I've been thinking of moving."

"Where?" said Isabel. The sky was dense, as if it might snow again, for real this time.

"Montana," said Jeannie. The dogs circled around her, ecstatic from the cold.

Isabel drank her tea down hungrily. There were clouds in her head from the night before. "Montana? Why?" Through the picture window, she could see her father moving around the living room, folding the afghan, straightening cushions.

When Isabel had gone to pack up, she'd discovered that all her clothes, lying neatly on top of the duffel bag, had been ironed sometime in the night. Her precisely folded jeans had creases in them.

"There's so much space there," said Jeannie. "It's quiet. And, you know, it's not like I'm going to stay here with Dad forever."

Jeannie drove Isabel to the train station in the Volvo. Their father sat beside Jeannie in the front seat. Isabel studied the back of his head, the careful parting of his gray hair, the red wool scarf tucked carefully around his pale neck. He sat quite straight, the seat belt running tautly over his shoulder. She hadn't said anything about the night before. Neither had he. When it came time to see the film, he would peer at the screen, and wince. Then he and Rachel would drive back down to Pennsylvania the same night, probably in this very car, which was clinking, Isabel noticed, just like the other one. What was that?

A chipped jelly jar, then another, rolled out from under the front seat. Isabel bent down and took a whiff. It was sweetish; Isabel looked at her sister. Jeannie's face, reflected in the rearview mirror, looked older this morning. There was a faint ridge on her cheek, from the sofa. She had a composed, but slightly blank, expression. One wet braid ran down her back, tied at the bottom with a shoelace. She drove confidently, easy with the manual steering wheel.

"I might go in just for a little while today," Jeannie said to their father. "Catch up."

He nodded. The glasses clinked from time to time. Outside, the sun played hide and seek with the roadway, always lighting the patch just in front of them, then ducking away. Isabel put on her gloves, pushing down on the woolly spaces between each finger.

"You should have taken what you wanted, Isabel," her father said, still facing forward. He coughed uncomfortably. "Dresses or whatever. Keepsakes."

Isabel reddened in the back seat. She put her hand over the corner of the album that was poking from the inside of the duffel bag, right next to the Simply Romantic bath salts from Rachel and her freshly ironed thermal shirt. Well, after all, she thought, guilty but determined. If she couldn't find the pearls. She was the one who needed it.

"Thanks," said Isabel.

She hugged them hard at the train station, first Jeannie, then her father, holding each one tightly, as if she might impress them upon herself.

"My big girl," said her father, slender and bony in her embrace. "You try to have some fun up there, Isabel. Why don't you have a hat with that short hairdo?"

"Hey," said Jeannie, closing the door that said GOLD CLEANERS: GOOD AS GOLD! "Let me know if you and Thea want a dog. Did I tell you Mouse is pregnant?"

Isabel silently admonished the train to go faster. There had been no answer the first time she called that morning, then it was busy. Death, she thought. Death to Cricket. It was her movie, her girlfriend, her house. Isabel would be magnanimous when she ushered Cricket out. Maybe, once they got rolling, Isabel would show Cricket how to hold a light or something. Isabel felt lighter and clearer this morning, as if a burden had dropped from her. Her doubts of the night before seemed like shadows. Today, there were no shadows. The sun was bright on the tracks. Her spirit was completely pure. They had a lot to do, she and Thea. She opened her journal and began making a list.

The train rattled along at its usual pace.

Carrying her heavy black duffel bag, Isabel ascended the stair into Penn Station, cracked and grimy and necessary as an unwashed coffee cup. Weary travelers sat on their suitcases around the station, many with wrapping paper and brightly colored bows visible in Macy's bags. Homeless people slept beside them. The station had a particularly frantic air, the travelers seeming more than usually desperate. Of course, Isabel realized, hiking the duffel over her shoulder, bath salts poking into her spine, it was Christmas Day. She hurried up the escalator and out of the station, treating herself to a cab with some of the cash her father had pressed into her hand in Pennsylvania. "Get yourself a nice haircut," he had said, although there was more than enough there for that. The city streaked by, traffic so light that the cab fairly flew to the East Village. New York had never looked as beautiful as it did to Isabel on this sunny Christmas afternoon. She was entirely grateful to be back in its wide and tumultuous embrace.

The cab sped past the playground, then lurched to a stop. SHAZ40! was newly inscribed on the front of their building in flaming red and yellow letters. Maybe the graffiti girl lived in the building, Isabel thought as she went inside. She hiked up the stairs to their apartment, dropped the heavy duffel to the floor, and put the key in the lock with mounting anticipation. She had so much to tell Thea, if she could get her off the phone.

Isabel didn't know why she was surprised, but she was surprised nonetheless, walking slowly from room to room, astonished. The heat clanged as always; the tin pie plates of water rested in the usual way on the radiator; but otherwise it was all different. It was all gone. Their furniture was crammed tightly into the front two rooms, like a collapsed house. The big, green vinyl recliner was wedged, springs up, into one of the doorways. Its vinyl footrest stuck out at a sickening angle into the hallway. The other rooms were, basically, empty. Also full: of lights, wires, boxes of half-eaten Entenmann's donuts, Styrofoam cups, cigarette butts, a banjo, and four wigs—all curly, Harpoesque. She didn't remember anything about Harpo wigs. She picked one up: it was flossy, red, polyester, and, as she quickly discovered, not her size.

The radiator spit softly. The sun was bright on the scratched floors, the Entenmann's boxes, on the video camera, set on a tripod, and an inscrutable trio of lights trained on the spot where the recliner had been, once upon a time. In its place, tacked to the wall, was a picture of a highway coming to a point as it disappeared into a desert landscape. A Harpo wig lay on the floor underneath the picture of the highway. Isabel felt a fluttering inside, a giddiness, tinged with anger.

The entire apartment, which smelled of Thea's Drum tobacco, had a peaceful feeling in the sun, as if relieved to have shed any obligation to be a living space—and wasn't it always too hot? or too cold? weren't the walls crumbling?—in favor of being this, a makeshift thing, a set. The odd thing was, it looked so much better, strangely gracious in the way ruins were gracious, larger and almost picturesque; the broken vein of plaster that had seemed depressing when there was furniture now had an interesting, sculptural cast. It would look good in a photograph; the right sort of disheveled person would look good posed before it. The abrupt half pipe in their bedroom now seemed evocative and eerie, like a disinterred bone. The light, tumbling unencumbered through the windows, had a new, rosy texture. She had never noticed that before. And although Thea was clearly not there, the apartment felt more infused with her presence than ever. For a moment, before Isabel began to wonder where her things were, she was pierced with love of Thea, surrounded as she was by the evidence of Thea, of Thea's ambition, visible in the rosy light, written on the bare, crumbling, suddenly picturesque plaster walls. Thea was an artist. She would get there. That was clear. Isabel could see, in the moment before she was really nearly blinded with anger, how much she had come to rely on that, holding fast to Thea's drive to carry her through, as if riding on Thea's broad back through deep water.

Her bow was nowhere to be seen.

Isabel went into the kitchen, which was a wreck, and put

on the kettle. A hand mirror with a dusting of white on it lay on the kitchen counter. Isabel tried to spell *Merry Xmas* in the white dust, but there wasn't enough. Thumbtacked to the wall was a note in strange handwriting. It said, "Patrick called. They need you 12/26." After some digging around behind the recliner, Isabel found the phone, reached awkwardly under piles of things to plug it back in, and called Patrick. His voice was a comfort to hear, full of mundane annoyance: he was so sorry, but they had to meet, Faith was being called to Tokyo, you know how crazy, but, well, it was her ball game, and didn't *he* have holiday plans? She would be there, Isabel said succinctly. No problem.

Thea didn't come back that night. After a while, Isabel unplugged the phone. She sat on the living room floor eating take-out rice and beans and an egg roll. Funny, she thought, that she had eaten the same thing for both Thanksgiving and Christmas, but it tasted so different the second time. Saltier.

Patrick said, "Are you all right? You look like hell."

"I'm fine," said Isabel, slamming shut a desk drawer. "I slept on the floor, so I'm a little cranky, that's all."

Patrick raised an eyebrow.

"Shut up," said Isabel.

There were just the three of them in the loft, which was dark except for a cozy light coming from Faith's office. Traversing St. Marks Place on her way to work, Isabel had felt an odd kind of excitement to be walking through the quiet, empty city. It was like being out at three A.M., four A.M., some secret moment in between light and dark. The wind whipped newspapers down the street; nothing was open except one deli, with one fat man behind the counter. Isabel bought a cup of tea and a greasy muffin from him. He was listening to what sounded like a game on the radio, narrated in another language. Isabel couldn't identify the language or the game; she ate the muffin as she walked, getting crumbs on her gloves. As she crossed a bright and deserted Fourth Avenue, its traffic light swaying in the wind, something akin to happiness rose in her. This morning, she did not miss the college town they had disdained. Patrick, who had the key, met her in front of the building that housed the Van Zandt Foundation, turned on the elevator with another key. It felt important to ride in the elevator with him, sleepy and irritated in earmuffs, on a day when most people were home eating too much. He had spent the holiday, he said as they ascended, making his costume for his New Year's party. "I'm going as Nancy Reagan," he said. "Red Bill Blass suit. A single strand of pearls. My friend Zoe's going to be Ronnie." Isabel said distractedly that she thought that sounded nice as she mentally rehearsed her arguments.

Now, Patrick, Faith, and Isabel sat around the glass-topped table in Faith's office. Patrick and Faith both had substantial stacks of files in front of them; Isabel had three: a woman who pierced her tongue with sewing needles, a theater group staging Proust by means of an elaborate arrangement of scrims, and the Friedrichsville players.

Faith opened an elegant silver thermos and poured herself some hot liquid that smelled like moss. She had on a little black beret over her thin, curly hair, a beret, Isabel had observed, that she always wore when traveling. A butterfly of eczema spread its wings over the bridge of her nose. She also had on glasses, because plane air dried out her contact lenses. Two silver suitcases, with Faith's trench coat thrown over them, rested next to her chair. In her glasses, Faith looked older and more serious; she looked as if she might be as rich as Isabel knew she was.

"Go," Faith said to Patrick.

Patrick dealt out his files like a dealer at a Vegas casino. "We talked about Pleasant already, I say ten; Schwartz, fifteen; the Duck Group, forty-five; Short, six; Yangtzee, thirteen; a bunch of little ones, here, here, here—fifteen hundred each; the Kings, thirty-two; and—don't get shirty, honey—seventy-five to you know who."

"He doesn't deserve it," said Faith, sipping her moss.

"It's good for us. They love him at BAM, that's our name in every program and every profile." Patrick was wearing his earmuffs around his neck, which gave him a sound-engineer sort of look Isabel admired.

"He's a Nazi," said Faith.

"Only aesthetically."

They held each other's gaze for a moment, then Faith nodded. "All right. But I think only twenty to the Ducks. We did them year before last." She turned to Isabel. "You seem to have been quite selective. What have you found for us?"

"Well." Isabel opened the file of the pierced-tongue lady. There was an eight-by-ten glossy inside of a big spiny tongue. "I thought maybe for performance art—three, I would say. She was a visual artist and began doing this kind of work a few years ago; what I think is interesting here is that the body itself is the material, her statement is very impressive, and she's the daughter of Holocaust survivors, so there's that too, which is working in a subtle way. All these issues of language and imprisonment." Isabel closed that file, opened the Proust group. "What's incredible here is the innovative use of lighting," she said, "which, it turns out, is really the way you can apprehend Proust theatrically—I went to a workshop of this and it was just extraordinary." She explained; Patrick and Faith nodded.

"Good," said Faith in her tiny, rich voice. She took the two files from Isabel. "I'll look at these on the plane."

"And then," said Isabel, holding the closed Friedrichsville file, "there's this rural, youth-oriented, community-based group that's staging *The Miracle Worker*—"

Patrick put his earmuffs on, as if to cover his ears. "Isabel—" he said in exasperation.

"Just listen." Isabel talked about *The Miracle Worker* for some time. She detailed the interesting resume of William L. Singer, but did not mention the girl with the wavy hair. "As an *eclectic* choice," Isabel concluded, "I think this deserves a place in the mix."

Faith elegantly twisted the cap onto the elegant silver thermos of moss. "No," she said.

"What?" said Isabel.

Faith took off her beret, fluffed her thin hair, put the beret back on. "No." She checked her watch. "The car should be here, I have to go." She gathered her trench coat and suitcases, shoved her pile over to Patrick. "Sweetie," she said to him, "you can read my scrawls?"

"Sure." He took his earmuffs off and glared at Isabel. "When will you be back?"

He and Faith kissed each other on both cheeks.

"Six weeks. In time to sign the checks." Faith held out her hand to Isabel and Isabel shook it; Faith's handshake was thin but firm. "And I'll see you, too, I hope," she said.

Isabel didn't say anything. Her happiness deflated. The rich, she thought, could be so careless. Like Thea.

When Faith left, the elevator clattering downstairs, Patrick said with a hint of impatience, "I thought we already talked about that one."

Isabel held the file against her chest, arms crossed over it. "I wanted to try," she said.

"Why?" said Patrick. "Why bother?"

"Because," said Isabel, then stopped. Why bother, indeed? "Because I think my life just fell apart," she said, and was instantly mortified, although Patrick seemed unperturbed. "Has that ever happened to you?" she said.

"So many times," he said. He reached over and squeezed her hand comfortingly. "It'll be okay, Isabel. She loves you."

"No," said Isabel. "I don't think she does, actually."

What was love, anyway? thought Isabel as she walked back home from the office in the afternoon. The Friedrichsville file was in her knapsack; she had a vague idea of writing them a letter, a nice note in a card. She loved the girl with the wavy hair, for instance, though she didn't even know her name. Isabel's big boots protected her feet from the cold, but she felt the wind on her face, and in her short hair. She did need a hat. What was love? Communication? Matching ski sweaters? A little yellow dog? Was it things in themselves, or the choreographed wedding bells at the end of the play? She had thought love was a dream they had together, a dream of a goddess, ironic and beautiful. But that goddess didn't seem to be working out. Maybe that had been her mistake, concentrating on Diana to the exclusion of the rest of the film, although now—now she wasn't so sure she was in love with Diana anymore. Diana was a myth.

Isabel stomped on a patch of snow, leaving a satisfying white boot impression. She was the one who had wanted to call her Diana, the Roman name, not Artemis, because of her own long-lost Roman house. Wasn't her Roman house a kind of love, and Lottie, and horses, wasn't it love for her to put on that horse head every night, waiting for the quick moment when Rebecca shone the light on her alone? Wasn't it love to stand there as a horse, painfully illuminated by Rebecca, in a moment that seemed to go on forever? And then all the rest of it, Thea's face in the dim bar light like the face etched on an ancient wall, her intoxicating dualities, didn't Isabel know already, on that very evening, that it would probably end up just like this? She could tell even then that Thea was not a woman who cared much for subtlety; she only felt things in the extreme. Romans and

Greeks: they never did get along. But Isabel had loved her anyway. What myth was that?

Isabel turned the corner onto their block; there was a clutch of kids were standing around on the playground, one proudly displaying a massive radio playing Grandmaster Flash. Ahead of Isabel were two figures in animated conversation, the shorter one carrying a pole of some sort. It took a moment for Isabel to realize that it was Thea and Cricket, with Diana's bow, which had been painted a particularly garish shade of orange. Cricket had tossed it carelessly over her shoulder, on a string; it bounced against her back as she walked. Thea was talking, making framing gestures with her hands. Cricket waved to the kids on the playground and they waved back. "*Feliz Navidad!*" called Cricket, and the kids laughed, bobbing their heads to the very loud thumping of the radio, like an enormous, thumping heart. Isabel's vision seemed to be blurring; sounds were blurring, too. For a moment she wasn't sure where she was, in what city. Was this the city of women?

Thea punched Cricket lightly on the arm. They walked on down the street past the building, on their way somewhere together.

Alone in the apartment, Isabel dragged out the little television and deftly hooked up the complicated array of wires—she, unlike Cricket, knew how to use equipment—but she couldn't find whatever it was they had shot in her absence. They must have had the foresight to take it with them. Instead, she found the videotape of herself opening birthday presents. She watched it with a cold determination to the end. "Oooh," the foolish, shadow Isabel said on the video. "Aaah!" She wouldn't be needing any of those things now: the light meter, the book about Mexico, and whatever happened to that 1950s archery book? Thea could keep the basketball. Thea zoomed in and out in a way that might have seemed loving if it had been a little less expert. On the video, Isabel held up the picture postcard of Diana and Thea lingered on it, coming in close until Diana filled the frame. The tightness of the shot made the picture almost seem real, Diana's robes fairly billowing, grainily. Somewhere behind the picture, Isabel laughed; there were party noises. The blender whirred in the background. "Celia! You pig!" said Isabel on the tape. Her voice sounded far away. Watching the scene as the afternoon light faded, Isabel wondered how that could have been, that Thea could have seemed to be looking right at Isabel when she wasn't really looking at her at all. The party noises echoed on the tape. Diana, tilting, then twirling to the floor as Isabel happily reached for another useless present, remained serene.

❧ ❧ ❧

At night, the lights and tripod and camera were like animals in the forest, peering at Isabel where she lay on top of the heap of blankets she had folded for a mattress, inside a sleeping bag. Outside, the kids were playing their radio, even though it must be so cold. They banged on the playground rides. The noises thumped restlessly for hours, echoing through the air shaft. The shadows on the walls from the streetlights below flickered on the walls, simultaneously fragile and solid. Isabel held up her hand in a patch of light, looked at her fingers, folded them, opened them again. She detested Thea and at the same time longed for her touch, the touch that had for so long matched her own. Her skin was missing. If Thea came back and touched her, just once, Isabel was certain she would get her skin back, and then she could go on, though she might not be famous now. The radiator clanged and hissed. The apartment was colder without Thea. Isabel didn't even have to keep the windows cracked open anymore.

When Isabel woke up on Saturday, at first it wasn't so hard, and then it was very, very hard. Because at first there were boxes, cardboard boxes from the bodega on the corner, and masking tape that didn't really stick very well. It was more like bad string. Isabel worked up a sweat, which was satisfying. She put her mother's ring on its fine gold chain around her neck, to make sure she didn't leave it behind. At first there were simple choices: was the green sweatshirt hers? Their one vase was definitely hers. She wrapped it in a sizable wad of the *International Herald Tribune,* then tucked it into its own box, which she labeled VASE. It took a surprisingly long time to deflate the basketball. After tripping over the recliner's footrest for the third time, she tugged at the recliner for a few minutes, thinking she would drag it back down to the street, where it came from, then gave up. She gave up on all the furniture, in fact. It was junk.

That insight made things much easier. Also, the fact that they had no pets. Thea was allergic. Isabel resolved to get a pet right away, perhaps Monday. Sitting on the bathtub cover, she began a list, writing at the top, *Call Jeannie about dog.* Or maybe a cat would be better, this being New York, mice being in every building. Isabel paused. The question of where exactly she was going fluttered briefly through her mind, but she decided with some firmness not to panic. She wrote, *Find apartment,* then, *Look in Sunday paper for listings.* That was wrong. She drew a little reversing arrow next to these last two and felt hugely relieved. She put down the list, picked up a fresh box, realized she was out of the masking tape that didn't even stick, and began to sob. She cried until she couldn't breathe, blew her nose on a dish towel, then cried some more, down at the bottom of the river where the fish didn't even go, and it was cold, and littered with sharp stones.

Still crying, she called Celia. No answer. Of course, she was in Vermont with her idiotically happy family. Isabel couldn't bear to call her own family, not yet. This definitely would not fall into her father's definition of fun. Susan. Stephen. Gary. Leslie, who had an answering machine. Those things were so alienating, Isabel thought, leaving a teary message. Why not just answer your phone? Anyway, it was Christmas weekend. No one was home; everyone was singing carols and drinking eggnog and getting everything they had ever wanted. In despair, Isabel unplugged the phone, carrying it back into the kitchen with her. She would take it when she went. Ha ha, she thought, blowing her nose again on the wet dish towel.

She would be gone by Monday morning, if not sooner. She would go to San Francisco; she would go to Celia's in Vermont; she would go anywhere, so long as it was far, far away. She hated Avenue A. It wasn't the beginning of things but the end. It should be called Avenue Z. She wondered with some anxiety how much it cost to go to San Francisco, then put the thought out of her mind. First, she had things to do. She picked up her list. *Masking tape. Kleenex.*

It hurt her that her bow was gone, but they h carelessly left the arrow lying on the floor. Holding one en of the arrow under her boot, Isabel delicately broke it in half and resumed filling one entire box with shoes. The box of shoes looked obsessive in a pleasurable way, like some sort of art project. The tiny plaster high-heeled one lay carelessly among them, as if it were real. Maybe she could cast them all in plaster. Maybe that could be her art. It was also good, she had discovered, it was comforting, to play the record player extremely loud. The Banshees, which seemed appropriate for the occasion. At last she understood just how the kids on the playground felt, with their enormous radio: *thump, thump, thump*. When you had nowhere else to go, you could live inside that sound.

She kicked a half-eaten container of donuts into the corner. Diana's sandals, Isabel's high-tops, and a pair of pumps she had worn exactly once, at graduation, all thudded into the box one by one. The music thudded. Her heart thudded, too, rapidly, with fear but also a weird excitement, like a creature that had been let off a leash and wasn't sure in which direction to run. Everything, both inside her and outside her, felt simultaneously too fast and too slow. She wasn't sure for a moment which was her heartbeat, and which the Banshees. Isabel got Thea's big flannel shirt from the back of the bathroom door and stuffed it into the box with the shoes, then taped the box shut and pushed it to one side. She realized she didn't even know Cricket's last name. Mendoza? Sandoza? Sandinista? She couldn't remember, although she was sure she knew it; she was just too upset. But she was also relieved not to remember Cricket's last name. It didn't matter who Cricket was.

There was nothing in the living room she wanted. She studied it for a moment, as if taking a picture of it with her mind. The Banshees wailed on. Isabel spent some amount of time casting about the apartment for the *City of Women* poster. It was hers, probably, but she couldn't find it. She thought of having breakfast, then lunch, but the thoughts passed. She fished her journal out of the duffel bag and sat on the floor, writing in Magic Marker, which was the only writing implement she could find. *I feel so strange, my head and my hands seem so far apart. I think I had a few things the wrong way. Perception. What was that part Ben was reading me about perception? On Monday I will buy some Hegel and try to find the passage, it might be helpful.*

I don't seem to own any socks. I guess they were all Thea's.

Crumpled Kleenexes were scattered all over the floor where she had dropped them as she went along. The boxes piled up, one by one, tilting an invisible scale toward departure. Who was going to carry them all? Isabel didn't know the answer, which bothered her tremendously.

She couldn't think. She couldn't think. The dry dark ran up her spine. Isabel went into the kitchen, put the teapot on the counter, then rinsed the white tracings off the hand mirror (they'd be sorry) and balanced the hand mirror against the teapot. Her face was very pale; her sweater was inside out. She thought of having dinner, but only got as far as bread and butter and salt. It seemed to have no taste. She washed it down with a beer, which made her lightheaded. There was the feather Thea had found, still lying on the bathtub cover. Isabel put it in her pocket. What had happened to that earring? Had she worn it to Pennsylvania? Over her ear, she saw in the mirror, there was a wayward strand of hair. She got out the scissors and snipped it. In the mirror, her head looked smaller than usual, her eyes larger. She held two fingers to her forehead. *I am here,* she thought. *I am here, I am here, I am here.* But why were her eyes so big?

Isabel's duffel bag was still resting where she had dropped it a light-year ago. She found the album, got it out, and sat at the kitchen table turning the yellowing pages of actors and actresses long since vanished from any stage. *To Cassie,* was scrawled on one, *We need more fans like you!* The autograph was illegible. Marvin someone. It was a small thing, but it was enough. The film stopped, tore, and burned to white.

⟴ ⟴ ⟴

From inside the closet, the temperature, the time of year, what record was on the stereo, who was on the playground, what place this was, whose boxes were packed or unpacked and who would carry them later—you couldn't see any of that from here, where it was very quiet, and very dark. Particularly when the door was closed. Isabel sat on the floor in the dark, leaning her head back against a stack of shirts and pants. In her hands were the pills; pills were in her pockets, and shaken into her sleeves, and scattered around her on the floor, which was hard and cold. She wasn't hungry at all, although she hadn't eaten in some time. And she wasn't tired, although at the same time she was so tired. Her muscles ached. Her hands were sore. But she was waiting, this time, until she got an answer. She pulled her knees up. *Come now,* she thought, or maybe she said it. *I dare you.*

She waited for quite a while. She waited until she didn't know if her eyes were open or shut; she waited until she was no longer sure how much time had gone by. Perhaps an hour, perhaps more. The pills ingrained themselves in her hand. She waited until the darkness within and the darkness without were one, a single vast expanse in which she was so much larger, and at the same time so much smaller, than she had thought. Far outside the closet, something thumped. Or perhaps that was her heart. It could be that way, her heart both here and there at the same time, like a ghost. Her heart and the heart outside pounded, as one. The darkness she had thought of for so long as her enemy pressed against her with startling intimacy. She clasped her hands together in the dark; a few pills dropped and rolled away. Her fingers felt like someone else's fingers, cold and thin.

It rustled in her ear; it slipped in. There was no need to say anything, even if she wanted to, which she didn't. Her tongue was full of needles. The thumping outside seemed to have stopped. A kind of roaring filled her ears and her eyes and her nose, lining her hands, encasing her skull. Something pressed her down, and down, something that was both outside her and inside her, stiffening her lungs and her veins and her nerve endings, pushing her down as far as she could possibly go, and farther still, until she understood, finally. How dark it was. How deep. How without mercy. Walls fell. She stood it; she needed to stand it; she needed to know. It was black, with one red spot. It folded and folded and folded and could not be unfolded. It ticked unbearably loudly, then did not tick at all. It was without sight or sound or speech; in a hallway a light went out, a door closed, good night, go to sleep, good night. Isabel clasped her hands together tightly, wordless and huge and tiny. A terrible pain suffused her, a soundless sound like the air after a chord has been struck and can no longer be heard. Then it was flat.

She could open the door, or not open the door. There was

no way to decide, because everything was flat, and folded, and could not be heard. She could open the door, or not open the door, and the two sentences were equally possible, they made perfect sense. This was not what she had expected, this niggling randomness, this simple pause, a single held breath in the infinite expanse of darkness. She suspected that now, even now, some vital information was being withheld. But the familiar breath held fast, waiting. It was waiting for her alone.

Isabel opened the door. The aspirin fell from her hands, from her sleeves. She wasn't sure if it was morning, noon, or night.

Isabel shook the can as hard as she could in the early Sunday light. The air came in through the windows, cold and smelling of incipient snow. It would definitely snow today. The little ball clattered. Isabel got a good grip on the white plastic button and spelled out each letter, making each one high and wide and indelible. I. S. She used both hands on the S. Then, like the beginning of an alphabet, A. B. She had to put the L in the corner, but that was all right, it looked right there, being cornerlike itself. And then WAS HERE—she got a little faster, a little more fluent as she went along. It was a plain, but satisfying, sentence. It would work. She scrawled the letters on the doorways and the windows, on the floor, over the video camera, over the lens, over the Harpo wigs, and especially on the beautiful ruined walls, and there were so many of them, she was glad she had bought more than one can. She was glad the bodega had been open. She couldn't live in these ruins, but they provided a good surface for writing in spray paint. The letters adhered easily, gleamed, fresh and shining, some red, some black, some dripping a bit, particularly the B and the two S's. The fumes were pungent; Isabel stuck her head out the window and breathed in the good, cold air. The sky, when she twisted her head up to look, was silver and heavy with a smear of light somewhere behind that seemed to spread out, illuminating the clouds. Bacon was frying in the apartment below. On the playground, someone yelled, "*Aquí! Aquí!*" There was the sound of a ball being kicked. The brick against her hands had veins of dampness, like a living thing. Isabel leaned on her elbows, breathing it all in. On a roof not too far away, she spotted a shaggy water tower she had never seen before. In the morning light it looked exotic, like a windowless round house in another country in the sky.

Isabel chewed on a cracker, which somehow tasted almost unbearably sweet. The rosy, snowy light poured in over the wreckage of spray paint and Harpo wigs and myriad little white fists of Kleenex; the light was sweet. Car horns sounded outside; the horns were sweet, too. Using the last bits of masking tape, she affixed the film script to one page in the album, the picture of the girl with the wavy hair to the next, then closed the album as well as she could with the help of a few rubber bands. Outside, snow fell in a thick white curtain. It fell over the playground, over the subways, over the river, over Avenue A, over buildings high and low, over the bell ringers in Times Square. Somewhere, it fell past the window where Thea and Cricket sat, looking at each other. Isabel gently set the album in a box. She took the ring on its fine gold chain from around her neck, wrapped it in a scrap of Kleenex, and lay that in the box, too, then closed the lid. She was done. It was a good thing she had had the presence of mind to plug the phone in, because just then it rang.

Later, much later, it often occurred to Isabel that she was lucky. She had never exactly thought of herself as a lucky person—on the contrary. But luck, she had discovered, was the sidewalk under her feet when she walked to work. Luck was the old rattling Van Zandt elevator, to which she now had the key. Luck was how many trees there were in the West Village, and how many new streets she hadn't known about, twisting and crossing one another unpredictably. Luck was the sound of Patrick's electric razor in the morning, and the three cobalt-blue pots of tomato plants she had lined up on the wide windowsill in her room. One was almost certainly sprouting.

The teakettle whistled. Isabel poured herself a cup of tea, then stared at the cup, wondering. The radio murmured. Isabel tucked her bare feet under her on the kitchen chair, tucked a lock of hair behind her ear, lit a cigarette. She really needed to stop smoking. She opened her journal. A feather from many entries ago fell out. It was iridescent and soft, an improbable shade of hot purple. She absently brushed it against her cheek. Patrick was out, so she had this moment to herself, and recently there was something, a desire that tugged at her, but it was elusive. Just begin, she thought. Begin with what you see, right now. She turned to a blank page.

She wrote the three letters—*tea*—and at once they seemed just the letters she had been looking for. They were the lucky ones, those three, standing alone at the top of the first page.

ACKNOWLEDGMENTS

I have been extremely fortunate to have as discerning readers of this book Bay Anapol, Lisa Cohen, Bernardine Connelly, Sheila Donohue, Abby Frucht, Steve Lattimore, Goldberry Long, Cammie McGovern, Laurie Muchnick, Peter Rock, and Diane WoodBrown, as well as my astute colleagues and professors at the Stanford Creative Writing Program. Carol Anshaw's inspiration, support, and editorial wisdom through the years have meant the world to me. I also owe a debt of gratitude to the intelligence and dedication of my agent, Jennifer Carlson, and my editor, Kathy Pories. Invaluable facts were provided by Charlotte Butzin, Karen Durbin, and Mike Pagano.

And none of this book would be possible without Robyn Selman, who is part of every word in it.